AF259091

THE LYONS' DEN

Kyle Michel Sullivan

Reimagined from the novel
The Seven Keys to Baldpate
Written by
Earl Derr Biggers
and
the play
The Seven Keys to Baldpate
Adapted by
George M. Cohan

KMSCB
Buffalo, NY

Third Edition
ISBN: 978-1-7376331-8-1
Published 2023 by KMSCB
Front cover photograph: Dan Skinner
Back cover photograph: Shutterstock
Cover design: Jam The Cat
Copyright 2011 by Kyle Michel Sullivan, dba: KMSCB

THE LYONS' DEN

Acknowledgements

Thanks to STARbooks Press for publishing the first edition of this in paperback and ebook, and to Brad and Sue for their backup. Additional thanks to Karl and Carrie for giving me so much support, even when I was being a Daniel.

Contents

About the Author

Other Books

In the Beginning There Was Tad

All right, let's just say it up front – Dan-O should never have agreed to help Tad ... excuse me, *Theodore J. Bentley, the Third* ... in the first place. But the way Little-Lord-Perfect rushed into the diner, breathless, light flakes of snow on his camel's hair coat, his ice-blue eyes projecting fear and need and horror on top of that tender little quiver he could get in his voice as he whimpered, "Danny, please, I have no idea what to do," well, I have to admit it would've breached the walls of any defense. Maybe even mine, and I hated his ass.

Okay, hated might be kind of strong, but I sure as hell didn't like him. Especially after what he'd pulled on Dan-O just six months earlier. You see, that's when Tad dumped him. After they'd been together for nearly three years ... okay, two-and-a-half, be technical! It left my guy unable to do anything but lie in bed for two days as he tried not to think, and the only reason he got back to life that quickly was his rent was coming due so he had to work or get evicted. Not an easy time, lemme tell ya.

But crap like that don't really matter to people like Tad ... excuse me, *Master Theodore J. Bentley, the Third*; he'd snarl in disgust without the full and flowing exclamation of his name. He was one of those young, privileged East-Coast-types who know from the cradle they're destined for great and glorious things. Meaning a producer in Hollywood, in his case; helps to know the shallowness of his aims. And man, was he putting everything he had into it. He'd already produced a cable movie using one of Dan-O's mysteries — *High-Heeled Moccasins*, featuring yours truly, Ace Shostakovich. But what made him a player ... someone who must be paid attention to, in Hollywood-speak ... was that he had also taken an option on two more of my guy's books – *The Dr. Pepper Tryst and Tristan* and *The Tangerine 42-D Cup Madam*. Both of them with a nice, solid little cult following.

And, again, featuring me.

Meaning, yes, I don't really exist except on the page or in the back of your brain. But if you think it's weird a fictional character's telling this story, you ain't seen what happened, yet.

Unfortunately, even having six mysteries published don't mean you make enough to live on in New York City. So while Tad was flying high playing Mr. Great-and-Glorious-Producer-Dude, my guy was still tending bar at two different eateries. And that's probably how things would have stayed if Tad's little problem hadn't reared its ugly head.

You see, as the Golden-One put it, he'd hired this way-too-pricey-twenty-one-year-old-Cheeto-eater, AKA: laptop potato, to adapt those two books into eight scripts for a cable series. Everyone Tad talked to swore he was the hottest screenwriter since Orson Welles, so who better to give him something high profile and eye-popping to show the money boys?

Tad finally got the screenplays on a Friday. And just knowing they would knock anybody's nose ring off, Mr. Brilliant arranged a drop-dead face-to-face with the yea or nay guy at HBO for the following Monday ... sort of a meet me, now, or I take it to Netflix kind of deal; being bilingual helps. Only then did he actually read the damned things, and that is when he saw his fledgling career crash and burn before his designer contacts.

Seems the Cheeto-eater'd had so little interaction with reality ... since birth, I bet ... he thought characters in movies were more real than real people were, especially when spitting third-rate film noir dialog that was dumb in the 1940s and doing crap that'd be idiotic even for a spoof of the mystery-thriller genre. But just as Little-Sir-Perfect was about to leap off the balcony of his multimillion-dollar penthouse, he remembered Dan-O worked weekday lunches, nearby, so raced over to waylay him.

Now he and my guy were seated in a downstairs booth in a back corner of the diner's faux black and white 1890s décor, right by the hallway to the restrooms. And having filled Dan-O in on his worse than death situation, Tad shifted into whine mode. "This means *all* the scripts are crap, all fuckin' eight of them, including the bible!" The bible not being that well-known book of Christian conflict but one that outlined the direction the characters and story would take; just keeping you up with the patois.

"C'mon, Tad," Daniel being the only one allowed to call him that, "I write books, not scripts."

"But they're based on your books! And you're the one who consistently informed me a story's a story."

My guy snorted as he snapped, "A script isn't a story, it's a desecration." Then he dug into his cheeseburger, served nice and hot, for once, by his buddy, Orlando, and which he was using as both lunch and dinner since he had another shift to work, that night.

"Danny, I told you from the outset," Tad growled, "you cannot fit a full two-hundred and fifty pages into an hour and forty minute movie without cutting some things. And you know, reviewers still said we kept very close to your story."

Didn't matter. So the movie had turned out nice enough, so what? It still wasn't ... well, it just wasn't right. I'd been made cynical to the max and Carmen ... she's my sexy secretary ... she was nothing but a sex toy, not at all like we were in the book.

Honest.

But Dan-O'd made enough cash off the rights and a bump in book sales to pay off a couple bills and move to an apartment that had fewer roaches, so he couldn't bitch too much. And since this series of screwed-up scripts were based on what he'd written, he probably did have a pretty good idea of what they'd need to work.

"Besides," Tad kept on with, "you're the one who's always said, and I heard it every time you were stuck in a plot, My characters'll work it out. Ace'll take care of everything."

"Which you said made me sound crazy."

"You did, but why stop now?"

Dan-O all but growled back, "I wasn't, Tad."

"Then why're you on Prozac?"

"I'm *not*!"

Not anymore, anyway. He'd stopped taking it three weeks before the breakup.

"Danny, the last time I was at your place, you still had a bottle in the bathroom."

"It's an old prescription and – whoa, whoa, whoa, whoa, wait, you went through my medicine cabinet!?"

"Yes. I was ... was looking for some Tylenol and ..." And all of a sudden, Little-Lord-Perfect could see in Dan-O's glare that he'd fucked up.

Oh, a little background here. He'd appeared at Dan-O's door a few weeks ago with a list of questions the Cheeto-eater had about the ...*Tristan* one, and he had used the bathroom twice while my guy was trying to understand where in the hell the damn questions came from since they had zero to do with the book he'd written. Then His-Majesty had said nothing concerning either the meds or the weirdness of the Cheeto-eater.

Well, Sir-Great-and-Glorious rolled his eyes in that way that always pissed my guy off, not so much because it was condescending or dismissive, but because he looked so damned good when he did it. Then he said, "Okay, fine, fine, I shouldn't have done that. And so what if I've seen you say things that would've put you in a padded room, fifty years ago? I know that's merely you being creative because I have seen it work. I never should have said that, Danny. I ... I'm sorry."

Which floored Dan-O and me, both. This dude was one of those people who never admit they're wrong about anything, and who have the looks, attitude and charisma to pull it off. Seriously, if he says the sky is green, it sorta-kinda is. Even when it's really blue. And if he says the world is flat – hell, not even the horizon would dare argue with him. But here was big, bad, beautiful Tad ... oops, *Theodore J. Bentley, the Third*; I keep forgetting one must have one's moniker correct, y'know and — oh, the hell with it; let him snarl ... here he was, allowing that he might have made a mistake.

That alone would've told anybody with even half a functioning brain that the bastard was up to something.

Anybody but Dan-O, of course, because as painful as the breakup had been, my guy still dreamed of getting back together with the creep. Which begs the question – why would anyone even want to be with someone so self-absorbed, even if he is good-looking? Jeez, even from the beginning, it'd been way too much of a one-way relationship, with Dan-O catering to the Glorious-One's every wish, including those he simply thought Tad had, as if he was the bastard's servant.

Well, the reason was just as simple, stupid and shallow as you might think; Tad wasn't merely good-looking, he was fucking gorgeous. And boy did he know it. If you bring to mind the epitome of every gay man's dream, no matter what his type – *that* was Tad. Period. End of story. And if you don't believe me, here's how Dan-O laid it out in ... *Tristan*.

"... But then, he was built by the gods of Greece, with a face so classic, cool and elegant, it was painful even to gaze upon him. And watching as he strolled along the beach in his scarlet, square-cut Speedo ... " One would never put a thong on a guy like Tad, nor flowery-designer briefs, nor would he be caught dead in board shorts; those were for fat Russians, Brazilians and boogie-boarder-boiz. " ... you could not help but sense the aura of a golden panther policing his lair, cloaked in the casual assurance that he could handle anything."

Yeah, be it male, female or Flipper. How he and Dan-O had ever wound up as a couple had been the source of endless speculation by one and all, especially since my guy was so his opposite.

Oh, don't get me wrong! Dan-O is not ugly, no; he just has ... well ... *nice* looks. Lean face. Crazy thick brown hair with eyebrows to match, hovering over dark sloe eyes. Smooth olive skin except for this sorta-kinda five o'clock shadow dancing across his jaw. A somewhat sexy scar along his left cheekbone. Put it all together with a bit of a hawkish nose, which dear mother insisted stemmed from his father's French-Portuguese heritage, and the fact that he was tight and trim, he had what you'd call a Joe-Above-Average kind of attractiveness. So why the hell an I'm-all-that guy like Tad would let a sorta-kinda guy like Daniel play high priest to his shining light for over two years meant only two possible answers to most people ... money or sex.

Well, since Tad was the rich one in the equation, the gossip was cast in stone and spread in glorious fashion by way of more than one flapping tongue ... who revealed they'd heard from somebody whose current lover had slept with another guy who'd been told by a friend of his that Tad was a lousy lay. And in the same breath, they'd pointed out that Daniel was reputed to have tricks up his sleeve that would turn the straightest guy to the pink side. Which he'd supposedly proven with a certain butch-action-actor he'd known. Who'd supposedly been so upset Dan-O had gone exclusive with Tad, he'd lost his sorrows in the arms of a porno god on that *other* coast, and promptly got outed. And who'd tried to un-out himself by getting married and begetting twins who actually looked like him, much to everyone's surprise ... including his, according to these self-same tongues.

But you still have to wonder: why would anybody want to fuck around with anybody who just wants to fuck around with them, in every meaning of the term, no matter how gorgeous they are? *That* is one of life's greatest mysteries. Yet that was Dan-O's wish, with reality making no hint of an appearance in any corner of his brain.

Dammit.

Meaning my guy was still just off-center enough to let His-Greatness wriggle his way back into Dan-O's hopes by capping off his plea with, "It's just, Danny, this series – it'll only be as good as the scripts I hand the jerks with the network, so they can mangle it with their notes and suggestions and stupid ideas and ... and, you ... you have your books out there, all nice and neat and selling steady and all yours and ... and all I have is my ass on the line, putting more of my investors' money into this project than I should've by hiring that twerp, and ... and the meeting's Monday! At noon! I can't change it; I'll look like an idiot, and I can't find anybody else on such short notice and ... and if you don't do this, I'm fucked. I'm totally fucked. My backers'll sue me, and I'll spend my life bankrupt, and I know I don't have the right to beg you like this, but you ... you have to help me, Daniel Bettancourt; you're my only hope."

Aw, jeez, the *Star Wars* reference!? That was below the belt! He fucking knew how special that movie was to Dan-O.

Sure enough, my guy jolted back to the first boy he'd ever loved, because *Star Wars 4* was the movie they'd seen on their first date. So what if it was just the super-slick re-mastered re-release version? Dan-O'd never seen it before, and it was one of his few pleasant memories. He and that kid had talked about it for hours as they kissed and fooled around, and he was sure they'd still be together if his own dear mother hadn't gone through divorce number three and marriage number four and moved him to Philadelphia. He'd resented her for years.

That made Dan-O bolt up from the booth and start pacing. Three steps up and three steps back, his hand rubbing the back of his head like he always did when he was threatening to get one of his headaches. I'd have jumped in with a few words of advice like, *don't do it!*, but he wasn't gonna hear me because Tad was still filling his head with shit.

"You're a good man, Danny. You've always helped me when I needed it. And I haven't done much in return, have I?"

You haven't done shit for him, you prick.

My guy grabbed some fries, still pacing as he said, "I ... I don't know the format, Tad."

"They're already in it. I have them here on a USB drive, with the program disk. All you need to do is upload it, then make the dialog work and the characters not suck."

"But I won't have the time. I have another shift, tonight, and I'm working all day, tomorrow, and Sunday brunch and ..."

"I'll get you out of it."

"Tad – shit, I need the money!"

"But your books're selling and ..."

"And royalties don't get paid for another month."

"Y'know, Danny, you really need to learn how to budget," Tad popped off, in his best big-brother tone of voice.

"This from a trust fund baby!" my guy snapped back as he flopped in the booth to focus on his quickly cooling meal. Made me happy to see him show the dick some backbone.

Tad stiffened. The one vulnerable spot in his life was that he would never have to work, if he didn't want to. Yeah, yeah, yeah, he'd always been able to live like he felt like or wherever he'd wanted, and everybody assumed he'd been handed his life on a silver platter and didn't understand how he had to bust his ass twice as hard to gain people's respect and on and on and – aw, jeez, if you got him going on it, he'd never shut up. But to my surprise, he jumped past the whining, for once, and went straight to his usual method of getting back on top.

"Okay, I'll add another thousand to my option on your books," he said in a quiet voice. "Up front. And you know, if HBO gives a green light, I have to buy the rights. Which means another eighty-nine-K." Then he took in a deep breath and added, "Of course, if they don't, the option expires and you don't receive another dime. Plus the books will be considered damaged goods so no one will want them, after that ... and ..."

And the son-of-a-bitch let his words trail off, with the

meaning obviously being, *play nice with me, or I take my toys and go home, and you get zero, zip, nada.* The dumb fuck. As if money mattered. You'd think he would've learned by now that my guy could live for a year on what most people wasted in a week. Shit, Dan-O had so few clothes and possessions and such minimal emotional support, it amazed me he was still human. Plus Tad knew damn well he was paying for mother's psychiatric care, not to mention his own therapy, thanks to her. That was why he was close to the edge by the end of each quarter, when a royalty check would magically appear in his checking account. Yet here was Little-Lord-Moneybags using cash and cruelty as bargaining chips. Make you feel as desperate as I can while I eat caviar, right asshole? Shit, the rich're different, all right; they're sociopathic motherfuckers.

Well – Tad's last comment startled Daniel into confused silence as he tried to figure out why the bastard was being so hard assed in his attempt to talk my guy into doing him a huge favor. In fact, he was so introspective, I think it made Tad nervous because after a minute he added, "Sorry, I ... I forgot about your mother's situation." Bullshit, bullshit, bullshit. "So ... there goes dumb-as-dirt-Tad saying the wrong thing, as usual." No shit there, Sherlock. "It's just, everything's been out of balance since we broke up."

Oh, no. He wouldn't dare go there.

"We didn't break up, Tad," my guy said, quietly. "You dumped me." Then he took another bite of his burger.

"I know," sighed His-Worship. "And I wish I hadn't."

He fucking *did* it! The son-of-a-bitch!

You see, that comment made my guy damn near stop breathing, waiting to hear the rest of it. And sure enough, Tad kept on with, "What if ... if this works out? What if we spend a week in ... in Bermuda? Just you and me? Away from all this snow. See if we can ... can start fresh."

"A week?" my guy whispered, not looking at him.

"Yes," Tad said, nodding. "Truth is, I miss you, Danny. I just haven't had time to let myself think about it. But if I get the go-ahead on this, it'll take a good ten days for the lawyers to pull the contract together and ... and we could ... you know ... just be together. On my Amex. Everything. Totally."

Oh, Tad always did have perfect timing. Book number six,

The Dirty Baker's Dozen, Plus 2, had just been published and was getting great reviews. It had even reached number twenty-four on the NY Times mystery bestsellers list and was trending higher, so Dan-O was almost on an emotional high. Gregory Taylor, his editor, predicted that by the end of the year he could stop tending bar and live the life of a real writer, since the new one was handing all my other stories a new life on the mystery shelves.

And yes, I do mean *mine*. Oh, all right, as well as Dan-O's, since I'm him and he's me. That's why we work so well together. Plotting the plot. Trying this secret path and that dark corner. Going left or right or up or down. Jeez, some of the arguments we'd have. And laughing fits. Okay ... maybe that would have put him in line for a lobotomy fifty years ago, but these days? A touch of schizophrenia helps a writer's career.

Oh, Carmen was part of it, too. In fact, he even described her as dark and pretty in a tender way, meaning she was a female version of my guy ... well, except for a nice set of, uh, headlights; but don't tell her I said that ... and she was always ready to jump in anytime I needed her. Wanna know why? Guess who Dan-O made me look like in the last four books? I already gave you a clue, from the passage in ...*Tristan*.

Right, I'm Tad's fucking doppelganger, except I have sensitivity, street smarts and savvy, along with an occasional love of alliteration, and don't ask me why. My patois is Dan-O's beast, not my own.

Tad knew, of course, and thought it was cute. As well as to be expected. He knew his value and accepted my guy's tweaking of my description as something that ought to happen, without question. I mean, why wouldn't someone want to make a guy like him the center of their universe?

But that was when things were hot and heavy between them. Then came the split, and I had to kick Dan-O's ass to make him finish proofing *Dirty Bakers'*... in time for his deadline. We'd only just made it, and that's because he didn't change anything. Which was unusual for him.

Look, don't get me wrong; I want my guy to be happy, and I really mean that. Just because he borned me to be a chick chaser instead of a noodle hound means jack shit. Everybody deserves to have somebody they can be one with. I got it with

Carmen, and for a little bit, Dan-O had it with Tad.

But that was then and Tad had gone, and my guy'd returned to living on nothing. But by this point he'd caught on to just how much nothing that was, and he hated it. And now here was Little-Sir-Perfect scrambling back into his life seeking support of both the physical and emotional kind, and the fact that Dan-O was letting him do it really pissed me off. Not that there's much I can do *about* it. I mean, yeah, I'm him and he's me so, my viewpoints ought to be his. But when you put up blinders for yourself so you can't see the truth of a scumbag, you won't see it. Period. End of story.

But not the end of this one.

No. This was just the beginning.

Well, when Tad offered up Bermuda as part of the deal, my guy did a U-turn so sharp, I damn near got thrown out of his brain. Then he whispered, "Don't joke about that, Tad."

"I'm not." And he had his best sincere look on.

"You ... you mean it? You and me for a week? Alone."

Aw, this was not gonna be pretty. My guy was already halfway into do-or-say-anything-he-had-to mode in hopes of getting the little shit back. And the bastard snapped to it like a cheetah snaps its eyes on a gazelle that's wandered too far from the herd and is about to become din-din. And that is when the stupid stuff started.

"Yes, Danny," he'd said. "A full week, just you and me. If this works. But you can't stay in the city. I don't want anyone to know about it, and you never could keep a secret."

"Yes, I can!"

The bastard ignored him and kept on with, "Besides, it'll help you if you're somewhere hidden, where you'll be alone and can work your magic to its best."

"I'll hole up in my place and turn off my phone."

"And order pizza and chatter with the pizza boy, if he's cute," Tad snapped, "and he'll chatter with *People* or *OK*."

"I never did that!"

Exactly, Tad! That was you, and you did it deliberately to spread this lie that the actor playing me was screwing the actress playing Carmen in *High-Heeled Moccasins*, even though they hated each other's guts. All just to generate publicity. Oh, but I forget – you're never wrong. And you always did suffer from selective amnesia, you little shit, especially when we're talking about things that make you look bad.

Tad pulled out his big-brother tone, again, and said, "Listen, buddy, we both know that once you get talking you can't stop and – no, no, no, Danny, you jabber, sometimes, and have no idea what you're saying."

Well, as much as I hate to admit it, that was true. But it's one thing to jabber about bullshit and something else to reveal crap that's really important. I mean, my guy's still got corners in his soul not even I have access to so I know he can keep secrets.

Daniel huffed as Tad whipped out his Blackberry-iPhone-egg-scrambler-and-maybe-even-coffee-maker to pull up his address book. "Got it! Use my father's place up by Bradleyville. It's on a lake, and it's closed for the winter. No one has a key to it except the caretaker, and he's an obnoxious old fart."

"Where is that?" Daniel asked, still not convinced.

"Near Middleton." Tad Googled a map on his iPhone.

"That's a good two-hour drive!" Daniel snapped when he saw it. "I'll have to work nearly non-stop to get done, as it is. When am I supposed to sleep?"

"Drink coffee."

"You have got to be kidding!"

Tad finally noticed Dan-O had his no-way-in-hell attitude on and said, "C'mon, Danny, it's just like college. Pulling an all-nighter to get that paper in on time sort of crap and living off junk food and ... and ..."

"I ... never needed to."

"Listen to me, I don't want that Cheeto-eating bastard to find out you're doing this until it's done, so it ... it has to be my father's place or ... or we drop the idea. And I'll forget about HBO and ... and see if I can pull together some more money for another writer to do what that creep should've done and hope it doesn't hurt me too much in my career."

Said with that fucking quiver, again.

Daniel huffed and paced about a bit, saying, "Will you at least drive me up, so I can start reading?"

"Can't. I'm booked to finish the edit on a project for a Tuesday showing, starting at six. I *will* be working on no sleep, this weekend. But I have an intern from NYU, so I'll have him drive you up in my car."

"What if *he* talks?"

"He's from Wisconsin; who could even begin to think that he knows anything? Does that work?"

That, my guy went along with. Dammit. So as Tad worked his magic in getting him off the schedule at his jobs without him getting fired, and called the intern, and wrote directions to this cabin, Dan-O skimmed the first script ... and damn near backed out of the whole deal. It was worse than crap; it was dog-meat.

"Shit," I whispered in shock, "he's got me soundin' like Mickey Spillane on acid."

"With a dash of Marquis de Sade," my guy muttered back.

Say what?! "Oh, dude, write that down; we gotta use it."

"Already did." He was barely paying attention to me.

"When?" I asked.

"*The Cadillac Criminal Mind.*"

"Aw, Jeez, we're repeatin' myself?"

"No, Carmen," he muttered. "It was her line."

Oh. Right. When she referred to this rich-but-nice-guy idiot who wanted to be a detective but got the patois down so backwards and bad, it almost got him killed. And she said it as only a girl New Yawk born an' bred could say it, "Listen, ya little shit, ya wanna play De Sade or Spillane? Make up yer mind an' stick wit' it for a day or two."

"Don't tell Carmen I did that," I said with a grimace. "She'll freak times ten." Especially since her English really is better than that.

"It is, so I won't," my guy smirked, reading my thoughts, since they're his own.

Then he and I both noticed Tad watching us, trying to keep a smile off his face as he said, "Merde, Danny, tu es si mignon quand t'es fou."

You are so cute when you're nuts?

Seriously? Backhanded flattery of the condescending kind in French 101?! When you're asking for a fucking favor?! Now I knew the bastard was up to something.

So it was all set, and Dan-O went to buy provisions at a drug store on the next corner. He exited with a nice full bag just as this skinny big-eyed kid named Paul pulled up in Tad's Cadillac SUV, which in the show kind of looked like an ice-breaker. His-Gloriousness insisted my guy ride in the back, like this was a cab, then only agreed to have Paul swing by our apartment because we needed to pick up the laptop.

"Okay, I guess you *do* need that," Tad grinned. "But shit, Danny, couldn't you have picked someplace to live that's more convenient to the freeway?"

"No dissin' my pad, Tad," my guy snapped. "It's the best I could afford."

Tad laughed, closed the door on Daniel and yelled at Paul, "Go forth, James! Quick on the pedal!"

To which Paul, in his infinite capacity for awareness, replied, "Huh?"

Tad just motioned him on and waved us bye-bye as we screamed into traffic, making five yellow taxis honk at us and drawing a torrent of nasty words from a couple of bike-shaws. Needless to say, Dan-O buckled himself in, tight.

That's when I nudged him and muttered, "Y'know, you really oughta write down that *diss my pad* line. Wasn't bad."

"It only works if I put someone named Tad or Brad into one of your stories," my guy muttered back, "and there's no way in hell I'm doing that to any of my books."

"*Our* books."

"Whatever."

"Promise?"

"Promise."

That's when we noticed Paul looking at my guy in the rear-view mirror, his eyes getting big. Dan-O just sighed.

Well, Tad's freakiness must've worn off on the kid, or maybe it was just his Wisconsin roots, or maybe Paul just gets antsy about double-parking, because when we got to Dan-O's building and we had to do that, he whined about it so much my guy just raced upstairs, grabbed the satchel that held his laptop and notepads and was back down in two minutes, flat. Meaning, he'd be stuck in black slacks ... old but nicely worn in; white cotton shirt ... no *T* under it, too clichéd; the comfy loafers he always wore; and a knee-length parka for the weekend. And while that look gave him a level of coolness that almost matched mine, it felt too much like a uniform and was not factoring into his happiness quotient.

As for me, well, since I can change on a dime, I was wearing the latest in cool-detective trench coats over your basic casual travel attire, which helps me feel as if I'm on top of the case. Being non-existent has its advantages.

The second we scrambled back in the Caddie, the kid gasped, "Parking enforcement!" and punched it into warp speed, skidding through the snow into traffic and nearly sending my guy to the floor along with his things. And the way he weaved in and around other cars, it took half an hour to pull laptop and groceries back together. Then in the so-called two-hour drive ... that took over three hours because Little-Lord-Perfect mis-programmed the GPS, keeping us on the 287 instead of following the 87 north, which none of us figured out until we were halfway back to the city ... Dan-O uploaded the last six scripts to his laptop, scanned through them and flew into what-the-fuck-land at the lunacy of how our babies had been abused.

For example, a bit was added where Carmen gets an anonymous tip in the ...*Madam* portion and races off to look into it without telling me. In direct violation of detective rule number one-oh-four. Which, of course, turned out to be a trap and wound up making her a hostage of the badder-than-bad guys, forcing me to risk life and limb to save her in a spectacular gun battle that belonged more in *Die Hard* than one of my mysteries.

"Are you fuckin' kidding me?!" my guy growled. "Now she's dumber than dumb."

It got worse. What did the Cheeto-eater have for Carmen's last line in the script? *You can be my private dick anytime!*

That was too stupid even for porno and set me to growling, "Okay, Dan-O, who can we contract to remove this dickhead's fingers, so he can never type again?"

"Gregory might know someone," my guy said, giving my suggestion a moment of serious thought then he murmured, "Man-oh-man, no wonder Tad needs help."

"That, or a fall guy."

"It's not my fault the scripts were written by someone with the emotional maturity of an aardvark."

"It will be if this don't work."

"Ace ... *any*-thing I do'll be better than this shit."

And boy was he right about that! Still. "You're talkin' a re-do of three-hundred-and sixty pages, Dan-O."

"I can make it."

"You just gonna cut and paste from the books?"

"On the first pass ... and second ... then polish."

"Rinse and repeat."

Dan-O looked up and blinked, asking, "What's that from?"

"An old commercial for shampoo. Saw it on *Comedy*

Central."

"At the bar, right. Meaning use the shampoo twice as fast to no effect. Talk about advertising to waste resources. That guy should've been throttled."

Of course, that's when we noticed Paul eyeing us in the rear-view mirror, again, his wide eyes even wider, his hands gripping the wheel so tight his knuckles were whiter than the snow. So Dan-O popped off with, "Don't worry; I'm only borderline psychotic."

"I know," Paul squeaked.

You *do*?

"How?" my guy asked.

"Mr. Bentley told me."

He *did*?!

"What *else* did he tell you?"

"Listen, I ... I'm straight. Okay?"

Dan-O chuckled. "Don't worry, we won't hold it against you; will we, Ace?" And he looked right at me to say it, meaning to Paul it looked as if my guy was talking to his very imaginary friend in the seat next to him.

The kid gulped and stared straight ahead. Pun intended.

I snickered, "I love it when you're wicked."

"Aw, shut up and get to work."

Thinking my guy meant him, Paul drove a little faster.

So I kicked back and started pondering the possibilities, peculiarities and just plain persnickitiness of the present project. Told you I liked to alliterate. It was looking more and more like this job was gonna be fun, and the only thing missing was Carmen, who'd refused to join us on the trip. She said she'd be around if we needed her, but I got the feeling she's really pissed at how she'd been made over and just wanted to see if we were going to leave her like that. Like she had no trust in my guy. Which made me halfway wonder if she was really off sweet-talking some other writer to put her in his book, just in case this blew up in our faces. Meaning, yes, we characters can be very fickle, especially if we feel we're being dissed, 'cause then we'll just get pissed, and so some will insist they find a new ... wrist ... to, uh, to be the artist – okay, so I'm not a poet!

Anyway, it was also good my guy wasn't driving, thanks to the snow. Traveling in that makes him even more tense than usual. It was nothing heavy, at first, just little flurries that got flurrier and flurrier and flurrier the farther away we got from the city. It didn't matter while we were traveling up this never-ending toll road because all it did was make the asphalt wet. But then we crossed the Hudson, and the snow started building into something mean and sticky. Combine that with the wrong-way fiasco, which meant getting off the freeway and tripping along this unplowed street that couldn't decide if it was a highway or a boulevard for so long, we all thought we'd missed the connection back to the 87, and the rest of the crap he read in the scripts, my guy was closing in on freak-out-pissed-off-gonna-kill-somebody mode. Seriously, Paul was starting to shiver in fear at the horrible things being considered for the Cheeto-eater. Then we almost got sideswiped by Mercedes and Dan-O started growling at the whole damned world just on principle.

"This is why I don't own a car! Everywhere you turn you're dealing with idiot driver, tolls, fees and added expenses." And on and on and on. Still, no bullshit on that. Why do you even need a car in the City? The mass-transit's great, and it costs as much as an uptown apartment to put the damn thing in a garage. And do not get either of us started on the usual traffic.

So now we were on the 6, and it turned into the 17 as we drove through an area of hills and turns and construction as occasional signs read, *Future 86*. Which reminded my guy of what they say in restaurants when they've run out of something. Which reminded him he'd had to wait tables while in college. Which he hated. Which sent him into a spiral of thinking it was an omen for how things would turn out in regards to the deal because he was probably 86'ing his future, and on and on. I finally had to remind him he had *NIN* on his phone, which he'd just upgraded, and then only because he had some left over from the Ten-K Tad paid for the option to my books – okay, *our* books. So he pumped up *Closer* and we rocked along.

Now I know what you're thinking, here – the idea of a gay man singing *I wanna fuck you like an animal* in a car driven though a nighttime snowstorm by a very nervous straight kid from Wisconsin ... well, it's hardly what you'd call the epitome of fun and games. But sometimes you gotta rock with what you got.

We finally turned onto a two-lane road that was dark and

damn near deserted. And the snow kept snowing, and the trees got thicker and even more foreboding, and the sky looked blacker than black until we passed over a hilltop and down in a picturesque valley of bleak, snow-covered fields twinkled the tender lights of Bradleyville, New York. And lemme tell you, the second I saw it, I knew this was the kind of place that ... well, while the chamber of commerce may say it's cozy and quaint, kids that live here probably see it as *the hell I wanna get the hell away from*, it's so terminally cute. And charming. And messy in its layout. Just your typical one-lane New England-style village.

Somehow Dan-O ... naw, better just call him Daniel, from now on, for clarity's sake ... anyway, since we'd made it alive Daniel lost his pissy edge and helped Paul find this ancient diner just off the main drag, where Tad said the caretaker'd meet us. We parked and walked inside to enjoy a blast of warm air, with Paul three steps behind my guy and still deep into wariness mode but obviously relieved to be around simple, sane human beings, again.

The diner was long, shabby and nicely cozy with a few folksy patrons and a cook-slash-waiter in a white chef's hat. It was all *so* clichéd, there was even a slice of apple pie sitting on a pie tray screaming, *I do a great à la mode with coffee. Eat me!*

Okay, let's test out your hypothesis, little piece of pie, thought my guy as he removed his gloves and –

"You that fool friend of Mr. Bentley's, come up here?" sliced through the air in a fingernails-on-a-chalkboard screech.

All three of us jumped around to see a five-foot gnome dressed in a massive green parka, thick gloves and a muffler, atop two spindly legs that were wrapped in tan ski-pants that then vanished into a pair of the biggest snow boots ever seen. Seriously, it gave the impression of an olive about to go in a martini, because all you could see of the person inside were two beady eyes that could easily be a hundred years old.

My guy nodded and asked, "Are you Mr. Serff?"

"Do I *look* like Mr. Serff?" the voice snapped.

Well, yeah, in that get-up.

The olive just kept on with, "He's in Boston. I'm the Missus. An' you're late."

"Uh, sorry, we got turned around. It ... it's nice to meet

you. I'm Daniel Bettancourt."

I couldn't resist adding, "Sancho Panza to the great and glorious Ace Shostakovich!" To which Daniel rolled his eyes, not in the snotty way Tad does but like he just plain can't believe I said that.

The old bat noticed said rolling of eyes and glared at him, thinking he meant her, then snapped "An' who else might ya be? Up here, this time of year at this time of night? All the best skiin's to the North. C'mon, let's get this done with." And she headed out, muttering, "Little fool."

Daniel followed her. "So ... I take it Tad explained ...?"

"Tad?" she snapped, all but kicking open the door. "That what he goes by, now? I knew him when he was just *Master Theodore James Bentley, the Third*, an' made me use every fool bit of that fool name."

Wow, looked like he'd always been a dick.

"An' yes, he did call," she snarled. "Couple hours ago. Asked ... no, *told* me to get the place ready for ya. Got pretty high-handed with it, too, like I's his employee. Like his poppa don't treat me all right and proper. Like I'm a fool. I'd of told him where he could go, but ya were already comin' an' t'ain't my way to let people die from exposure. Not 'round my parcel of the woods, anyhow. T'ain't polite."

And I swear, she really did say *t'ain't*. Twice!

We were back out to the snow before she even seemed to notice Paul and snorted, "You the driver?" The kid's eyes got bigger, if that was possible, and he nodded.

Daniel jumped and said, "Sorry, this is ..."

She cut him off with a wave of her hand and focused on the kid. "You're set up at Bradleyville Inn, down the end of the street. Tell 'em Wendy sent ya."

"I didn't bring any clothes or stuff," Paul said.

"They got a laundry."

"I don't have any money."

The gnome glared at my guy. "Give the kid a couple bills."

"Me?!" Daniel yelped.

"He brought ya up, didn't he?"

Dan-O snarled then forced himself to pull a twenty out of his wallet. "Charge everything you can to the hotel bill," he said as he slapped it in the kid's hand. "If there's any cash outlay, I'll take it out of Tad's hide."

Yeah, just try and get it back from Mr. Moneybags. Half the reason he's got such a nice bank balance is he never spends any of his own.

"Now get your things," Mrs. Serff snapped, cutting my thoughts off, "an' toss 'em in the back, here." Then she climbed into a four-by-four with this massive snowplow of a front bumper that would've been the perfect car-crusher at a monster truck rally. Seriously, it even had fold-out steps going up to the sideboards, so the old bat could reach the cab.

"Paul, will you be okay here?" Daniel asked, eyeing the truck with what did not amount to certainty.

"I'm not staying the night," he snapped as he opened the Caddie's door.

"Ya are if ya don't want to get snowbound halfway back t' th' city!" snapped the old bat as she settled in behind the truck's wheel. "They're expectin' four feet, and our snow cat ain't goin' looking for ya. Now let's get goin'. It's cold!"

Daniel reluctantly pulled his satchel and bag of groceries from the SUV and climbed aboard as Paul huffed and looked around and tossed out a few hesitant *dammits*, and finally aimed the Caddie up the street, headed for the inn.

Well, away we went in the other direction, tires spitting snow with abandon. And I have to say – while I may've thought my guy was getting into something out of control before, now I knew it for a fact.

We were doomed.

Goin' Serffin'

We roared along a dirty white road that vanished into darkness beyond the thirty-foot range of the headlights, fog lamps and maybe half-dozen mean-beams fixed on a bar over the cab. Sitting on a child's booster seat so she could see over the steering wheel, Mrs. Serff drove like a bat out of hell as Daniel jiggled and jostled about and wondered how the hell she reached the gas pedal and clutch. Twice, she slammed the plow down when we approached a drift built up across the road, ignored the brakes and sliced right through it. Fortunately, my guy'd buckled himself in, after a lot of effort. My guess was the belt hadn't been used since the truck was new, twenty-thirty-forty years ago), and he had a death grip on his satchel.

The road curled and curved and dipped and rose and crossed frozen creeks and skimmed next to hedges grown to be fences, all now topped with inches and inches of snow, before it disappeared the moment we curled through a thick glen of trees. And that is when we finally skidded to a halt in front of this L-shaped, Alpine-style, two-story cabin. Its roof was peaked with snow and a pair of windows flanking the entrance from floor to ceiling were so opaque, they seemed more like caves leading to the River Styx. Referencing Greek mythology, here; Google it, spoken in my condescending Tad-manner.

"All righty, then," Mrs. Serff snorted as she pulled the hand brake and jumped out. She turned on a flashlight that was as big as she was and headed straight for the front door, cutting through white powder that was up to her butt as if she was an ice-breaker.

Daniel climbed down and glanced around, taken in by the gentle hints of beauty from the countryside and the idea of black, snow-laden evergreens pointing straight up to the darker-than-dark sky. The barest suggestion of moonlight filtered between small breaks in the thick clouds, offering just enough illumination to reveal two similar cabins a bit farther down a gentle slope that led to a frozen lake. The ice on it tried really hard to gleam in the vague light before it was covered over completely by the white stuff, but no go. All three cabins were dark and silent while the forest rustled and groaned from quick bursts of wind.

"Ace," he whispered, his imagination filling in details the shadows hid, "where do I know this place from?"

"One of your nightmares?" I snapped, not at all happy we were here.

"Yeah, maybe," he murmured, vaguely.

And I kicked myself. He'd gone through a nasty patch of those after having his mom committed, and never mind it'd made his life one hell of a lot saner; he still felt guilty over it.

"Well, come on!" snapped Mrs. Serff from the front porch, one of those long, inviting types that would be perfect on a summer's evening. "Ain't no need to freeze to death. Not yet, no-how."

Daniel nodded and plowed along the trail the old bat'd already left. It was still not easy, and by the time he hit the first step, his shoes and pants legs were soaking wet and his lungs and nose hurt from the icy air he was gasping in.

She pulled a key from her pocket and unlocked the main door then pushed it open with a slow, vicious creak that would've sounded just right in a 1930s horror film. She glared at it as she entered.

"I tol' Homer t' WD-40 that," she snipped, her voice an echo in the darkness. "That kind of nonsense sends a signal to transients the place could-might provide shelter, like a coyote callin'. That brings down property values. Look what happened in Hollywood! California, not Florida. They litter the place an' fill abandoned buildings. Same for Venice. California, not Italy. Saw that when I was there ten years back. Ain't no transients in Italy. Saw that when I was *there*. Just Italians all over, 'less you consider Albanians an' Bosnians what come across the Adriatic on boats, twenty years ago, like them Cubans and Haitians did here, thirty years back. Or was it forty? Hmph, they count as immigrants, or can you call them transients, too?"

And I do not think she drew a breath during that jumble of words. All I could say was, "Ya wanna talk about jabberin'?"

"Point out the obvious," my guy muttered back – then slipped on some ice right by the door jam and skidded in after her. He managed to keep his balance and a grip on everything, but only barely.

The old bat just glared at him as he straightened up and shoved the door closed with his butt; it didn't dare be anything but silent while she was watching. By this point she was well into the place and shining her flashlight all over as she said, "So here we be, Mr. Bettancourt, though why we be here's pure foolishness, if ya ask me. Dead of winter in a summer place. Power all off. Nobody 'round for miles and miles. I can't figure it. Course, if I could, I'd be rich as a fool."

She sure wanted to make sure we got her point, for sure.

"I don't ski," Daniel said, still huffing from the exertion of not crashing to the floor.

"Anymore," I sniffed, looking the place over.

"Good fer you," snapped Mrs. Serff as she headed for a fireplace. "Less of a crack at breakin' your back. I'll start a fire. Cozy up the place."

"Dream about it," I said, "unless you're torchin' the joint."

That's when Daniel finally got a look around, and he near groaned. Inside was as dark and silent and cavernous as it'd seemed, outside, with wood beams lifting the vaulted ceiling up so high it vanished into the shadows. Steps led down from the entry deck to an open living space that focused on this massive flagstone fireplace that had a flagstone ledge around the hearth and some dusty frames and knick-knacks propped atop a flagstone mantelpiece. Talk about consistent. A couple couches flanked it, both protected by dustsheets, and a long dining table sat by a set of French doors. Sheets also covered it and the eight chairs with it. The last of the furniture was a quiet lava lamp on an end table, uncovered and still.

"I haven't seen one of those since we lived in Chicago," he murmured. During mom's second marriage to a broker in the Mart. My guy'd loved watching the slow globs of color drift up and down like happy little aliens trapped in a snow globe and had mentioned that to her. And the response he got was, "You read too much science fiction. Try this." And she'd handed him a Jackie Collins novel.

I smirked. "I think she was hoping you'd get off on the sex

scenes."

"Didn't work," Daniel whispered, almost chuckling.

A wide wooden staircase angled up behind the chimney to a bridge-like landing that looked out over the main room. It led to a door by a hallway. Behind the landing, the tall windows that flanked the entrance were hidden by thick drapes cascading to the floor. The basic feeling was weirdly gothic, despite the architecture being more Frank Lloyd Wright than Wilkie Collins.

Yeah. Perfect place to write, Tad.

"Any kindlin'?" Mrs. Serff muttered as she pulled the hood back on her parka. Man, she really was close to a hundred years old. She squatted by the hearth, found an old magazine and tore out several sheets to crumble up. After tossing them under the grate, she took a couple of logs from a pile and blew clouds of dust off them. It glittered as it drifted down, thanks to the flashlight's beam, reminding my guy of the fairy dust from *Peter Pan*.

"Dan-O, could you get any more clichéd?" I smirked.

"Nope," he whispered as he headed for the table.

Mrs. Serf all but crawled into the chimney to see if the flue was open, then came out with perfect smudges of soot on her cheek and nose. She cast a furtive glance back at my guy and saw he was setting his things on the table, so she innocently pulled out a lighter. And a cigarette. She set a page of the magazine ablaze then lit up the cancer-stick before putting flame to the kindling. She aimed her smoke at the fire, in ecstasy, thinking she'd put one over on us.

She couldn't have been more wrong. My guy has this way of observing people so they never know they're being watched, and he'd seen it all in the reflection of the glass in the French doors. He'd also noted they opened onto a deck, and what view he could see was magnificent. As for Mrs. Serff's sneakiness, he just shook his head. He didn't care about smokers; he'd been one himself till Tad went into uber-whine-mode with, "I always smell it on you." So he quit. Cold turkey! Just another offering to His-Grandificence in hopes he'd make his day. It's enough to make a fictional character give up on their human contact, despite the fact that the human contact still let that ... oh, shall we say, *fictional* character have a smoke or two, himself, in his books. Not like they did in the Forties, where every damn conversation was over a Lucky Strike. Nor was he so hooked he couldn't drop it like Daniel had. Honest. He just kept getting written up as using a smoke to think. Sort of like my guy was doing it, himself, by proxy.

So Daniel shrugged it off, pulled his parka tighter and tried a light switch. Nothing. He pulled out his cell phone. No bars.

"Well," I said, "Tad wanted you isolated."

"No shit," Daniel sighed, shaking his head. "He was supposed to have the power on by the time I got here."

Mrs. Serff huffed at him, hiding the cigarette. "On a Friday night? In that snow? Only a fool'd think that'd happen."

I cast Daniel a near smirk. I was getting more and more right about this, though I still couldn't figure out the why and wherefore. Just like one of my mysteries.

Hmm, something to file away for later use. *The Case of the Creeping Creeps*? Nah, have a color in it. *Crimson Creeps*?

"You should've just said you'd use this place then holed up in a hotel," I snorted as Daniel opened a door by the table. It revealed steps leading down to a deep black basement. "More time to work; room service at your fingertips; no stress."

"How would we have blown off Paul?" he asked.

"Threaten to blow him and tell. He'd run like a rabbit."

Daniel just sighed, his silence pointing out the obvious: that we'd really been backed into a corner by having that kid along. And I know, I know, Daniel'd asked for a driver, but still I had to wonder, *How does it make sense to drive a hundred miles to work in a dump that has more drafts than a Hollywood screenplay?*

"At least it has character," he said.

"Of the mean-assed kind," I snapped. "Hey, I like that line; write it down."

"Already used it."

"When?"

"*The Tangerine Forty-two D-Cup Madam.*"

Shit, he was right. Only on that occasion I was referring to what was, seriously, a huge bra that actually did hold forty-two tangerines and was the final clue in the kidnapping of a Macaw worth eight hundred thousand dollars, thanks to the two flawless diamonds it'd swallowed while eating the slice of – ready for it?

Tangerine that they'd been hidden in!

"At least I'm quotin' myself, this time."

"Good," he said, then did a fake sniffing around, hiding a smile. Deep down the nicotine urge was tickling, and he wanted no temptation tossed his way. "Do you smell cigarette smoke?"

Mrs. Serff quickly tossed the last of the cigarette into the fire and rose with a huff. "Who're you talkin' to?"

That's when the logs popped and crackled to life.

Daniel smiled at the sudden noise, remembering that second husband's home on Christmas mornings, when the man would turn on the lava lamp, start a fire up, and they'd roast marshmallows, over and over. And things had been really nice for a few years.

"Nobody," he whispered in answer to Mrs. Serff.

"Tell that to a hundred-thousand readers," I chuckled. "Followers on your blog and stuff."

The old bat huffed then tossed another log on the blaze. Daniel joined her to warm himself.

"Oh, that does feel good." But there was something in the back of his brain suggesting some more serious déjà vu was going on. He shook it off by looking around. "Water heater?"

"In the basement an' it's 'lectric, an' Homer keeps it empty in th' winter."

Daniel noticed a rotary-style phone in a nook by the hearth, so he tried it. A happy little dial tone greeted him, to his relief.

"Would you fill it, Mrs. Serff? I'm calling Tad."

"That's a fool thing t' do," she snarled. "It'll freeze over."

"We'll have power, or we're out of here," he said as he dialed. "My laptop's battery's on half-life." Meaning the deal would be off since Tad hadn't done his part. Cool. Maybe this'd turn out all right.

The old bat snorted and stomped down into the basement. "Fool thing t' do. Just have t' empty it. But see what happens when you do a body a favor? Well you can be sure, I'll never do nothin' for nobody never, again." Then she shot back at my guy, "An' I'll bring up some lanterns. No way in hell're you keepin' this. It's worth forty dollars!" And she shook the flashlight at him just before she vanished into the darkness with it.

"Y'know, there's a word for broads like you," I sighed.

"Yeah, *broad*," Daniel said, absently, as the phone finally began to ring. "From *The Dr. Pepper Tryst and Tristan*."

"Damn good case," I said, strutting. Oh, that was our third book, about a series of murders meant to start up a drug war. Combining it with *...Madam* should've worked since Tristan, this gay friend of Carmen's who got caught up in those murders, was in both books and knew the crazy old bat. But the Cheeto-eater'd made him this faggoty asshole in the scripts who's on the wrong side of the law and ... and y'know, I'd just about decided we really did need to kill that fucking laptop potato for no more reason than to spare the world another line like, *Don't bitch at me, you bitch*, aimed at Carmen by the gayer-than-fuck bad guy. I should pop back into the ether and ask the fates to go rattle the fucker's pterodactyl-sized brain.

That's when I realized Daniel was looking closer at one of the framed items on the mantelpiece. He rested the phone in the nook of his neck and picked it up to wipe off the dust, and it turned out to be a photo of Tad in college. Damn, he looked even better back then, if that was possible. My guy gazed at it, stunned, then let his eyes wander about to watch the blaze send dancing shadows across the room.

Not good; I could feel a blue mood building in him, which always popped up whenever he let himself realize how perfect Tad was, looks-wise, anyway. Which fed into how imperfect he was in his own mind, basically. Which segued into him beginning to see he'd jumped feet first into God knows what, and now uncertainty was threatening to take complete control.

So I strutted over to say, "Y'know, you could boil water for coffee on that fire. If this joint's got a kettle."

"Hm?" Daniel looked at me with this little-boy-lost look that could make even the ice in Tad's veins melt, then he nodded. "Oh. Yeah. Hot, uh, toddy does sound good, right now. I brought tea. Packets of lemon. Honey. You think there's a wet bar? Maybe some bourbon or Irish whiskey here?" *Any*-thing alcoholic.

I shrugged and started looking around. Normally I can sniff out a bottle of booze in no time, but nothing was looking promising. Then the phone stopped ringing, and we heard Tad's I'm-getting-into-a-panic-so-you-don't-want-to-see-me-like-this voice screaming, "No, match-cut A and D, not C!" before he snarled into the phone, "What?"

The word blasted into Daniel's ear, and he almost dropped the phone but caught it just in time and gasped out, "I'm here."

"Shit, Danny, you took long enough."

"It's snowing. Your directions were wrong. And power's still off."

"Oh, shit." Tad yelled away from the phone, "Sandy, call Vince at Con-Ed!" then growled into it, "How bad's the snow?"

"They expect four feet, but Mrs. Serff has a killer plow."

"To put it mildly," I snorted.

"Will you be able to get back to town?" Tad asked.

Daniel shrugged, as if the twerp could see him. "It's supposed to stop by morning. Just in case, she mentioned a guy in town has a snow cat. And if Bradleyville Inn's got WiFi, I can e-mail them to you."

"You don't have an Air Card?"

"I never needed one."

"Shit, Danny. Okay, but I must have them by ten am, Monday, ready to print. My meeting with Grissom's at noon."

"You will."

Tad's voice took on that big-brother tone, again, that made me want to throttle the son-of-a-bitch. "I mean it, buddy, there is no extension on this deal, so if you're not one hundred and ten percent sure you can do it, tell me now. I don't want to be calling HBO at ten-oh-five with some lame-assed excuse."

Daniel took in a deep breath. One time, just once, he'd asked for an extension on his deadline for a book, and Gregory had said fine. But Tad had the memory of an elephant, and such a nice way of using past moments to cut you down without seeming to mean to. All my guy could say was, "No question in my mind."

But I could feel the uncertainty still building in him, so I added, "We'll make it, Dan-O. I promise."

Tad chuckled. "You really are saving my life, here. And freezing that cute little butt off to do it. So if this does work out, it's two weeks in Bermuda. How's that?"

Oh, that little snake. Making promises my guy needed to hear so he'd stay focused on the job.

"I really do miss you, Danny. Miss having my own private schizo-boy." He chuckled, and I had to roll my eyes. I pretty much suspected half of Tad's attraction to my guy was the spice this supposed schizophrenia added to the relationship. In fact, things started going bad once Daniel'd started on Prozac and become more even-keeled. Because my guy turned out only to be depressed, not deep into a brain melt. Just because nobody else can see or hear me doesn't mean that I'm merely a figment of his split personality; I'm as real as unreal can be, dammit.

Then it hit me – Daniel was off Prozac. Could that be the reason Tad's come sniffing around, again? Add back the spice?

Daniel just nodded. "Let's ... see how it goes."

"It goes how Tad wants it to," I muttered, and BAM, the lights came on! Daniel jumped. I nodded. "See? See?!"

"Lights're on, Tad."

"Sandy, never mind!" he bellowed away from the phone.

"I better get started," Daniel said, softly. "Oh, I'm calling on your land line; there's no cell phone-age up here."

"What? Shit, I don't have that number."

Daniel noticed a number on the phone's rotary dial. "It's Jackson-five-two-one-nine-two."

"Jackson?"

"Like my grandmother's phone," he said, smiling tenderly. "So this'd be five-five. They used names for prefixes before they went all numbers."

"Now we're numbered before we're named," I said.

"Got it," said Tad. "Shit, Danny, I'm beginning to think you're priceless."

Naw, sometimes my guy can be had for just the promise of a kiss and a roll in the ...

Oh, shit.

Oh, man, I shouldn't have thought that.

Daniel, buddy, hey, ignore what I said and – aw, shit; too late. Now he's chasing his tail down memory lane, right back to this Halloween party, three years ago, where he was done up as *New-Spock* and feeling just as anti-social while standing on Gregory's balcony overlooking Central Park, inhaling the fourth of a dozen cigarettes, downing his third-too-many beer and overindulging in a nice full plate of the I'm-way-too-serious-for-you dip and chips. Excuse me, olive-artichoke-brie-pâté and rosemary-rusk wheat toast brushed with light extra-virgin olive oil. Seriously! Still, it was different from the Mac & Cheese or peanut butter and jelly he had to eat, every other night.

Anyway, he was off in a corner of the patio having a quiet discussion with me about the final polish on *The Dr. Pepper Tryst and Tristan* before he sent it in to be laid out when what should stroll up but this tall, golden warrior in Spartan garb, looking as airbrushed and perfectly buffed as all those doomed soldiers in that disgustingly anti-gay – hell, anti-anything-but-perfect-white-butch-heterosexual-male movie based on that stupid anti-anything-but-perfect-white-butch-heterosexual-male comic book ... excuse me, *graphic novel* ... from a few years back. Of course, Daniel noticed he was coming, and also noticed every queer and straight female eye in the joint was locked on what was probably the world's most amazing ass wrapped in a tight leather loincloth.

Daniel figured he'd just get smiled at and brushed off if he said anything, so he said nothing, but then Sir-Perfect stopped beside him, leaned against the railing and stuck out a hand.

"Hello, I'm Theodore J. Bentley, the Third."

Daniel had to make himself remember that when a hand is offered, it's only polite to shake it. So he did and somehow managed to reply, "Daniel."

"Bettancourt. The writer, right?" And he grinned as if he'd said something truly clever.

Of course, Daniel chuckled to let him think he had, and then nodded. "There's those who wouldn't agree with you."

"No, I've read your work. They're idiots."

"On that, I'd agree." And Daniel offered him a real smile.

"It's odd, but I thought mystery writers were supposed to be geeky men trying to prove they have a dick or pissed-off women wishing they could cut their husbands' dick off. You fit neither profile."

"Thanks. I think."

"It's a compliment," he nodded. "And an honest appraisal."

"Wow," Daniel almost gasped out. "Uh, I ... I can't tell if you're being blunt or flirtatious."

"I don't flirt. When you look like me, you don't have to."

"Now you're being arrogant."

Tad smiled. "Gregory warned me you're the honest type."

"Not always," Daniel all but whispered out.

Tad shrugged. "No, you're right. But it's just a tool, to let people know they can't use me."

Okay, so the guy told the truth about that. So what?

Daniel shifted to take in how perfect everything about Tad was. "Are you saying you've been used?"

"People tried. I wanted to act, but there're plenty of idiots out there who think men like me haven't brains enough to know when they're being manipulated into bed. Even by friends and family. And all for the promise of jack shit."

"That's too bad. And too typical."

"I agree. The problem is no one would give me a chance, otherwise, not even on soaps. Apparently, I'm not a good actor, so I don't bother, anymore. I take it you were used, as well?"

Daniel shook his head. "People don't get that close to me." Which was bullshit; he had been. Big time.

"Why's that?"

Daniel cast him a wicked little grin. "I'm trouble."

Tad laughed. "You don't look like the type."

"Oh, no, check with Gregory. He'll give you the advance word. Shit always happens around me. You know that plane that ditched in the Hudson?" Tad gave a wary nod. "My fault. I was taking pictures with a flash and blinded the lead goose, and he led his gaggle straight into the engines."

Tad gave a burst of laughter. "You had me going, there."

"I'm serious," Daniel said, letting a twinkle in his eye hint that he really wasn't. "I'm doppelganger to Gladstone Gander." See where I get my alliteration? "If you touch me, all hell breaks loose." And he put that last bit out there like a challenge.

"What's a Gladstone?"

"Disney cartoon character."

Tad's perfect grin widened with a chuckle and he said, "Vous êtes trop drole."

Meaning, *you're real funny*, in basic French. Well, don't bother trying to show off, buster; my guy knows French and Spanish, both, with a dash of Deutsche, just for the hell of it.

Then Tad leaned in closer to rub a thumb up and down the nape of Daniel's neck. "Don't see any hell, yet."

My guy gulped, feeling explosions in every part of his body from being touched by this Mega-god of masculine beauty. "It, uh, it's a cumulative effect," he said. "Give it time."

"I have a better idea," Tad whispered. "Let's pretend we're in Vegas." Which made absolutely no sense, but then he leaned in and kissed Daniel, and any need for explanation dropped forty floors to the pavement.

All right, as should be obvious by now, I do not like Tad. Haven't from the second he sauntered up, shooting off sex appeal like it's his original concept. I figured he had forty-seven secret reasons for going after my guy like he did, and I still think so, but since I'm not real I can't be jealous, can I? What I can be is honest in saying that for all his beauty, Sir-Great-and-Glorious could not kiss worth crap. He rammed his mouth against Daniel's as if he was trying to bite into it and shoved his tongue inside as if trying to gobble my guy's tonsils off the back of his throat. And I hope that sounds disgusting enough. Not because it's man-on-man but because it's just plain rough and clumsy and a tad painful. Pun intended.

How-*ever*, Daniel didn't give a shit. He let the oral assault take him over and make him an instant horn-doggie. Then when Tad whispered, "And that's just a down payment," that led them straight to Daniel's bed, in Queens, where my guy showed the dick exactly how a dick should be dealt with. Which had stunned Tad so much, he'd actually stayed till the next morning. And let Daniel fix him brunch. And talked!

About what? We can get into that later; what mattered was how Tad answered when Daniel finally had the nerve to ask him why he'd come up to him.

"Your look," Tad whispered, still high on all the times he'd ... oh, let's just say, *found nirvana*. They were lying side by side on the bed, Tad on his back, my guy on his side tracing his fingers over the man's torso. "I've always liked men who're tight and trim, with a bit of hair on them."

Daniel chuckled. "*You* fucked *me* for *my* body?"

He'd looked at Daniel and given him a brutally honest look of appreciation as he said, "No. It's your eyes. They stopped me cold. So innocent and lost. Like a little kitten." Then a grin slashed across his face as he rolled on top my guy. "Who knew you were such a wildcat in bed?"

They'd laughed and tussled and kissed and hugged and got back to doing the mutual satisfaction thing, and things were damn near perfect for nearly two years. Daniel popped out *The Tangerine Forty-two D-cup Madam*, *The Cadillac Criminal Mind* and got way into *The Dirty Baker's Dozen, Plus Two*, so I kept my distrust on mute. And that was hard, believe me.

Of course, all of this flashed through my guy's mind in the space of a nano-second after Tad's last comment, so all he did was sigh and say, "Later, Tad," and hang up the phone. And he didn't move, his eyes focused on Tad's photo, his mind slipping into this total no-think zone he uses as his safe place.

And I hate it when he does that! Because then I can't connect with him, and I got no idea what the hell's going on in the back of his freaky little brain, and it makes me nervous. So I jumped in with, "I think he's up to somethin', Dan-O. I'm serious! Tad's tryin' to screw you up on this deal. It don't make sense, none of this does." And he knew it as well as me.

That helped him shake off his mood and say, "Ace, I ... we don't have time for paranoia. I made the deal, so I have to live up to it and ..."

"Who in blazes're you talkin' to?!" stabbed at us both!

We jumped around to find Mrs. Serff at the basement door, a lantern in hand. Damn, even I'd forgotten about the old bat.

"Oh, stop that foolishness," she snarled as she stormed in. "It's just me. And it's supposed t' be just you up here, too."

"It ... it is," said Daniel. "Me and me alone."

"Except for me," I smirked.

"Don't sound like it," she said as she set the lantern by the hearth. Then she started yanking sheets off the furniture in a flurry of dust particles.

"I ... I was just working something out in my head," Daniel said, putting the photo back.

"Uh-huh. Heater's fillin'. Water'll be hot in an hour."

Daniel moaned. "I won't get started till nearly eleven."

"You're lucky the pipes ain't froze! But that's what ya get for comin' so damn late. Drivin' in that storm. Night all 'round ya. Some people're just nuttier 'n squirrel shit."

Okay, maybe I needed to re-evaluate my attitude about her because she was coming up with some kick-ass comments. So I nudged my guy, and he nodded and quickly wrote it down.

"Right," he said. "If there's a stove, I could make coffee." He went to the table and grabbed the bag of groceries.

Mrs. Serff tossed sheets in a closet as she said, "'Course there is, an' it's 'lectric."

"Okay. Where?" he asked, wandering back to the hearth to

set the bag down.

"The kitchen," she said, "is to the left. Like it's always been. Didn't 'Tad' tell you nothin' 'bout nothin'?"

Daniel pulled out a jar of *Nescafe* and closed his eyes, fighting his temper. The old bat was finally getting to him. "No. He didn't."

She was about to close the closet door when she stopped and cheerfully said, "Y'know, brandy might be better."

Daniel sighed and looked at her. "Mrs. Serff, right now I would kiss you for some brandy." Shit, *any*-thing alcoholic.

She glared at him. "Don't let my Homer hear you say that; he'll beat you t' a pulp. And don't you think just 'cause he's eighty an' got a wooden leg, he can't."

Daniel set the jar of instant down, so he could rub his neck and head and face and fight the headache he felt coming on – until she pulled a squat, clear bottle of mahogany-red liqueur from the closet. Which made him jolt the moment he saw it. Because it was *Dvin Brandy*. His grandmother's favorite after-dinner drink.

"Since Churchill loved it," she'd said, and she'd idolized the man. In homage to her, he'd used it in all of his books.

"Where'd that come from?" he asked, shaken.

"Here," the old bat snapped.

"Did ... did you bring it?"

"Hell, no! I don't drink." Then she smiled. "Much. Cups're in the kitchen, too. First cupboard t' the right."

Stunned, Daniel hesitated then forced himself to return to the table, grab his satchel and wander up the steps to a door directly across from the entrance. I stayed with him, because he was beginning to chase that deja-vu tail, again, and I wanted to stop him before he got dizzy.

Through the door sat a huge, dusty kitchen that was state of the art – forty years ago. A massive island with a stove sat in the middle of the room, pots and pans and utensils hanging above it. A sink was across from it, under a window, and the other side had a refrigerator and freezer, with miles of counter space and plugs enough for every electronic appliance you could ever want. Only thing missing was bottles of wine in the floor-to-ceiling wine rack, right next to a very empty wet bar, dammit.

He didn't bother to turn on a light, now that the moon was

sending some vague beams in through that window; no drapes on this one. He just set his satchel on a counter and grabbed a pot from above the stove and opened the cold tap, which grumbled like a thousand year-old man before spitting out rusty water. He let it run for a minute to clear it then put his hand under it so the sharp cold could bite into his skin.

That slapped his mind around to give me my *in*. "Too bad Carmen's not here. She loves Brandy Alexanders."

"That ... that was just for ...*Tristan*," he murmured. "She went straight cognac in *Cadillac*..." Then he focused on filling the pot.

"Prob'ly why she talks drunk, half the time." And she did, seriously, but don't tell her I said that.

He set the pot on the stove and, after trying three knobs, got it to heating. By this point, confusion was settling in, because he was back to wondering why the lodge looked so damn familiar. And how could a bottle of *Dvin*, which was damn impossible to find anymore, have shown up here, of all places?

"It's just a coincidence, Dan-O," I said, taking off my trench coat before I hopped onto the counter by the sink. "Detective rule number three-eleven – the obvious can mean nothing. C'mon, this is Tad's dad's place. I bet the old guy just decided to try it out thanks to your books, and he does have the resources to bring a bottle in from Russia. By courier, if he wants."

"Then why. Is it in a closet. Instead of the bar?"

"Nothin's in the bar, buddy! So why come clear in here to get a sip when you can keep it closer?"

"That ... just doesn't make sense."

"Neither does Nana drinkin' it, 'cause she was Norwegian, not British. And why'd they stop makin' it? And why'd they start, again? You can drive yourself nuts with *why*."

"But this house ..."

"C'mon, it's got the same floor-plan as thousands of other places. It's just remindin' you of one you been in, is all."

"Yeah ... yeah, right," he said, closing his eyes and nodding as he slowly regained control. "Oh, man. Doesn't take much to freak me out, these days, does it?"

"Dan-O, this is a pretty intense situation. I just wish I could offer more than creative support."

"I know," he sighed. "It's just ... Ace, I dunno, I'm just so tired. So fucking tired of working non-stop. Of living on nothing, day after day after day. Sometimes I even feel like I'm vanishing into my work with no anchor left in reality. Shit, I'm closing in on thirty, and what do I have to show for it?"

"Six books, one movie, eight crappy scripts."

"And a partridge in a pear tree," he chuckled as he turned to look at me ...

And this OLD MAN GLARED AT HIM THROUGH THE WINDOW!

The guy had a beard that flew in all directions and wild hair under a white knit cap that made him look like a chrome-dome Santa out to slaughter both naughty and nice.

Daniel yelped and backed out of the kitchen. I rolled my eyes and followed him to the door.

Mrs. Serff was tossing the last sheets into the closet as she glared around the door and snapped, "Now what?"

Daniel nearly stumbled down those stupid little steps. "There's somebody outside!"

She snorted, "Oh, just the hermit."

We both popped off with, "Hermit!?"

"As in *Herman's*?" I added. Musical group; Google it.

"That's what I said. Don't ya listen? When Homer's away, he follows me 'round."

"How?" my guy asked. "Does he have a snowplow, too?"

"Prob'ly hangs on a rope and skis behind hers," I said. And wasn't that an interesting image?

"Don't be silly," she snapped then headed for the kitchen, the coffee and brandy in hand. "Knows all the shortcuts, is all. Now you listen to me, young man, you don't leave coffee on the hearth. The beans're baked just fine, an' more roastin' does 'em no damn good. Trust me. Used to make my own coffee from them imported beans till they got so damn expensive, an' if you get 'em hot 'fore grindin' them, kills the flavor. No, instant coffee oughta be kept away from heat. Lasts longer an' adds to that aromatic smell." Then her voice disappeared with her through the kitchen door. Again, without drawing breath.

Daniel looked at me as he tailed her back into the kitchen, wondering, "Do I go on like that, when I jabber?"

"Dan-O," I said as I followed him in, "compared to her, you're mute."

Just inside the door, she grabbed two funky-looking cups from the cupboard and rinsed them out. "Pick your choice," she snipped.

They were from a Momma and Pappa Bear set. What? No Baby Bear? That is completely incorrect! How'll we know when it's just right?

Daniel chose the Mama Bear mug and noticed the water was boiling, already, the steam dancing up to drag his mind back to drifting, again. So I nudged him and said, "Laptop."

He nodded and pulled it out of the satchel along with the AC adaptor/recharger.

To keep his mind even busier I asked, "What if you add this to the story?"

"This?" he muttered, absently, plugging everything in.

"Isolated cabin," I said. "Snow storm. Hermit."

He looked at me, confused. "Story's set in LA, and we don't have time to change it or …"

"What is?" the old bat snarled.

Daniel looked at her. "Huh? Oh, the scripts I'm writing, uh, rewriting are set in Los Angeles."

She gave Daniel a glare that would've knocked a buffalo on its tail. "Scripts? You come up here to write?" Daniel sort-of smiled and nodded. She kept on with, "This time of night?! What kind of fool notion is that!?"

"Don't look at me," I muttered, looking at the ceiling.

"Wouldn't have hurt you one bit to stay in Bradleyville till mornin'."

"Yeah, have a beer at the inn," I snickered. "Freak Paul out by demonstrating how to milk a frozen heifer."

Daniel fought back a chuckle, pulled out his note pad and wrote in it.

Mrs. Serff eyed him. "You laughin' at me, young man?"

"No, ma'am. Never." And he said it in such a casual manner, it doused her pissy-fiery attitude. She huffed and turned back to the coffee as he finished writing and kept on with, "I just had a funny thought and had to write it down so I'd remember … it …"

And his voice trailed off as he watched her dump spoon-load after spoon-load of instant in both mugs. Seriously, I was getting a caffeine rush just watching her.

"These people and their money," she muttered, "think the whole world's here for their pleasure."

At that, I had to ask, "It ain't?"

"I'm sorry, Mrs. Serff," Daniel said. "I didn't realize this was such a ... an inconvenience."

"Inconvenience?" Mrs. Serff snapped. "Gettin' me out of a warm house in the dead of night to take care of somethin' that don't need doin' till the mornin', that's nothin' more than an *inconvenience* to you?"

"Oh, back away from the broad, Dan-O," I murmured. "Sometimes niceness just adds to the trouble."

She kept on with, "You gonna tell me you didn't get half froze just walkin' between the truck an' the door?!"

"Oh, yes," my guy said. "I did. A bit."

"Got a storm blowin' through an' the weather service says it'll get down to zero, but they're as big a fool as anybody, so it'll get colder, you can bet on it."

"You're right, Mrs. Serff."

What could I do but sigh and say, "And while we're at it let's apologize for the snow. Damned indecent of it to fall in February! *What* was it thinking?"

The old bat looked out the window. "Clouds're breakin'. Gonna get nastier cold 'fore I'm to home."

Daniel almost said something, but kept quiet.

She huffed and muttered then turned her glare back to him. "You really a writer?"

Daniel chuckled in that way he's got, like it's a joke on him. "Well, I do have six books out, and my second one was made into a cable movie. *High-Heeled Moccasins*?"

"Never saw it," she said, handing him his cup. "Sounds trashy." She tried her own, then added more brandy.

He took a sip of the coffee, and his eyes nearly curled back from the strength of it. "It was," he choked out.

Hey! "Don't diss my book, buddy!"

"Movie," Daniel gasped.

"Oh." Right. That was.

"Water too hot?" Mrs. Serff asked.

My guy politely nodded then was able to croak, "They, uh,

they're murder-suspense-mysteries involving Ace and his sexy-secretary, Carmen O'Brien, in all sorts of adventures as they ... oh ... *enjoy* each other's company."

Oh, uh, did I not mention the part where Carmen and I practice the *Joy of Sex*? All over the place? In some very weird ways. Who'd have thought a guy into guys would know so much about guys into girls and girls into guys and, as it turns out, girls into guys into guys and ... uh ... well, you get what I mean, right?

"Screwin' around, huh?" the old bat snorted, cutting off my own tail-chasing, and I'd swear I caught a twinkle in her eye as she said it. "Sure, nothin' sells like a slut. Warmer by the fire."

She led Daniel back into the main room, leaving the *Dvin* by the sink. I stood by the kitchen door to guard over it.

"Ya just had t' come up here t' do this writin'?" she said.

"We didn't know it was snowing," Daniel said, sheepishly. "And the fact is solitude does help me concentrate."

"Dude," I moaned, "any more solitude, and you'll be a monk."

"You see, as you've seen," he kept on with, "I talk to my characters. And they talk back." Glare pointed at me, here. "That's why I need to be alone. Don't want to get dragged off to a padded room."

"Again," I snapped.

"At least," he said, "I'd like to avoid it till I've finished what I need to do."

"Uh-huh," the old bat said, giving him a once over with her evil eye. "Well, alone's what you'll get an' plenty of it."

Bullshit. I motioned to Daniel and said, "What about ...?"

"That hermit," he nodded.

"Oh, he'll follow me back down the hill," Mrs. Serff snapped, waving him off. Hmph, maybe he does snow-ski behind her. Then she glanced at her watch. "Dang, it's near on ten o'clock. Homer'll be home, soon, so I'd best get goin'. An' he'll be here eight a-m Monday mornin', on the snow cat, like Mr. Bentley wants, t' take you down. An' he won't like it one fool bit more'n I do." She gulped down the rest of her coffee, how, I have no idea, then set the mug on the mantelpiece and headed for the door, pulling her parka back around her like a cocoon.

That's when I had an idea. "Get the key; lock the doors."

"Why?" Daniel asked me.

"It might shut me up about Tad pullin' shit to mess you up."

He scrambled after the old bat. "Uh, Mrs. Serff, Mrs. Serff, just one more thing. Are there any extra keys to this place? Tad doesn't have one."

"He don't 'cause mine's the only one," she snarled, as if it was so obvious only a fool couldn't see it.

"Could I have it?" And he gave her his best puppy-look.

Didn't help. And so what if by this point nothing but her eyes were showing, again? She still was able to shoot out enough of an evil little glare to make us both cringe. "Why?" she snapped.

"Uh ... in case I need to leave for a little bit," he said, "and I ... I want to lock the place up. Keep out transients. You never know; they may have come up from Venice. California."

She huffed, but handed the key over. "Cain't see nobody goin' nowhere in this storm, but here ya be. Now you keep in mind — you lose it an' Homer'll have to change the locks. If he's gotta do that, he'll beat you to a pulp, and just 'cause he's eighty an' got a wooden leg, don't you think he can't."

Dang, I was getting to where I wanted to meet this Homer.

"I'll take good care of it," Daniel promised.

She huffed, again, and opened the door. It CREAKED like a cat whose tail got stepped on, so she turned her glare on it and growled, "Now don't you start." Then she turned her glare on my guy, huffed, "Nuttier 'n squirrel shit," and headed out.

When the door closed behind her, it did not dare be anything but creak-free.

I breathed a massive sigh of relief and proclaimed, "Blessed silence!"

Daniel locked the door and returned to the fire, saying, "Makes you feel better, huh?"

I leaned against the stone mantelpiece and shrugged, "It's the part of you not trustin' Tad that's makin' itself known; my part of you not trustin' him's been there since day one."

"Did it have to be that way?" Daniel sighed. "Couldn't you have given him at least half a chance?"

"Like you'd give a snake a chance to bite you?" I snapped.

"Don't," he whispered. "Just ... don't. Please."

He eyed the framed portrait of Tad, and I could taste the conflict in him. And I just don't get it. I mean, he's like this ... this wary cat that really wants that piece of tuna the nice human is offering but remembers the last time it went for a nibble it got kicked across the room but it's really hungry and the fish smells so good but it knows damn well that if it gets too close it's going to be boot to gut time, again, but it still finds itself getting closer and closer and ... shit.

What really gets me is part of the reason I'm here is to stand between him and that boot, so he won't be sent crashing to a place he never wanted to come back from. Be like the guard dog of his psyche. And even though I'd been working overtime trying to do it, right then I felt like I'd only been half successful, because it was obvious this was headed for a bad experience.

Of course, it didn't help that I crashed the party after dear Mother almost got him committed. Meaning yes, he really has seen the inside of a padded room. If I'd been around, earlier, I really do think I could have used her melodrama to build him a better firewall against the world.

You see, since my guy was the steady one in the family, he was given control of Mom's last divorce settlement, despite being just nineteen. She got a nice monthly allowance, which husband number five figured was cheap since it gave him back his sense of normalcy, but only Daniel could access it to get extra funds if she needed them. And all went well for a few years – until he found out he'd been lied to. Twice. Once for a hernia operation that turned into a facelift for a new beau; the other to pay off her therapist that wound up as a trip to Cancun. After that, he'd wanted documentation for her calls for cash, sending her into a fury worthy of Alexis Carrington, *Dynasty*'s diva-slash-bitch. The over-the-top tirades continued for months, kicking him just enough off balance to where people wondered if he was the one losing it.

Of course, his sole sister being off in her vague chemical reality, during which she'd vanish for a week every few months in a modern version of *rinse and repeat*, added to the burden. But then one day mother and sister, despite detesting each other when sober, got their warped little brains on the same page, dressed up like blond-Barbie-bombshells with push-up bras and six-inch heels and convinced an attorney that the faggot-son-and-brother's mind had left him. My bet is they looked under *Homophobes-R-Us* to find the prick. Then they appeared before a *born-again* judge who totally agreed and issued a court order, and the next day, the sheriff grabbed my guy from his language lab at Philly and chucked his butt into a state facility for *evaluation.*

It took doctors maybe seventy-two minutes to figure out he was fine, considering, but seventy-two hours to convince that fucking judge. By that point, dear mother's lawyer had broken open the settlement and she and sister had split the cash. Then both had gone the vanishing route, leaving said lawyer and judge to answer for their stupidity.

It was while Daniel was being evaluated that I popped into the picture. He was screaming at everyone and no one, "I'm not crazy; I just need a new reality!" Which I felt was a fairly interesting way to describe the situation. And never mind his own low-key psychosis, which wasn't so much schizophrenia as just wanting *friends* around that he could talk to any time of day or night. In secret, of course. Sometimes a touch of insanity is all that keeps you sane. Anyway, that's what gave me a way to ... oh, let's just say, *introduce* myself and ask if I could tell him a story.

To which he responded, "Anything to get my mind off this crap."

"Okay, Dan-O," I smiled ... and the name came from him. He'd watched an old episode of *Hawaii Five-O* the day before that had a big butch actor holding a young, slim, attractive soldier hostage during a stand-off with Jack Lord and company, and Dan-O'd had an, oh, let's just call it *a nice dream*, that night, with him as the soldier and the butch actor as a savior instead of a bad guy and ... well, 'nuff said about that.

So I told him about this guy who's about to be executed for matricide. Got his total focus, with that. But three days before the needle goes in, a girl he knows talks me into investigating the murder. It takes me no time to learn the DA's office withheld evidence from the defense. Seems the murder weapon was found stuck in a *Jell-O* mold that was otherwise smooth and untouched and sitting in the fridge. CSI had taken the knife out, and it had his fingerprints and some of her blood on it, so that's all they'd cared about. Problem was they never mentioned the *Jell-O* was made just minutes before she was killed; she'd called a friend to ask how long it needed to be in the mold before she could remove it, so it hadn't had time to set. Meaning it was plopped on a plate and the knife was placed in it at least four hours later. While her son was in another part of the city dealing with a traffic cop. And he didn't get home till after her body and the knife were found. So there's no way he could have done it.

Naturally, the DA's office fought reopening the case, and two judges agreed with them, but just hours before the needle went in, I figured out it was the District Attorney who killed her. They'd been screwing around, and she'd wanted him to leave his wife. So after arguing, she'd wound up dead, then he'd used his office to frame the son. Why put the bloody knife in the blue *Jell-O*? He figured it'd make the kid look crazy, so anything he said would be suspect. Then they'd pushed for the death penalty, just to be consistent. Of course, the killer suffered a supremely spectacular death when he tried to escape; his car ran a light and got broadsided by a truck carrying ... and let us have a drum roll please ... jelly donuts! Who wouldn't chuckle at that?

I had a pretty good idea Daniel'd know how to keep it fun and frisky by adding a layer of insanity to it that I couldn't. And I really think working on the characters and motivations was the only reason he kept from slipping into cloud-cuckoo-land before that judge accepted the doctors' recommendations.

Meaning, yes, he maintained a grip on reality by working in a fantasy world. Gotta love the dichotomy.

So that's how *Red Knife in Blue Jell-O* sprang into being, and he's the one who gave me my voice – sharp, cool and snarky. Then as all the legal issues were being satisfied, which wound up getting that judge removed from the bench, we wrote it and it was accepted by the first publisher he submitted to – Gregory Taylor's house. He loved the slick mixture of sex, suspense and slapstick. We've been a hot team ever since.

Now don't get me wrong. I'm not taking sole credit for keeping my guy in the realm of the sane; Carmen helped, too. Where he found her ... well, they won't tell me; but I don't care because she's all Yin to my Yang. Of course, therapy also kept him in balance, until he began to subconsciously understand how bad things were becoming between him and Tad and wound up on Prozac. But no question, if he hadn't had me and Carmen to steady him, he'd never have made it to his twenty-fourth birthday.

Oh, did I happen to mention that Halloween party where he was *New Spock* – it was that particular birthday? And that he was the guest of honor? Meaning yes, he was born on Halloween. Figures, right?

So right now, he was sort of caught in the middle of this slow-moving river, waiting and wondering which way to paddle his boat.

Obviously, my being wary as shit about the bastard wasn't working, so I decided to try a new tactic and said, "All right, Dan-O, maybe I'm wrong about Tad. I mean, yeah, I'm always right in my books, but that's not reality, so ..."

Daniel nodded. "So let's just get down to the writing."

Probably not a bad idea because the blues were starting to wrap around his brain, again. So I went all chirpy.

"Okey-doke, how's this? ...*Madam*'s partly set in the mountains an' snow near LA, right? So trap me an' Carmen in an isolated cabin. Winter storm. All cozy an' fun, till this hermit starts killin' people in the other cabins!"

He gave me a look of pure you-have-got-to-be-kiddin'-me before he said, "Ace versus Jason? And you really think that'd be better than this crap?"

I smirked and said in my jokiest voice, "Can't be worse."

He caught the facetiousness and almost smiled. "Jeez, you're an asshole, sometimes."

"No, *you* are, since I'm you and you're me." And I batted my eyes at him.

"No shit," he muttered, but I could tell he'd at least stopped the tail chasing and returned to the better part of himself. "Okay, cut and paste," he continued. "Story as is."

"I don't think that'll be enough once we're rid of the lousy parts. What if we slip in that new one about politics as a wrap-around? Make me undercover as the hermit, remembering these other two cases. They could all tie in together. That'd work over eight episodes."

He just frowned. "Which new one?"

"The one with the payoffs and crooked sheriff."

"*The Cocoa-Butter Conspiracy*? That's set in Miami. No winter down there; just palm trees and empty condos."

He sipped some coffee, grimaced and headed for the kitchen, taking Mrs. Serff's Papa Bear mug with him.

I followed, saying, "So? Detective rule number one-fifteen – crooked politicians are everywhere. And you already been workin' on it for months; we could lay it on in a snap. As for the sex. Me an' Carmen? Playin' in the snow?" And didn't that bring a wicked angle to my dangle?

My guy just shook his head. "You'd get frostbite in places you don't want."

"Would not," I said, "not 'less you wrote it that way."

"I speak from experience," Daniel sang as he rinsed out the Papa Bear mug, poured in half his coffee then added hot water.

Oh, did he ever. Going skiing in just his boxer briefs at Vail in the middle of a snowfall a lot like the one blanketing the outside now, all just to show Tad that he would. It'd taken him the rest of the weekend to warm up.

He grinned at the memory then tasted the diluted coffee and grimaced. "At least it'll keep me awake. I'd better take my shower, now."

He checked the laptop, still charging, of course. Then he grabbed the *Dvin* with one hand and the cups with the other and headed back into the main room.

I followed him over to the dining area, murmuring, "You could always forget about this biddy-baby-bath-time."

"I've been working all day, and it'll relax me and – shit!" He gave me a look. "I didn't even grab a towel or underwear."

Uh-oh. "Dan-O, it won't hurt you to go au natural for a weekend."

"Be ripe and ready on Monday morning. Right," he sighed. "Dear God, what I sacrifice for my art." We both chuckled at that. "Maybe there's soap and a towel or something in the bathroom, and I can just go commando. Wash my briefs out."

"Carmen'll like that."

"Don't I know it?" he said as he turned off the lights.

I followed but stopped by the fireplace. "You think she'll ever show up?"

"I hope so. It'll make things easier."

"Tell her you'll put back in a bit where she watches Tristan and another guy have at it."

He started up the stairs then stopped said, "I dunno. I had some readers freak over that, in ...*Madame*. Not so much about the guy-on-guy action but because she got off on it."

"Play it for laughs," I said. And put her in the mood for lots of fun with me.

"I might," he snickered, "just to hear HBO try to cut it without offending Tad."

Yeah, one thing I had to give Little-Sir-Perfect – he was one of those, *Okay, I'm queer, so what?* dudes. Not enough of them, if you ask me.

Daniel smiled at the thought, nodding. "What I'd like to know is how'd the Cheeto-eater explain cutting it?"

"The scripts were so crappy," I chuckled, "Tad probably didn't even notice, yet."

"He will, eventually," smirked my guy. "Man, I'd love to see that."

I leaned on the banister. "Maybe he'll let you peek in."

Daniel grimaced, still smiling.

Oh, did I not mention Carmen also likes to sneak in and watch my guy and his guys in bed? He'd let me, if I wanted to, he gets off on the fake-voyeur idea of it; but I'm not a noodle-hound, so I'm not into that. However, I think that's why she joined my guy's world, because he lets her be just as kinky as she wants. But don't tell her I said that.

Daniel chuckled. "Can you hear me explaining it? *Hey, Tad, did you know I invite phantoms into the bedroom to take notes as we fuck?* And that's on top of me talking to people who aren't there."

"Hey, hey, hey, I am so here. I'm you and you're me."

"So let's talk to me about fixing the scripts, okay?"

"All right, all right. I'll get to work while you're relaxin'; but you're gonna wish you hadn't said you'd do this."

"I already do. But if it ... if it gives me a chance to get back with Tad ..."

Aw, that was fucking pathetic. Of course, I didn't say it, but I didn't need to. He knew what I was thinking.

He sighed, slumped a little and quietly sighed, "Times ten," in answer, then he continued upstairs.

Damn, I felt like a dog, opening the door for those blues to sneak back in. Because as much as I dislike His-Greatness, I have to admit he had made my guy happier than anyone since his grandmother.

Like on their six-month anniversary, he'd picked Daniel up after work and driven him straight to The Hamptons. To a five-thousand square-foot *cottage* on the beach. That's when we found out his real family name is Little-Lord-Moneybags.

Now, Daniel'd already taken the weekend off to spend at Tad's million-dollar condo, treating him to nonstop massages, something the twerp loved to receive from my guy, and sex in every which way you can imagine, so this sudden change in plans took him by surprise. As did entering this bungalow to find it bursting with baskets of fruit and cheese and baguettes and wines and meats and candies enough to keep them powered up for the whole weekend. Then he'd swept Daniel up in his arms ... like Rhett did to Scarlet in *Gone with the Wind*, just before he raped her ... and carried him into a bedroom drenched in honeysuckle.

"Like around your grandmother's home," he'd whispered.

My guy couldn't speak; he just breathed in as deeply as he could, remembering lazy summers on her back porch as a breeze passed over the tiny flowers and smothered him in their aroma, bringing back the tenderness he'd received from the one person he knew had loved him, unconditionally. So when Tad lowered him to his feet and wrapped his arms around him and nuzzled his neck, from behind, with complete affection, Daniel'd started weeping, he was so happy.

Of course, Tad thought he'd fucked up and started to whine about how hard he'd worked to get everything right, but Daniel stopped him with the longest, tenderest kiss he'd ever given anyone. Okay, so maybe I'm prejudiced, but seriously – my guy knows exactly how to do that to the max effect. None of this chewing-of-the-mouth crap, just lips barely touching. Noses softly shifting from side to side. Hands caressing up, up, up Tad's back to mingle fingers in his hair. Nine times out of ten, not one damn thing more was needed to get any guy ready for ... oh, let's just say, *the main event.*

He'd started to undo Tad's shirt, but after one button, the guy stopped him and, for the first time, undressed my guy, slowly, slowly, lingering in areas they both loved, providing him with sensations almost as intense as he'd been giving, bringing both of them to the point where even the softest breath from one or the other sent shock waves through their bodies.

They'd only left the cabin once, that weekend, and that was just to splash about in the icy, gentle surf, naked and laughing. Until a cop appeared and they had to scramble back inside. And on the drive back to the city, Daniel was completely at peace.

Aw, shit.

Suddenly I could see what this was all about – that's what my guy wanted back. He didn't give a damn about Tad's beauty; it was the sharing of a life and the support, both real and imagined, that he'd had with Theodore J. Bentley, the Third. The feeling that he was loved. That someone besides his grandmother ... someone had really, truly loved him. And brought him contentment and happiness. Even if just for a little while. Isn't that something we all dream about? All need a little of?

And I was so busy hating on Tad, I hadn't seen that till now? Shit, what the fuck is wrong with me?

I watched my guy slip into the door to the left of the stairs, and I thought, "Okay, Dan-O. I get it. I finally get it. And I want you to have joy in your life, again, so I'll drop the firewalls and do whatever I can to make it so. But shit, buddy, does it *have* to be with Tad?"

Man, I really did wish I could've stopped thinking that the fucker was up to something. But this whole setup just reeked of it. So what I did do was promise myself that if that son-of-a-bitch wound up hurting my guy in any way, I'd find some way to rip his fuckin' heart out.

Of course, that meant I'd have to find it, first.

Yeah, won't that be the trick of the ages?

Daniel paused to glance around the dark bedroom. The curtains over the windows were open, and a soft light offered just enough illumination to show it held nothing but a naked bed flanked by Oak nightstands and an Oak vanity dresser with an oval mirror. Very faux-rustic. He set the coffees and key on the dresser and eyed the brandy. Finally, he said, "Fuck it," and sipped some, coughing at how sharp and perfect it was.

"Churchill had the right idea," he croaked. He took another sip, already feeling warmer.

Okay, so now I'll bet you're wondering how I know all this even though I stayed downstairs. Simple. Carmen. She always knows what my guy's up to in his ... oh, let's just say, *private time*. And I've got a direct line into her, when she wants to be around. Meaning, yes ... she'd finally joined us and was doing her watching bit. Besides, I knew where this was headed, and all I could do was shake my head at how obvious he was being in trying to postpone the writing, like all writers do until they get started.

He sipped more of the *Dvin* and leaned against the window to look up at clouds. They were thickening, again, swallowing up the last hints of the stars. He gazed at the snow as it whispered down to lay another blanket over the trees and rolling hills for as far as the dark would let him see. The moon mooned the earth one last time during a break in the sky-cover, increasing the magic of the moment, before letting the world slip back to dark and slumbery.

Daniel's mind drifted back to that trip to Vail. Tad driving a rented Jeep up a winding mountain road in the middle of an evening storm so much like this, going too fast, as usual, with Daniel fighting to keep his nervousness from showing.

Tad still noticed. "I know how to handle snow," he said in his big brother tone, even as they skidded and nearly wound up going over the side of a cliff. "Hell, I could snowboard before I could walk."

"Yeah, but does the car know that?" Daniel'd only half joked back at him.

"Metal and plastic don't think," Tad laughed.

"You never met my grandmother's Buick!"

Tad chuckled and kept going, even after they almost hit a deer and skidded in three full circles before traction was regained. Daniel laughed, near hysterics from the exhilaration of surviving. Right then he knew life with Tad would never be dull, that's fer dang shure.

So they made it. And who'd ever have expected that after two lessons, Daniel'd be better on skis than Tad? Or expected the sight of Tad snowboarding down the slopes in that scarlet square-cut Speedo would have been so damned erotic? That's why Daniel'd nearly gotten his bits frostbit – to show Tad he could be just as crazy. And who'd have known that their nights would solidify their love affair so intensely ... well, intense on Daniel's part ... that nothing else mattered?

All right, I'm not being fair; it was hot for both of them, at the time. Tad was super attentive. Real aware. And always surprised at how high Daniel could keep taking him. Which is probably why on the last night there, after they'd made love and were blissfully tangled up in bed, Tad had looked at my guy so intently, for the first time Daniel seriously thought this I'm-all-that Adonis was in more than mere lust with him. And when Tad traced a gentle finger down the scar on Daniel's cheek and softly asked, "How'd that happen?" – Daniel had to remind himself to breathe, the guy's voice was so filled with concern.

"Uh, shaving," Daniel had replied.

Tad tossed off his patented half-cocked grin and snorted, "Bullshit."

"No shit. With a straight razor. I was researching how men got clean chins in the twenties, and it's amazing more throats weren't cut considering how tight the angle had to be when you were slicing off hairs with what was, effectively, a butcher knife."

Tad had laughed and kissed the scar. And Daniel would've died for him, right then and there.

All I could think at the time was it's a damn good thing I'd already built a pretty solid firewall around my guy to keep him from admitting the scar actually came from a fight with his sister. That would have meant explaining when he was fifteen and she was a wild and crazy bundle of just-turned-thirteen hormones and chaos, in one of their more physical confrontations she'd pushed him through a patio door that had pre-safety-glass panes. Then she'd laughed as he tried to stop the bleeding while his dear mother had merely rolled her eyes, grabbed a towel and snapped, "Now we have to get it fixed!" And then called 911. When they saw him, the paramedics said it was a miracle he hadn't been slashed to ribbons.

And what had dear Mother's response been? "Nonsense, this boy doesn't have that kind of luck."

Yeah, true maternal love slathered over a nice helping of psycho-sibling rivalry.

That had happened during husband number three, the holy-roller. Seems little sister was furious the SOB wasn't as interested in her as he was in Daniel. This was as my guy was getting the idea that the little moments of bonding step-dad loved so much were becoming just a bit too hands-on, Jesus on his shoulder or no. But when he'd finally let mom know, all she'd said was, "And I thought the bastard was boring. Changes my opinion."

For about six months. Until Daniel found first love, and mother found new excitement in a Maserati, and #3 found he had no choice but to divorce her since she threatened to turn him in for attempted child molestation. Then #4 got dumped when mom met a Rolls Royce twice her age and four times Daniel's and ten-million times anyone's bankbook. Who then wound up begging my guy to take over the family and the money he was settling on said mother in order to be rid of her and back to his life of Pez collecting.

Needless to say, family life had been downhill from there. Yeah, by this point he knew it's always better to bring up the family psychoses after you know each other one hell of a lot better. So much for being Mr. Honesty.

"And now comes self-flagellation," Daniel sighed. "Talk about your basic mystery. Why does this crap always come up just when I need my focus the most?"

The moon peeked between the clouds, again, catching his

eye. The elegance of the vista before him made him smile. He loved winter. How clean it was. The air so crisp and real. The snow sharp and true. Maybe he'd blow off Bermuda and ask Tad to join him up here. Try to rekindle the perfection of that Vail weekend. Get back on skis, again. Besides, they hated fags in the Caribbean, and why would anyone want to go anyplace where only their cash was welcome?

"Easy," he whispered, "Tad loves the beaches in Bermuda, and we want him to be as open to me as possible."

So another sip from the brandy. And another sigh. And another step closer to the blues.

And that's when Carmen made her move, whispering in from a shadow behind him, a tall, exquisite set of feminine curves wrapped in a slinky negligee, her lovely face framed by hair as shiny and black as a raven's feather. She folded her arms over my guy's shoulders to kiss his neck with such tenderness, it hurt. He almost let himself lean into her.

"'Allo, Dan-yell," she whispered, her voice thick with a Caribbean Spanish lilt as her elegant fingers drifted around to the center of his neck. Her words took on a soft purr as she continued with, "How you are?"

Daniel stopped her and chuckled. "C'mon, Carmen, you know I'm gay."

"Only in your mind," she purred. "In my mind, all men are open to me. And if *you* put this in my mind, then it must be in *your* mind. And since we share this mind ..."

"Your point being?"

She sighed then smiled. "Oh, so it is through me, you only see all men as toys to play with."

He shook his head and whispered, "One of my dreams."

"But me, you never will dream about?"

"I couldn't take you away from Ace. He needs you."

Yeah, right, pawn your disinterest off on me.

She softly giggled. "Then let us dream about this." She stepped back and waved a hand. And who should appear from the shadows, naked and perfect, but ... drum roll please ... Tad.

Yeah, big surprise.

Daniel sort-of grimaced. "No, I've got so much to do." But those powerful arms circled around to open my guy's parka and tickle his nips through his shirt. Then those perfect lips brushed his ear as those beautiful hands guided his coat off.

Without a thought, Daniel turned to kiss him long and deep. Tad had learned a lot from my guy, at least in Daniel's mind. So he gave as good as he got.

Oh, and just for everyone's edification, I'm still not the one describing this; it's Carmen feeding me the info, hence the nicer voice. I mean, I don't really care what my guy does with anybody, so long as it makes him happy. I just let myself Zen and wait till all is said and done and process Carmen's upload in a more abstract manner. It's the straight guy in me.

What does sometimes jolt me into the middle of everything is Carmen. Man, can she get going when these two're hot and heavy, be it in reality or jack-off fantasy. And at that moment, her motor was revving at thirty-five-hundred.

She traced her fingers across both their faces as she purred, "It is only for to help you think, Dan-yell. Twice as fast will you write. So much deeper will you go. Remember how you make me the one who loves. The one who dreams. The one who seeks beauty in life. Ace never can understand me. He is too much the rabbit boy in love."

Wait a minute! That jolted me into post-Zen, Carmen!

"But here," she whispered, almost giggling. "Now. With him. There is only beauty, no? The line of his face. The caress of his hands. The touch of his lips. The feel of his body molding to yours. All is so right. So real. So pure."

Daniel sighed from the emotions building in him as Tad unbuttoned his shirt. Carmen backed away, her breathing deep and ragged, just like my guy's.

"This is why you give to me life, Dan-yell," she continued. "This is why you give to me song. To do what you will not do. To be as you will not be. So, to me you give everything, okay?"

Tad lowered Daniel to the bed in this perfectly smooth, romantic, swooning motion.

"No, I ..." my guy said, breathless.

"Shhh," was her response. "We end this soon, and then we make it me to lead you through the story. It will be so much the good. We tell how I come over from Cuba. Learn to be who I am, in the streets of Miami. To fulfill my deepest desires."

Daniel frowned, "Wait, you're from the Bronx."

"I think that change in *The Cadillac Criminal Mind*, no?"

Daniel tried to rise on the bed, but Tad pushed him back down and whipped off his belt and pulled off his shirt.

"No, it ... it was a ... a cover, remember?" he whispered, fighting to keep from losing himself in Tad's insistence. "You ... helped Ace infiltrate a gang of heroin smugglers in Yonkers. He saved your life ... and that other guy's and ..."

Carmen broke into her perfect Bronx snarl with, "Son-of-a-bitch, that's right!" She jumped over and flicked Daniel's forehead with a finger.

He jolted. "Hey!"

"I went through *Dirty Baker's Dozen*... talkin' like some stupid bitch from Havana, and you never said a word! Don't you listen to me?!"

"You sounded fine!"

"Like hell. Even Ace noticed, an' he's a fuckin' idiot!"

Hey!

"You let me make a fool of myself, Daniel Bettancourt," she snarled. "What kind of respect does that show me? And me your best creation!"

Again, hey! What about me?! I'm right here, now, in the corner, and it's not my happy place!

She ignored me, as usual, snarling with a wicked grin, "Well, now we're gonna punish you, but good. Right, Taddy?"

She swatted Tad's ass, so he shoved Daniel down. Flopped on top of him. Crushed him to the bed. Yanked off his pants. Traced his lips down Daniel's quivering belly as Carmen slunk back in a chair to watch, her motor now up to red-line.

Which is when any good horn-dog should make his move.

So I snuck behind her and whispered in her ear, "I'd say that's as safe sex as you can get," trying to keep from alerting Daniel to my arrival.

She gave a deep, throaty little giggle and wrapped a hand around my neck in that way I sooooo love, where her nails dig into me just a little. But he still heard me and snapped, "This chatter is non-conducive to a satisfactory ..."

"Speedy?" I sniped. I know, but I couldn't help myself.

"... Result. So shut up or go."

I smirked then Carmen and I began fading away to have our own little party in the cosmos, but not before I saw Daniel turn Tad's perfect face back to him and muttered, "Now, I'm all here."

Tad smirked, kissed him, grabbed his briefs at the sides, yanked them off and slung them into the shadows. Which I'd seen him do, in reality, and was still scarred from. Well, as scarred as a straight fictional character who inhabits the mind of a gay writer can be. And now you know why I always close my eyes and ...

"Jeannie – fresh-as-a-daisy.

Just love – how-she-obeys-me.

Does things – that-just-amaze-me so. Tah-da-dah."

It was the theme song to *I Dream of Jeannie* being sung in as off-key a manner as one could and still be thought of as singing!

Outside!

In the snowstorm!

And headed this way!

Of course, Tad vanished and Daniel bolted up and grabbed his pants to hide just how close he was to ... oh, let's just say, *a satisfactory result*. And once again, I felt a flash of pride at how he'd endowed me with his dick and not Tad's.

And I don't really need to get into the why of that, do I?

Anyway, my guy was freaking out at how he couldn't find his shirt or underwear in the dark, so I popped in with, "Calm down, calm down, it's probably just that hermit."

"No," he muttered, "Mrs. Serff would've kept him away."

"Why?"

He had no answer to that.

The singing became humming, and was just as crappy, like a third tier audition on American Idol.

"Have you seen my briefs?" Daniel gasped, panicked.

"C'mon, Dan-O, Carmen's the only one who sticks around to watch you and Tad, whether he's really there or not."

"Where'd she go?"

Sure enough, she'd vanished. "I think she's cheatin' on us with another author ... all this crap about her takin' over my story, the two-timin' tramp, but don't tell her I said that."

My guy rolled his eyes, pulled on just his slacks and crept out to the landing then froze as he heard the long, screaming CREAK of the main door opening, and then that crappy voice sing-humming that stupid song ...

Until it stopped.

Which is usually a great big moment of, Uh-oh.

Daniel carefully peeked down at the living room as he heard the door close with another huge CREAK. Then came way, way too much silence.

Finally, a big dumb ox of a guy, bundled solid against the cold, a red-and-white-swirled knit cap on his head, looking kind of like a peppermint candy, like the ones in those cellophane wrappers and ... oh, never mind. Well, he carefully entered the room, his eyes locked on the fireplace. He looked around, uncertain then checked the closet.

Daniel quietly kept tight against the shadows, so we could barely hear him snarl, "Son-of-a-bitch! My brandy."

Okay, now that *is* a great big moment of WTF?

The guy backed over to the phone, picked up the receiver and carefully dialed a number, his eyes sweeping the place, looking like a wary weasel.

Daniel fought to hear him speak.

"Max?" the guy whispered. "It's Haddon. I'm at The Lyons' Den. There's a fire and my brandy's gone and – no, the fire's in the fireplace. Has Costello already been up?" He checked a manila envelope in his pocket. "But that fire's fresh, and I got the only key to this place and – wait, Max, you did change the locks? ... You swear?" Then his shoulders dropped. "Right, that hermit; I forgot about him. There goes my brandy. ... I'm hidin' the package in the secondary spot. Tell Costello ..." He started to get angry. "But that freak might find it." He huffed and snarled, "Okay, okay. If you're sure he's in town. But the next drop's at the secondary spot, no buts. ... Right." He hung up and headed for the kitchen.

All Daniel could do was mutter, "Are you kiddin' me?"

I popped in from a shadow, now dressed in the perfect suit, of course, and asked, "Why not? Isolated cabin. Closed for the winter. Perfect place for a spot of criminal misbehavior."

"But tonight?" his voice soft and strangled. "Tonight!?"

"Right," I nodded. "Does seem opportune. So what do you think Tad's up to? Oh, and why is that lunkhead drinking a fine brandy like *Dvin*?"

Daniel just waved me silent.

I leaned on the banister and looked about the room. It was dark, the only light dancing out from the fire, but I caught a glimpse of the grocery bag and that reminded me. "Your laptop. It's in the kitchen." I rolled over to lean on the banister with my elbows. "If he sees that, he's gonna search the place. That might prove awkward."

"No shit. I need a weapon, just in case."

Not a bad idea. I cast a glance down at the hearth and the bin holding its tools. Daniel nodded and quickly crept down the stairs. A couple of them creaked, but he didn't stop; he just snuck over to the fireplace to grab a poker.

But the second he had his hand on it, Haddon sauntered in from the kitchen, saw him and pulled a pistol! "What the hell!"

Daniel jolted and raised his hands. "Whoa, whoa, whoa, I'm not armed! I'm not ... uh ..." Oh, right, except for the poker in one hand. He dropped it.

"What're you doin' here?" Haddon yelled.

"Spending the weekend," Daniel said. "What's going on? Who're you?"

"Never mind that!" the guy snarled. "How'd you get in?"

"Through the front door."

"Like hell! It was locked an' I got the only key!"

"No, you don't."

Haddon huffed. "Do so."

"I don't see how because that's how I got in and ..."

"Bull! I bet you broke in and ... and ..."

"Don't be silly! Check for yourself. My key's on the dresser, upstairs."

The guy hesitated, uncertain. "Really?"

"Yes," Daniel all but snapped. "Which means your buddy lied about changing the locks and ..."

"Oh, Dan-O!" I groaned.

"Wait. You listened in on my phone call?" Haddon asked, incredulous.

"You shouldn't of said that," I half-sang to my guy.

Daniel nodded. "Yeah."

Haddon fumed. "That was a private conversation between me and a friend of mine! I can't believe you! Sneakin' around and listenin' in on people like some peepin' tom! Do you know how impolite that is?!"

I jolted and looked at Haddon, because the one positive thing Daniel was very sensitive about was being polite. And I didn't blame him. Sometimes good manners are the only thing that keeps you from crashing into a cartoon version of a Tasmanian Devil.

"Impolite?!" Daniel snarled. "*Me*!?"

Haddon huffed, a bit less certain, apparently because Daniel was not reacting in the way he'd planned. "Uh, yeah, you little sneak!"

Daniel advanced on the man, me pacing him as he snarled, "I am the epitome of good manners. Emily Post was seared so deep into my synapses I couldn't even consider being impolite, and you're claiming I've done something that is completely contrary to my genetic structure and socio-biological make-up?!"

Wow, he ought to get pissed off more often. That was good.

"Uh, yeah!" said Haddon, then he added, "I think."

"No, he don't," I said, trying to keep Daniel from spinning into that snarly little beast.

He still growled, "And me wanting to know who's breaking and entering into this property has no bearing on it, whatsoever?"

Haddon was taken aback by the comment and actually thought about it. "Well, yeah, I suppose that would mean something else besides a breach in etiquette." Which he pronounced *edi-quit*, which even I knew was wrong, "And – wait, wait, wait, wait, wait! I ain't B-an'-E-in' nothin'!"

"Then who gave you a key?" Daniel snapped. "It sure wasn't Mrs. Serff, and this isn't your place. Oh, unless it's Tad's dad's."

Haddon frowned. "Wait, who the hell're Tad's dads?"

Daniel blinked and said, "What're you talking about? There's only one and I never met him, but …"

"Well, if you don't know him," Haddon snapped, "then how the hell'm I supposed to know him?"

"Huh?" Daniel looked at the man, lost for a moment. "But I do know him."

"You just said you didn't," Haddon said.

"I did?" Daniel blinked. The dude was right; he had. "Oh. No, I know Tad, that's what I meant. This place is his father's, not yours, and I wondered why he would give you a key."

Good cover, buddy.

"He didn't," said Haddon.

"Then where'd you get it? 'Cause Tad doesn't have one."

Flustered, Haddon muttered, "I just got one, that's all!"

"Just got one," Daniel said, rolling his eyes. "Right."

"Well, yeah! That's ... that's how it worked."

Daniel moaned, "Oh, come on, cut the stupid act."

"I don't think it's an act," I said, quickly peeking into the man's ear and waving my hand on the opposite side of his head. Just as I figured, totally empty.

"How else could you get a key," Daniel kept on, "if not from Mrs. Serff or Tad? Are you so lost in your lying you can't tell when it's obvious you're lying?"

Haddon jumped up and down, furious. "Hey-hey-hey-hey-hey-hey, you got a lot of nerve, sayin' that when I got a gun!"

Daniel shook his head. "That's a pistol. A revolver, to be more precise."

Which he knew. Husband #3 had thought showing Daniel the Christian way to shoot-to-kill would be a great way to get closer as step-daddy and step-boi, and no, that is not a typo. Daniel was almost willing to accept the innocent explanation of his plan ... until that forty-year-old man started fondling the pistol as if it was a substitute for something else. That got to be more than a little creepy.

"I know that," snapped Haddon. "I mean ... I ... listen, if you don't tell me who you are, I'll kill you dead!"

"Kill me dead"? Daniel turned to me. "You're right; he is dumb."

"What?" Haddon hissed. He looked around. "Who're you talking to? Somebody else here?!"

Daniel grimaced. "No! I, uh, I'm talking to you. To say *kill me dead* is a misuse of the English language and hardly the mark of an intelligent man, let alone, a polite one."

Now that bugged me, so I grumbled, "You let me misuse it."

"Proof of point," Daniel muttered.

"Hey!"

"Okay," snarled Haddon, "then how 'bout this point?!"

He bolted over and shoved his pistol between Daniel's eyes. My guy froze. In the pistol's chambers were what looked so much like real bullets, they probably were. Which took this whole thing into a whole new realm.

"Oh," he said.

"Right," sneered Haddon, nodding his head like a monkey in heat. "This pistol's got some serious damage in it. So does that prove who's in control?!" Daniel said nothing. Haddon's nods grew sharper, making him look like a hyena. "Uh-huh. Uh-huh. Now you tell me, who the hell are you?!"

Daniel let a weak smile cross his face. "Ace," then added in a stronger voice, "Shostakovich."

I had to laugh at that. "Dream about it, baby. He's probably heard about me and ..."

"Why're you here?!" Haddon snarled.

Oh. So. He hadn't. The ignorant little shit.

"To write. The ... the owner let me use the place."

"You must think I'm a real idiot to try that crap on me," Haddon sneered.

"Oh, no *think*," I sneered. "We know."

Daniel sighed. "Look." He pointed to the hearth. Haddon stepped back and glanced at it. "Those're my groceries, and my laptop's charging in the kitchen. And my footprints're outside and I was ... prepping to take a shower when you showed up."

What a way to put it, but at least my guy got Haddon back to hesitating.

"Wait, you really know the guy what owns this joint?"

"Yes. C'mon, I'll even show you my key." He started for the stairs.

Haddon jumped back to being threatening in his danger-puppy mode. "Hold it!"

My guy froze and Haddon patted down his pants.

Daniel jolted. "What're you doing?!"

At that, I had to roll my eyes. "Frisking you, you idiot."

"A bit too much like he's with the TSA, if you ask me!"

"I'm no queer," Haddon sneered.

"Careful!" Daniel snapped. That was another sore point with my guy, though he didn't usually get as freaky over that word as the *F* one, and we ain't talking *fuck*.

"Just gotta make sure you ain't armed," said Haddon. "How was I supposed to know you go commando?"

Daniel slammed back to incredulous and motioned to his lack of shirt and shoes. "Where can I hide a gun?"

"You mean a *pistol*, right?" Haddon smirked. "So maybe you got one in your room."

"Fine, search the room then get the hell out of here!" Daniel snapped in a way that really impressed me. Looks like jack-off-icus-interruptus is a great way to get him into his own danger-kitty attitude. I'd have to remember that.

"I will," the guy said, then stopped. "I mean, you show me where it is." He shoved the pistol against Daniel's back.

Daniel sighed and led the man up the stairs.

I stayed down by the fire to watch, because ... well, to be perfectly honest, something about this was weird. Like the guy was pretending to be a crook but couldn't keep it straight in his head. Daniel'd had a problem with a character like that in *Dirty Baker's...* – a scally-boy named Jem. He'd planned for Jem to be the bad guy but the little shit kept doing shit that wasn't right for it, to my detective mind. Daniel and I fought over it till I finally figured out the problem – Jem was covering for an older woman he loved, whom he was sure was innocent but who turned out to be the real killer. What made it funny was, even with all the proof I pulled up, Jem didn't believe she was the devil's own bitch till she nearly killed him, too. This dude, Haddon, he had the same lack of certainty about his goal and yet the same focus, and it made me nervous, for some reason. Hell, I could easily have thought he wasn't real, he was so all-over-the-place.

I got jolted back to *now* when Haddon jabbed Daniel with his pistol to keep him from entering the bedroom. They were on the landing by Daniel's door.

"Not so fast, buster," the guy said. "You're awful eager to get in there."

"It's where we want to go."

"Just 'cause I want you to go in there don't mean I want you to want to go in there."

Say what?!

"You stay out here where I can see you," the cretin snarled, like something out of a Jimmy Cagney movie.

Daniel sighed to the heavens. "Fine. Fine. Whatever you say. Just get done and get out of here."

"Dan-O," I moaned, "we both know this creep ain't goin' nowhere till he's taken there."

Daniel nodded as Haddon entered the bedroom, turned on a light and searched, keeping both the pistol and a half-wary eye on Daniel. He found the key and picked it up, confused.

Daniel just stood there. Watching! Like a fool!

Oh, now I'm saying that!? Thank you, Mrs. Serff!

This was really too much. I strode up the stairs, shaking my head.

"Dude!" I snapped. "One minute you're in his face while he's got a barrel pointed between your eyes; the next it's all standin' around wonderin' what to do! Why do I let you write me!?" I flicked the door's knob then yanked at Daniel's pants leg. "Secure the door then call the cops, idiot."

"He has a weapon," Daniel muttered.

I sighed, "And that's a real door made of real wood, not one of those fake things. If he's trapped inside, you're safe."

Daniel took a deep breath and nodded, understanding. He noticed Haddon was wandering over to the bed, where the parka lay, so he stepped just out of eyesight, quickly slipped off his pants and made a loop in one pants leg.

"Quick an' dirty," I said. "An' tight."

He nodded, hesitated, then yanked the door closed, looped the pants leg around the knob, pulled it tight and tied the other pants leg to the banister!

Haddon slammed against the door, pounding on it as he yelled, "Ace, open this door! Open the door, dammit, or I'll shoot!" He yanked at the door, but it barely gave an inch. He pounded on it some more! Yanked at it, again! The pants tore in the crotch but the door was definitely tied closed.

Daniel laughed and scrambled down the stairs to grab the phone, then he dialed 911.

Haddon's voice trailed after him, screaming, "Ace, you son-of-a-bitch, I see it was you took my brandy, too! You know how hard that shit is to find? I'm gonna get you, you bastard!"

Yeah, and your little dog, Toto, too.

Daniel snarled into phone, "Hurry up. Hurry up!" But it kept ringing and ringing and ...

The front door screamed open, behind him!

Maybe ... Maybe not ...

Daniel yelped and spun around to find one of those good-looking, level-headed, boy-next-door types entering, wearing a Navy Pea Coat, jeans and boots, with a red muffler around his neck and a cap with ear muffs hiding dark blond hair, all of which was noticed by my guy in two-tenths of a nano-second. The dude looked at him, startled, this sweet deer-caught-in-the-headlights expression on his face. Daniel's choice of words, not mine, I swear.

"Oh, uh, look," he said, "I dunno what you're expecting, but this is pretty presumptuous!"

That's when Daniel remembered he was ... oh, let's just say *swinging in the wind*. He quickly covered himself with the phone receiver, which didn't exactly make things look better, from some angles, though I did catch a quiet giggle from Carmen, the little kinkstress.

"What – who're you?!" my guy managed to gasp out.

"I ... oh, damn," said the other guy, "you're already here. I thought I'd beat you up."

All right, the sound of that, we did not like.

Then we heard branches of trees noisily smashing about in anger before something landed hard, outside, accompanied by Haddon yelling, "Son-of-a-bitch!!" We all jumped.

"Uh-oh!" hit both Daniel's and my mind.

That's when a voice loud enough to be heard in Hoboken shrieked out of the phone, "'Mergency operator! What's your 'mergency!?"

Daniel slammed the phone down then he and I raced up the stairs and tore the pants off the doorknob. Literally, since they were already half torn at the crotch. We bolted into the bedroom to find it empty. The bathroom door was ajar, so we scrambled in there to see the window was wide open, Haddon's pistol on the floor and the outer panel of the shower curtain pulled off the rod and lying halfway out the window, with both keys gleaming on the deep blue material. Along the wall opposite the tub were a sink and non-stop mirror. Oh, and I simply have to point out – the inner shower curtain was covered with hand-painted cartoon fishies, a la Dr. Seuss mixed with too much psycho-Dali. So if this was Tad's bathroom as a kid, it explained a lot.

Daniel grabbed the gun and keys then looked out the window. A tree branch pressed against the house, the snow brushed off it. Daniel's parka was tangled in the branches, halfway down. Snow at the base of the tree was messed up, too, with footprints leading off into the darkness. Haddon was gone.

"Obviously, he's not hurt," I sneered. "Must've fallen on his head."

"Dammit," Daniel snapped, slamming his hand against the window jam. "Why'd he take my coat and leave the pistol?"

"Looks like he dropped the weapon," I offered. "As for the coat, I don't think he wants you followin' him."

"Shit, I should've figured he wouldn't just stay here."

Which made me feel dumb as dirt, since I'm the one who talked him into doing this, so I said, "C'mon, I didn't think he'd do a runner, and I ... I'm better at this than you."

"Big comfort." Daniel snapped as he yanked the curtain in then closed and locked the window. Finally, he checked his pants. They were torn in half. He glared at me.

I huffed, "I ain't the guy that didn't grab an extra pair."

"I wouldn't have needed them if it wasn't for your ..."

"*Your*!"

"...Hair-brained idea."

He stormed back into the bedroom, found his briefs and pulled them on then he looked around, sighed and strode back into the bathroom to grab the outer shower panel since it was opaque cloth. But then I saw the design it had and grimaced.

"Dude," I said, "there's green seaweed and pale bubbles on it!"

"It's this or I go downstairs in my tighty-whities."

Point taken. So he wrapped the curtain around himself, like a sarong, then he pulled on his shirt, plopped the keys in its pocket and exited, pistol in hand, looking dangerous. Which he was, because when he gets pissed, he doesn't always think as clearly as he should. And that is always a big load of *Uh-oh*.

As he descended the stairs I stayed on the top step, and yes, I was pouting. I mean, it's not like I meant for his pants to get ruined, and really it was his idea as much as mine, so why was he all pissed me?

The dude saw the pistol, smiled and raised his hands in mock surrender, saying "You've got a whole arsenal here."

Daniel frowned. "Excuse me?"

Oh, come on! "Dan-O! Not even you are that dense!"

The dude grinned and said, "I just meant ..."

"Yeah, okay, I got it," said Daniel. He held up the pistol and added, "This isn't mine. Belongs to the guy who escaped."

The dude blinked. "Escaped?"

"Yes," said Daniel. "He was holding this gun ..."

"Pistol," I snapped off.

"... Revolver on me," Daniel continued, with extreme patience. "So I tricked him into going into the room then locked him in. He climbed out the window to get away ..."

"And you're gonna tell some guy you don't know the whole story," I sniped. "Not even Carmen's that dumb!"

Carmen popped in from a shadow, now wearing a skirt, blouse and those six-inch heels that drive me nuts. "You callin' *me* dumb?!" she snapped. "After some of the crap you pulled?!"

I tried to wave her off with, "Not now."

"Yes, now," Daniel muttered. "Keep him busy."

Carmen forced me to look at her and began to talk, but truth is, I didn't hear a thing she said; I was focused on Daniel and his latest search for stupid behavior, since he obviously had no awareness of just how dangerous it was to trust anybody who looked that good in a pea coat.

The guy eyed Daniel. "Keep me busy?" he asked in a half-amused voice.

Daniel turned back to him. "Huh? Oh, uh, yeah ... uh, no, no, not you. The guy upstairs. Kept him busy doing, uh, stuff and ... and ... "

"Did I interrupt something between you and him?"

"Huh? No! No, that's just – things happened that weren't supposed to happen, and I wish hadn't happened, but I was just thinking I ... I think I ... I ... uh, why're you here?"

"To see you," he said with a despicably charming smile.

"Me? Why?"

"To discuss the rewrite job you're doing."

Daniel sat on the arm of a couch, wary. "Tad sent you?"

"Tad?" He gave Daniel a way-too-deliberate *who's that* look as he said, "I don't know a – oh! Theodore J. Bentley, the Third! You call him Tad. This is so cool." He pulled out a note pad and wrote it down. "I thought he hated that."

Daniel watched him, even more confused. "What is this? What're you doing?"

"Making notes," the dude said, absently.

"About what?"

"You."

Daniel shook his head in disbelief. "Excuse me, but am I supposed to know you, or something?"

The guy looked up and smiled, a bit embarrassed. "Oh, right, I am so sorry. I'm Cervantes Lee, and I write special interest stories for *The Bradleyville Weekly*."

"You have got to be kidding me," Daniel said, nonplussed.

"No seriously. Here, I'll show you." He pulled an iPhone from an outside pocket. "I can access my articles."

Daniel didn't move. "That won't work; no cell phonage."

The guy blinked. "Oh. Right. Well, I …"

The landline rang and they both jumped at the sudden sound. Daniel snarled and grabbed it. "Tad, did you send …?"

A loud, gruff voice cut him off. "This is Sheriff Candelaria. My operator says somebody tried to make an emergency call from this number, but they got disconnected."

Daniel grimaced as I scrambled down the stairs, leaving Carmen by herself, in a huff. "Dan-O, think – you get the sheriff involved you're lookin' at five hours of who did what, where, how an' when. The bastard's gone, he don't know you know anything an' you still got your schedule."

"What if he comes back?" my guy wondered, aloud.

I rolled my eyes. "He probably thinks you're callin' the cops on him, so he won't. An' if he does, kill him."

"You think I could?" he asked me, not joking in the least.

"Sure," I said, kind of surprised. "You got the arsenal."

"Right." Then he said into phone, "Wrong number." He set the phone down and turned to this Cervantes character. "Okay, now you have to go. I don't need another distraction."

"Distraction?!"

Yeah, buddy. Trust me; I've seen my guy around your type before, pre-Tad, and it don't bode well. Unless ... whoa, unless it means he gets interested in you and drops His-Gloriousness. Oh. All right. Possibilities here.

"You know what I mean," said Daniel. "I have to get started writing and ..."

"But I just arrived," said Cervantes, "and it's snowing ..."

The phone rang, again. Daniel jumped and backed away from it. "Will ... will you answer that?" he asked. "It may be the sheriff, again."

Cervantes frowned. "Sheriff?"

"Please? Tell him ... just tell him nobody's home."

The dude reluctantly picked up the phone. "Yes?"

The same gruff voice said, "This is Sheriff Candelaria, again. I was talkin' to somebody, but they got disconnected. Is everything all right?"

Well, aside from the fact that we were now deaf because he was talking so damned loud you could've heard him in *Cleveland*, we were fine.

Cervantes put his hand over the receiver and turned to Daniel. "Weren't you trying to call the sheriff?"

"No! Uh, no. No, no, no. Wrong number."

"Hello?!" said Candelaria.

Cervantes grimaced. "But that guy, upstairs ... "

"Is gone," Daniel snapped. "And talking about it'll put me even farther behind, so tell him I ... I ... I went to Rochester, and I'll deal with it Tuesday."

Cervantes said into phone, "Uh, yes, we're all fine, here."

"You sure?"

"Sure as snow, sheriff," Cervantes said, then grimaced.

"Oh. I see. Sorry to bother you. Have a good night."

Cervantes hung up the phone. "That was wrong."

"Sounded fine to me," Daniel said.

"I know Sheriff Candelaria," the dude said, absently. "He may recognize my voice and wonder why I didn't identify myself when he called, or tell him I was coming up here."

Daniel frowned. "Why would you have to tell him?"

He looked at my guy with such lovely innocence, I could feel Daniel tickled by a lovely touch of distraction-ville. "And did you notice those green eyes?" I whispered, nudging Daniel even closer. "And the fair hair dancing about his head? And that square chin? And that neat body just visible under that pea coat?" All for his benefit, of course; anything to kill the Tad urge.

"This place is abandoned," the dude said. "If somebody saw me looking around and called him ..."

And wasn't the expression on his face so nice and open and inviting and ... and ... wait a minute, the joint's abandoned? That don't make sense, so I had to jump in with, "This is Tad's dad's pad, Dan-O."

Daniel nodded, muttering, "And he's got a caretaker."

Cervantes bopped over to say, "Oh, the Serffs just keep watch on things, in case the homeless try to settle in. Since the owner's never here. That's why it's listed as abandoned – so they'll keep a sharper eye on it."

And what a nice, neat, easy explanation. All right, what the hell's going on? I nudged my guy, getting wary.

He nodded, absently, the asked, "How did you know I'd be here, Mr. Lee?"

"Cervantes. Van to my friends." And offered up a clean, open smile.

Which pushed me deeper into conflict zone. Yes, I wanted to be rid of Tad, and a dude like this would be perfect to shift my guy's focus away from the prick, but it just plain didn't feel right.

Of course, by this point, my guy couldn't help but say, "Cervantes. Such an unusual name."

Oh, man, not a good sign.

Van's smile became a grin, which I noticed made him even more endearing. "My folks' favorite book was *Don Quixote*, what can I say?"

Whoa, whoa, whoa, whoa, whoa, whoa, whoa! *Don Quixote*?! What my guy thinks is the perfect novel? You're not just named after the author, you're also referencing it? Wait a minute. "Dan-O, something's wrong about this!"

He just nodded.

The guy offered his hand, saying, "And you *are* the reason I'm here."

"Really?" Daniel said, as wary as I was, but still doing the handshake thing.

"Sure as snow," said Van, taking off his coat, flopping it on the back of the couch, and looking even more fit and fantastic under a Gansey sweater. "I know a guy you work with, Orlando, and he overheard you and ... Tad, is it? He heard you discussing rewriting eight scripts in time for a meeting on Monday, and he called me since I'm up here in Bradleyville because it sounds exactly like what I need, Mr. Bettancourt, especially since if you lose, he says you have to pay Tad Bentley a hundred thousand dollars."

"Well, that's not right," said Daniel. "And, it's Daniel. I won't be ready for *Mr.* Bettancourt till I'm ninety."

Van's grin became a nearly tender smile, and his eyes stayed focused on my guy's. "Daniel. Makes it even more like in the Bible."

"Huh?" Daniel said, then he remembered and added, "Right. In the den of lions."

"You know the book?"

"Some of it."

Which was nonsense. My guy'd read it from cover to cover, including the begets. He wanted to see what hubby #3 was all about and quickly realized that the whole idea of hypocrisy and nastiness about gay men in general ... not to mention divorce, shellfish and suits made from a wool-cotton blend ... was way too easy to play around with when you wanted to, and that was exactly what the bastard was doing in his quest to be *best-buds* with his step-son.

"It's a good name," said Van. "It has strength. Control."

Daniel almost laughed. "That makes me its antithesis."

"I dunno about that," Van said. "Daniel. I've done some research, and you seem pretty strong to me. But you see, that's the reason I'm here because I figure you're going to win, and if I have the scoop, I can sell the story to US Weekly or People and get my own career as a writer going, and since I knew where the only key to this place was kept, I rushed up here to let you in, so you wouldn't freeze looking for it, but the snow slowed me down, so it's a good thing you knew how to find the key; I'd hate to be the one to write about you freezing to death, which would not be a very auspicious beginning to a writing career, unless you like obituaries, which are fine, in and of themselves, but I've already done enough of those, and I'm loathe to do another one. Especially yours."

"Jeez," I muttered, "does anybody up here ever breathe in when they talk?"

Apparently not, because he still managed to add, "So, why'd you put it back?"

"Put what back?" Daniel asked, distraction mode making its reappearance.

"The key," said Van. "Why not keep it with you?"

Daniel frowned and showed him a key, in answer.

Van jolted and said, "But that's the key I have."

"Not possible," said Daniel. "Trust me." And my guy's gears shifted from distracted to wary, which made me a little happier. Give us time to think things through. Then Van showed Daniel his own key. My guy huffed. "That's three. Mrs. Serff said there's only one."

Van blinked. "Oh, uh, she must not know about the others."

Uh-huh. That old bat didn't know nothing about nothing.

"No kidding," Daniel snapped then he started pacing. "So what's going on, here? This is supposed to be a private cabin in the middle of nowhere."

"Oh, it is, in the winter," said Van. "The skiing's to the north."

"Then why've I had two visitors in twenty minutes?"

"Um," Van said, nice and blank, "that is kind of weird."

"Weird my ass," I sniped. "My bet's on Tad being up to somethin', an' this guy's part of it." Sometimes it's best to just let the obvious do the talking, know what I mean?

"You're right," Daniel muttered, his pacing going faster, talking more to himself than to Van. "I *should* have stayed in New York. At a hotel! A sign on the door saying, *Do Not Disturb*. Operator holding calls. Room service at my disposal."

"Don't forget access to the bellboys," I added, sweetly, remembering a certain tryst on his first visit to New York with an Italian stallion named George, that included champagne and strawberries dipped in chocolate to celebrate the release of our first book. I had to cover eyes and ears, both, on that one, even as I got the relay through Carmen, whose motor hit red-line in nothin' flat! Whooh. That was the weekend that solidified my guy's decision to leave Philadelphia and live the life of the Big

Apple.

"But no," Daniel kept on. "I had to buy into Tad's suggestion this would be better, a hundred miles better, which in and of itself makes so little sense any idiot could've seen how dumb it was! Shit, I'm beginning to think the phrase *screw-up* uses my photo as an illustration."

"No, you just get the kick for trustin' a prick," I said. "Again."

"Right," Daniel said straight to me. "You're right. Every decision I make that makes sense when I make it turns into a great big disaster when I put it into practice, thanks to ..."

"Daniel, come on," Van said, cutting him off. "I think you're being kind of hard on yourself." Well, at least the sound of his voice ended the pacing. The dude continued with, "Besides, it seems this cabin would be the perfect place to write. Quiet, comfortable, isolated."

"Not," I snarled, sweetly.

"Wait'll you see the view, in the morning," said Van as he tossed a log on the fire. Then he sat on the hearth's flagstone lip, the image of sexy earnestness. "It is perfection."

Of course, Daniel noticed and watched him, but at least he was still wary about the guy. Which could be either good or bad, for my purposes. Or both. Hell, I didn't know, right then. Dammit.

Van kept on with, "Imagine it on a cool summer evening, as fireflies dance in sunset air and laughter echoes from the other cabins and mingles with the soft aroma of hamburgers and shish kebobs roasting on grills. Birds sing, joyously, as they nest for the night and owls call upon waking, their tender melodies combining to bring you a peace that can be felt only once or twice in a lifetime."

Oh, shit. That last line. "He's quotin' you," I said.

Daniel nodded. *The Dirty Baker's Dozen Plus Two.*"

Van grinned. "Read the whole thing. Reminded me of here."

He read my guy's book? And he's using it to calm him down? Okay, that didn't sound like somebody who was up to no good. And he even connected with it, seemed like. Confusion, thy name be *Van.*

"But it's set in ... in Scotland," my guy murmured.

Then he took in a stunned breath and looked around. Holy shit, that was it! This house damn near fit the description of that resort, right down to the Gothic curtains! The room began to shake for Daniel. Y'know, there's coincidences and there's coincidences, and then there's something else goin' on!

"Who cares where it's set?" Van said, forcing my guy to sort-of wander back to reality and look at a pair of warm green eyes focused straight on him. His face open and honest. I was glad for it, but at the same time I could see this Van guy was doing some serious seduction here, all earnest, gentle and supportive with a don't-I-look-fucking-gorgeous-sitting-in-the-firelight-with-no-other-lights-to-distract-from-how-romantic-it-is pose. He kept on with, "Their hills seemed like my hills, and the tenderness of your description brought forth memories I'd forgotten. You see, I grew up here. Had my first kiss on a hearth just like this one in a cabin just like this. And my first heartbreak."

Daniel sat on the arm of a couch, close to him, now caught by Van's golden glow. "Who ... who'd be dumb enough to break your heart?" he asked, even though his mind was still swimming.

"Oh, someone I thought I loved."

"Someone," I muttered. Gay code meaning a guy. Meaning no question he was after something and figured the best way to get it was to aim for Daniel's dick.

My guy nodded. "Of course." He heard it, too, and was just as confused by it, so like a security blanket, Tad's image flashed into his mind's eye in all his beauty to help him take a step back.

I was both relieved and wanted to scream! Here's the perfect dude to get Dan-O away from that jerk, and he's turning out to be just as worrisome as Little-Lord-Hotness! Shit!

"What do you mean?" asked Van.

Daniel looked away. Well, maybe it is best to keep in wariness mode, for now; easier to deal with than distracted. But what startled me was my guy was hurt. Actually hurt because some dude he'd met five minutes ago wasn't proving to be completely, totally worthy of his trust?

That sounded a bit too needy.

"I didn't mean anything," Daniel said to Van. "It's just the one aspect of my life that matches yours. In a way."

"Yeah? And I figured you for the heartbreaker."

I snarled at that. "Will you give it a rest?! We got the four-one-one on you, so let us catch up and figure you out, first."

Daniel gave a short laugh. "Right." He made himself look around the cabin, the freak-out moment drifting away to be taken over by remembering a lot of lodges were laid out like this. After all he'd used his memory of the one in Vail for his template in Edinburgh, and the one he'd visited there had turned out to be so close to his vision, minimal changes in the details were needed to make it work.

"Uh, you're right, Van," he said, "this would've been a great place for me to finally have a little peace."

"Of course," Van said, then hesitated. "Wait, I ... I don't understand what you mean."

"Oh, nothing, really. I just have this chaos that follows me wherever I go. Runs in the family. My sister had it, too, till she got married a few years back and stopped talking to me."

Van blinked. "She stopped talking to you? Completely?"

Daniel nodded. "Just over a year ago. She found her peace, albeit in an acceptable form of delusion."

"I still don't understand."

"Born again," my guy said. Van grimaced. "And she won't let me near her because now she's got twin boys, and she's afraid queerness is as contagious as the chaos."

"You have got to be kidding me."

Nope. Bitch actually got a restraining order against my guy to keep him away from her family, using his three days in the nut house and the fact that he now had a male lover to justify it, the fucking – oh, even the *C*-word's too good for her. Once again, she found a judge who hated fags. Amazing how many there are, now, thanks to the GOP and their rabid dogs. So he did all the paperwork and filed the forms. Then when Daniel came to visit, at sister's invitation, no less, he'd been served at the airport. And the sheriff who did the serving said, "You go anywhere near them kids, you faggot, I personally will kick your faggot ass into jail, you got me?"

Daniel caught the next flight out. And I can't even begin to tell you how deep this ripped into him. I honestly think the only reason he didn't toss himself off a bridge or buy a pistol in that gun-worshiping state was that Carmen and I, both, were there reminding him he needed to finish proofing *Cadillac Criminal Mind* and had started *Dirty Baker's...* and leaving them undone would've been the wrong thing to do to us. Plus, at that time things were still good enough with Tad to make him long to be back with him, much as I hate to admit it. So that had propped him up until the humiliation and hurt could slip far enough into his shadows to be manageable.

"Never assume I'm kidding, Van," he murmured. "But maybe it's better that way. The chaos still follows me. And keeps driving people off. Like I'm a budding *McMurphy* from *One Flew Over The Cuckoo's Nest.*"

"Like your DNA wants you back in that padded room," I joked.

Daniel just sighed.

I jolted. Shit, he took it wrong, like I meant it as a slap. "Dan-O, c'mon, I was just goofin'," but it was too late; it had vanished into that part of his brain I was never allowed to visit. Shit. Aw, man – here came that fucking blue phase, again.

"Have you always been so down on yourself?" Van asked, his voice carrying real concern.

Daniel shrugged. "Never known much different."

Van looked away from him, frowning. "That ... that's too bad." Then he took a deep breath and looked back at Daniel to say, "But you know, some people say that chaos is good for creativity."

My guy and I both chuckled at that one. "Then I should be Shakespeare," he said.

"No, seriously, Daniel. Have you ever considered Orson Welles' speech as ... as ... oh, what was it? As Harry Lime, in The Third Man. How'd it go? Uh, something like, *Under the Borgias was murder ...* Uh, give me a second ... I'll think of it ... " His voice trailed off as he worked his memory cells.

Daniel smiled at him and murmured, *"Like the fella says, in Italy for thirty years under the Borgias they had warfare, terror, murder and bloodshed, but they produced Michelangelo, Leonardo da Vinci, and the Renaissance. In Switzerland they had brotherly love. Five hundred years of democracy and peace. And what did that produce? The cuckoo clock."* Daniel now gazed at Van, impressed. "You know the movie?"

"I love the classics," said Van, and I think for the first time he was being honest. I think. "That one was brilliant."

"And you think that quote applies to me?"

Van looked straight at him and said, "Daniel, your books – no, your writing holds a style and depth of character that is just plain phenomenal. Parts of *The Dirty Baker's Dozen Plus Two* bordered on poetry."

"Oh, *what* do you *want?*" I wailed with frustration. "Just tell us!" Because it was getting to be more and more obvious he was up to something and yet harder and harder to make my guy care!

"I dunno," Daniel just sort of smiled then added, "I mean, thanks, but I don't think that's really …"

"But nothing," Van cut in. "What about when Ace first arrived at that summer resort and saw those four old women in the lobby?"

Wow, he really had read the book.

My guy grinned and said, "The battleship and her attack group."

"Who sniped and gossiped in whispers just loud enough to be heard by the people they were talking about."

"Because that was the only way they could prove they're still effective in this world."

"The subtlety of your description was breathtaking. I could just picture how they dressed and sat and ... and could almost hear the mocking tone in their voices. And thanks to their careful choices of words, I began to feel as if I could easily be the next victim of their casual cruelty."

Daniel slid down the side of the couch to sit on the floor, pistol still in hand, the key going back into his shirt pocket, him doing that thing where he watched Van without seeming to.

The guy kept on with, "When it turned out their gossip was the motive behind a brutal murder, the way you connected their cold-blooded maliciousness to that evil made the hair on my neck stand on end. And then, even after they knew what they'd done, for them to deliberately brush it off as meaningless, it ... it suggested that they, themselves, had once been victims of the exact same maliciousness and felt they had to carry on in the same horrible tradition, if only to prove that what happened to them was not pointless."

Daniel let a hint of wonder cross his face. "Nobody's ever said anything like that to me, before."

"And all in one breath, too," I snipped. Sorry; couldn't help it. That's how I'm written.

"That's inexcusable," Van said.

"I am proud of the book," Daniel said, almost bashful. "Even though it's darker than my others."

"I think it shows your evolution as a writer."

"Thanks. Y'know, I stayed in Edinburgh for a week to research it. It was the first time I could afford to do that."

"Really?" Van asked. "But the detail in your stories ..."

"Oh, you can find anything you need online, these days," Daniel sighed. "Except the truth of a place. The reality of it. You have to actually be there to know that."

"Well, I guess your books were catching on nicely, by that point, weren't they?"

My guy shook his head. "I still have to tend bar. It's just, that was the first time I got an advance, so I splurged on the trip. Wasn't a good idea, financially, but ..."

But he didn't really care because he'd really needed it. The problems he was starting to have with Tad had made it hard for him to concentrate on the story, so me, Carmen and a few other members of the ether-sphere wrangled a really great deal for the trip into his frame of reference, and he'd said, *Fuck it*, and bought the package and packed his bags before he could change his mind. And it jolted him back into the story in a way that did make it deep and dark and close to brutal, in some ways. And he'd gotten the best reviews, yet, for his work. Talk about zero need for regrets.

"Did you climb Arthur's Seat?" Van asked.

"Yeah," said Daniel, smiling. "Once. As a man twice my age made three trips up and down those wickedly crooked steps."

"Yeah, right," Van chuckled.

"No, seriously," Daniel said, looking straight at him. "He was like a mountain goat. On his third trip down, I asked him what he was doing and he said he was training for a hike in the Himalayas."

"Wow, that'll do it."

"So you've been to Edinburgh?"

Van blushed. "No, but I want to, some day. I'm big on all the legends of Camelot and Scottish history. My ancestry."

Daniel chuckled. "Tales of honor and valor and decency. So out of date."

"Never were," Van grinned, then he finally seemed to notice my guy was wearing nothing but his shirt and that way-too-goofy shower curtain. "Daniel, aren't you cold?" he asked.

My guy just shook his head.

Van motioned to his coat. "If you want to wear that ..."

"No, really, I'm fine."

Which was a great big pile of bullshit. He was cold, and he would've loved to take Van up on his offer, but he couldn't quite settle things in his mind, yet, about Van, so couldn't quite make himself accept anything more than words from this guy, yet. Even though deep down he really felt it would be the right thing for him to do. Which made no sense to me, but you can't argue with instinct.

"Then sit on the hearth by the fire," Van said.

Daniel looked at him and had to allow that his eyes were gentle and caring, and they seemed as if they could be trusted and would never hide from him. They seemed to honestly care about him.

And that is when he noticed that fucking frame on the fucking mantelpiece with Tad's perfect fucking face in it, and he had to look away because suddenly he felt like he was being disloyal to the fucking shit! "No," he said, "I like it here."

Van shrugged. "So tell me, with a talent like yours, why do you write books like *Ace Shostakovich*?"

Uh, what? Excuse me? "Let's not go there," I muttered through clenched teeth.

"Why not?" Daniel said, sending me a snarky sneer then casting Van a sideways glance. "I gotta pay for therapy in some way."

"Okay, then why make this bet?" Van asked. "I mean, it really does sound as if you could lose a lot of money."

"It's not a bet."

Van nodded. "So what is the payoff?"

"Oh, something I'd been dreaming about," said Daniel, suddenly embarrassed. "And now I'm wondering why."

Oh? Really? Good, buddy. You keep right on wondering.

Van gave him an encouraging smile, hoping for more.

Daniel looked away. "I just don't feel like discussing it, right now. I've already talked a lot more than I intended to." And he cast Van one of his hurt puppy looks.

"Okay," said Van, almost seeming to encourage him. "When that's done, do you think you might want to stay up here? Write some more? Find a new voice?"

That tore it! "Hold on!" I snarled. "I'm Dan-O's voice."

"And you never shut up!" Daniel muttered, startling me.

Of course, Van thought Daniel meant him. "Oh, I'm sorry. I hope you don't think I talk like this all the time."

Daniel cast him a confused look. "Huh? Oh, no, uh, no, listen, Van, fair warning, here. I have ... well ... discussions with my characters and sometimes I can get carried away."

Van hesitated. "You can?"

My guy nodded.

"That was going on while you and I talked?"

At that, Daniel just smiled.

"Well," he said, then added with a sweet smile, "they also say, there's a fine line between genius and schizophrenia."

"And he's danced over it so many times," I snarled, still unhappy about him snapping at me.

Daniel sighed. "Why am I not surprised you'd say that?"

"C'mon," I sneered. "He's puttin' down the work that kept you sane."

"I'm being objective in my opinion, Daniel."

"Thanks," Daniel said.

"Dan-O, you know damned well the little bastard wants somethin'. Can't you wait till you know what it is before you listen to him?!"

He glared at me, irritated, and snapped, "Wait – what's wrong about suggesting that I could write something fresh and real? Human. Honest. About something meaningful?"

"Like a freak lost in his freakiness?" I snapped back, now more than a little pissed off. Again, that's how I'm written.

"I ... have no doubt you could," said Van, uncertainly.

Daniel jolted and looked at him. And BAM! Hurt puppy cranked up to a hundred percent and he almost let tears into his eyes. "No?" he whispered. "None?"

"At all." And Van looked so adorable saying it, Daniel

damn near got up to go over and kiss him. But being the loyal fucking mutt that he is, he remembered Tad and why he was here and made himself stand and move away from the guy.

Oh, this was driving me nuts! SHIT!

Van noticed and rose. "So," he continued, "can I stay and get your interview, since you've already given me a good down payment on it?"

Oh, and here it comes, the great big *Ah-hah*! "The son-of-a-bitch," I sniped. "It was all just a nice, sweet line he's been offerin' up. He wanted your story, an' he got you to give him every damn bit of it, with just a dash of sweetness on the top. You fuckin' idiot."

Daniel tightened and whispered, "Yeah."

That jolted my focus sharp back to my guy, and suddenly I felt like dirt. Because his heart had dropped straight to his feet, and I'd helped push it over the edge. I mean, yeah, right, he had no reason to feel so let down; after all, he'd only just met this character. And seriously, falling for so obvious a ploy to get an interview was stupid to the max, and I know, I know, I keep bouncing between using this guy to get rid of Tad and seeing him as a threat, and I don't know why I couldn't settle on which way to go except, to be honest, something about Van scared me, a little. Hell, a lot. So I'd happily shoved him away, hard. And by doing it I'd ripped Daniel up.

And yes, I also know, it's really a case of Daniel hurting himself. That I'm him and he's me and all that psychobabble. But did I really need to twist the knife, like that? Because I was finally starting to see that something more was going on with my guy than just wanting Tad back. Something more than just sharing and caring. Somehow it was deeply tied to a part of his inner world that he'd never let me see, and lurking behind it was this ... this new sense of fatalism that was really beginning to spook me. For the first time, I was afraid for him.

Of course, Van didn't know any of that. He thought Daniel was talking to him, so he chirped up with, "You mean it? I can stay and watch?"

Daniel sighed and turned to him, hiding his pain behind a gentle smile. God, he was something. Even when his feet've been yanked out from under him, he can still be all Mr. Polite to people. It was something I'd always admired in him and wished he'd given that little detail to me. Especially while dealing with Carmen when she's on a tear.

"Sure," he said. "Why not? After what happened with that guy, maybe I do need a watchdog."

"Woof!" Van said, all but bouncing. "So who was he?"

"I dunno," Daniel said, pulling the curtain tight around him. "But he had a key to the cabin, hid something somewhere and called a guy named Max about someone named Costello."

Wait a minute! I jolted back into full-Ace mode to grab my guy by the ear and scream, "Dan-O, I fuckin' told you to …!"

"You don't mean Max Benitez and Josephine Costello?"

I looked at Van and continued with, "Dude, you should tell him everything."

"I dunno," said Daniel, wary. "Why?"

"Josephine Costello's the mayor of Bradleyville. Max Benitez is her executive assistant. There've been rumors of a payoff on a bid to repave the downtown streets."

Wait a minute. "Bradleyville's tiny," I said.

Daniel nodded and asked, "Is the job really big enough to bribe someone for it?"

"The town's the county seat, so also has discretion over who gets county projects, which can add up to millions. And if the state likes your work, there's an even better chance at top quality jobs."

"Oooooh," I said, purring at Daniel, "this sounds like a job for meeeeeeee."

Daniel rolled his eyes. "Don't you wish?"

Van blinked. "Don't I …?"

"Nothing," Daniel said, forcing himself to focus on the here and now. "This isn't anything I really need to know about. I have to get to work or I'll lose everything."

"So is this how you normally write?" Van asked, looking him up one side and down the other.

Daniel blushed. "No. No, I ... I am getting kind of cold."

"Pants help keep you warm," said Van, trying not to smile.

"Point out the obvious," Daniel smiled back as he started to climb the stairs, then he stopped and could not help but look at Van in a way that was so wistful, it hurt. "I just wonder if it's a mistake to let you stay."

Van blinked. "How do you mean?"

"It's just," my guy said, "until I'm caught up in the story, I'm easily distracted and you ... well ..."

"So I *am* a distraction? I really am?"

Oh, what a great big moment of bullshit. Flirting with my guy then giving him your nicest smile as he's walking up the stairs, knowing full well the light from the fire dances across your face in a manner guaranteed to make anyone take notice, be they gay male or straight female ... and where did that come from, Carmen? I heard her giggle, the bitch. Playing with my mind even as I'm playing with Daniel's. Still, I had to admit Van's a good-looking dude, and I'm not into guys but now I knew Carmen was of that opinion, too, and ... all right, I grant you it gets pretty confusing, at times, trying to keep track of who's interested in what, where, how and when but ...

A key entered the lock to the French doors and cut off my jabbering. We jumped, and Daniel had to grab his curtain to keep it on.

The doors opened slowly, silently. Then an old, old man in a plaid wool coat and yellow britches, with a wild beard and white knit cap on his head peeked inside and saw Daniel and Van. His eyes flared and he bolted into the room, slamming the French doors closed behind him as he snarled, "What in Sam Hill're you two doin'?! This ain't no bathhouse!"

Daniel and I instantly recognized him.

It was the hermit.

Let the Chaos Commence ... Sort of

"You, too?!" Daniel exploded.

"Me?!" the hermit yelled back. "What do you mean me?"

"I mean you because I'm looking at you and I'm talking at you!" Daniel snarled as he stormed down the stairs towards the old fart. Van gently held him back by grabbing the tail of his shirt. My guy kept on with, "What're you doing here?"

"I live here!" he snarled back.

"*Live* here?!" Daniel nearly sputtered.

"Nice of the old bat to tell us," I snapped.

"Yeah," the old man sneered. "It's my home in the winter. Summers I'm at my igloo on the North Pole. Don't like heat."

Van peeked around Daniel, asking, "You have another key?"

"No, I got the real one! The old man gimme it the day he died – or was it the day after?"

"What old man?" Daniel asked.

"The father of that little twerp down in New York, that's who!" And he all but spit.

Daniel blinked. "Tad's dad's not dead."

"You so sure?" the hermit snapped back.

"Uh, I ..." Well, no, since we'd never met the man. Daniel frowned at the old guy. "So you know Tad?"

"Know him?" sneered the hermit. "I hate him. Him and all his faggot friends."

Oh, shit. If there was any word that'd cut past my guy's polite-mode, it was that *F* one ... and we ain't talking *fuck*.

Daniel raised the pistol and snarled, "Don't you even think about saying another word, like that, 'cause I'll shoot you back to last Friday!"

Wait a minute!

"That's my line from *The Cadillac Criminal Mind*!" I said.

"I know!" Daniel snapped.

"Know what?" the old man sneered.

Now it was my guy's turn to hesitate, but then he tightened up and said very calmly, "That you're leaving. You'll have to stay with Mrs. Serff for the weekend and ..."

"The hell I'm goin'! I got a key!"

"An' I raise you by three, you ol' fuck," I snapped, "so you're outta the game!"

But before Daniel could gather his thoughts enough to let his politeness filter kick in and him not repeat what I said, another key was heard! This time entering the front door lock and cutting me off, again! Talk about WTF!

"This baby makes five!" I wailed.

Daniel leaned against the back of the couch, exasperated.

The key kept struggling to work the lock, so the hermit snuck up to a window and peeked out a curtain. He huffed and whispered in a snarl, "It's a woman! I hate women!"

"Is there anything you do like?" asked my guy, absently.

"Chipmunks," said the old man. "They's quite sociable an' polite, if you got some walnuts."

My guy just rolled his eyes.

"Tell you what, Daniel, let me handle this while ..." said Van.

"No, you two hide in the kitchen."

Hermit glared at Van. "I ain't goin' nowhere with no ... !"

Daniel quietly cocked the pistol, warning in his eyes. "I mean it. You say that word one more time ... "

Van stepped between them. "Daniel, I'm the guard dog, remember?"

"And it's my space that's being invaded. Besides, I'm the one with the arsenal." And he held up the pistol, then un-cocked it, for safety's sake.

"So let me have it, and I'll send her on her way."

Excuse me?

"Dream about it, buddy," I snarled.

Daniel just sighed, "I'm supposed to give a gun to a guy I just met?"

Van shrugged. "Okay, uh, why don't I go in your room?"

Daniel nodded. "First door on the left."

Van quietly jumped up the stairs. Daniel watched his powerful legs leap three steps at a time with no effort. Didn't hurt that his butt looked really nice in those jeans. Then he thought about how casually Van had been willing to take over the situation, making him seem like a take-charge kind of guy and – wait, what was that odd bulge at the small of Van's back? Under his sweater? My guy looked at me and I nodded.

"Pistol in a belt holster," I sighed. "Looks a lot like the one I had in ...*Tristan.*"

"Shit," Daniel whispered.

No shit. So Van had a pistol and wanted this one, too. Not cool. Hidden weapons always mean they're up to no good. Detective rule number one-forty-seven.

The old man backed into the kitchen, giving a disdainful huff at Daniel, but my guy paid him no attention. He just wandered over to the table and sat on a chair in a shadow with a sigh.

Well, it was time for me to shift into super-hyper-wariness mode because if I didn't, Daniel might still blind himself to this guy's plans, faults and issues, too, just like he had with Tad. And that was with the dick being up front about everything and laying it out on their first night, between rounds one and two.

Man, what a sight that was – Mr. Moneybags lying next to my guy on his single bed in his single ... uh, that's a one-room apartment for those not up on New York tenement living; about the size of a small bedroom, with a bathroom, mini-fridge and hotplate, costing twice as much as anyplace else on earth ... while Daniel was still half in his costume. Seems that'd turned Tad on in a surprising way.

"I really want to fuck the new Spock," he'd whispered between kisses at the door.

"All cool logic, except when he's in heat," Daniel replied. "So how do you know he'll live up to your expectations?"

"I don't," he'd growled back in the sexiest voice God ever gave man, "but leave on the ears, okay?"

Daniel was too lost to even think, so he'd just nodded. Then Tad actually tore the rented Starship Tunic open and back off my guy's shoulders, and yanked his pants to his knees, and ripped away his briefs, and tossed him on the bed, and did exactly what he said he wanted to do in moves that were so quick, fast, sharp and electric, he'd finished off by the time I gathered my thoughts enough to look away and let Carmen do her reporting thing. Then as he lay on top of my guy, his breath heaving, their bodies crushed against each other, their sweat mingling in ways that made the moment even more weirdly erotic, he'd whispered, "That ... that was for me. Next one ... that's for you. That's for you."

Of course, Carmen was seriously impressed. "You're addin' this to ... *Tristan*, right Danny?"

And he'd barely been able to nod in answer.

Tad finally rolled off Daniel, and they'd lain side-by-side for a good ten minutes before he roused himself to begin tickling the hair on my guy's chest.

All right, so it was just a couple minutes, but when you're sitting around waiting while nothing's happening, it seems like forever, all right?

That's when Tad *happened* to reveal he was an associate producer for an indie film company in Queens.

"We've done a few things for cable," he'd said as his fingers drifted over the hair on Daniel's belly. "And my boss is great. He said he'd let me produce a project if I brought him the right one."

Of course, I caught on to what was what, here, and nudged my girl to say something but she shushed me.

"What's he looking for?" Daniel asked, enjoying the moment too much to worry about paying for the torn tunic.

"Tough-guy mysteries."

See! See!? So I just had to pop up beside Carmen and bark, "Like mine?" Of course, the second I saw what she'd been enjoying, again, I snapped my eyes closed.

Then opened them back up. Because the picture of these two lying in shadows cast by a low-key lamp propped on his desk that was facing the wall, Tad leaning on one shoulder and gazing at my guy, Daniel looking back with pure wonder, it was close to artistic.

Of course, Carmen then wrapped her hand around my neck and whispered, "Don't even think about goin' to the pink side."

"No worries, baby," I said. "You're the only pink for me."

Of course, Daniel also caught on to what Tad was leading up to and smiled, saying, "There's lots of them out there," not yet willing to accept that what the prick was really telling him was exactly why he'd just fucked him and that he wanted to fuck him over, but in a less-than-fun way. And yes, later he told my guy he'd done it because of his eyes, and there was truth behind that, I'm sure, but this was probably the truer truth.

"That's true," Tad said, nodding. "But I read that one about the knife in the Jell-O and *High-Heeled Moccasins*, and I think the *...Moccasins* one would be perfect for us." Of course, those were the only two we'd published, so far. Anyway, Tad's hand kept drifting lower and lower in its soft tickling, getting Daniel going, again. "Or maybe even your new one; the one about the pop."

"How d'you know about that?"

"Friend of mine owns a mystery bookshop," he said as he shifted to lie atop Daniel. "He got an advance copy."

"But how? I'm still doing a final polish."

"Who cares?" Tad said then bit my guy's left tit, and I mean hard enough to hurt. "Ready for seconds?"

And then he nuzzled Daniel's chest and proceeded to prove exactly how second rate he was in bed. Seriously, the guy couldn't have got a hot-to-trot priest who'd just got out of the seminary off, he was so clumsy in the ... oh, shall we say, *oral department*. I don't want to get too graphic here because at that point I did close my eyes and got it all from Carmen, and she was much better in the viciousness.

"He acts like he's chewin' gum, for cryin' out loud," she'd laughed. "Like he's never sucked on a lollipop in his life."

Which didn't matter so much to Daniel. He just took over and showed Tad what making love was all about, taking him places he'd never been before and starting their relationship off just right. And since he liked being with Tad and making the prick happy, *High-Heeled Moccasins* got made, and got good reviews, and did well in the aftermarket sales, and brought Daniel his slightly-larger apartment and a queen-sized bed and let him not have to wonder about making his rent, for a few months.

All right, a year. Jeez, get technical. He still had to work to pay for his mom and his bills on a month-to-month basis.

And now he was falling into the same pattern. But at least this time he was fighting with himself over whether or not he should fight it. So it was time to bring in someone who could help him make up his mind – Little-Lord-Perfect, wearing that scarlet Speedo, looking even more tan and glorious than usual. He bolted out of a shadow by the French doors, snarling, "Danny, why're you talking to that ... that *Cervantes* person?"

Daniel rolled his eyes. "Not now, Tad," he whispered.

"No, no, no, yes, now," Tad snapped. "I can't believe you're thinking of ruining everything for some man you just met!"

"I'm not."

"Oh, please! After knowing him ten minutes, you're spilling your life story to him when it took you nearly two years to start telling me, and you wouldn't have then except for that phone call from your sister and ..."

"And look what happened."

"Well, if you'd have let me know she was a born-again freak, I'd never have told her we're lovers. I thought you'd be happy I was owning it."

"Is that why you started pulling back?"

"Is that why you started having those blow-ups? Is that why it took you three months to tell me you're on Prozac? What – am I supposed to tie myself down to someone who's crazy?"

"Tad, please," Daniel sighed. "Will you just shut up?"

"Danny," he snapped, "you promised to keep this deal quiet, but he *is* the press and you're telling him everything."

"He already knows about it."

"So? Even when a promise is broken it needs to be kept."

Daniel spun on Tad, irritated. "Y'know, in my fantasies, you never speak, and *that* is why."

Which is when Carmen came floating in to say, "C'mon, Tad, it's easy to figure this out. Danny hasn't been with nobody since you dumped him."

"No, no, *I* didn't dump him," Tad snapped. "*Tad* dumped him!"

"An' your point is?" she snickered.

"That it's beside the point!"

"No, it's ignorin' the point that the guy's got an ass on him that'd make the butchest dyke join wiener world."

Talk about politically incorrect ... but Daniel did not contradict her.

Carmen sighed and caressed his cheek. "But, baby, let's get real. He is playin' you."

Tad smirked and nodded. "Absolutely. He's here for a story, that's all. And you'll let him ruin us both."

"You really wanna tie yourself to another dick like that?" Carmen purred.

"I never did that," said Tad with his best puppy dog look.

Daniel sighed. "This you. But not the *you* you."

No shit, Dan-O, and – wait. What was that? Are you finally acknowledging Tad was always a dick? Very good!

"But doesn't that make me perfect?" Tad asked.

"Yes," Daniel said. "As a right hand man."

"Now just a minute, here!" Tad huffed.

"No, now go away."

Tad would've argued more, but the front door finally CREAKED open, cutting him off. Carmen pulled him back into the shadows just before an absurdly elegant woman of thirty-going-on-twenty, wrapped in a massive fur coat and wearing the latest in designer boots meant more for Park Avenue than up-country entered. She force-freed her key, shoved the door closed with an even louder CREAK and an attitude as nasty as Mrs. Serff's, then headed for the kitchen.

Daniel sighed and hit a light switch. "This help?"

The woman jolted, saw the pistol and raised her hands.

"Okay," my guy continued, "I'm sure you'll excuse my wondering, but why are you here?"

She just eyed him and asked, "Are you with Heinz or Costello?"

Daniel frowned. "I'm with Tad. Are you?"

"The men in my life have names like Jesse or Luther or Cornelius," she said. "I can't imagine even knowing a Tad, let alone admitting it."

Hey, I kind of liked this broad.

"Yeah, sometimes I'm sorry I have to admit it, myself," said Daniel.

She looked my guy over, all but licked her lips and started advancing on him, like a lioness stalks her prey. "How did you get in?" she asked, her voice as sultry as a cartoon seductress.

Daniel held up a key. "With one of these. And I'll bet you thought you had the only one, didn't you?"

"No."

"Oh."

Hmph, honesty. Whole new tactic.

"Did you notice that you're wearing bubbles?" And her voice held insinuations only a deaf man couldn't figure out.

Which flustered Daniel a bit. He responded with, "I got a better question – who *are* you?"

She smiled. "Are names so important?"

"They help one keep track of people. Mine's Ace."

I still had to bark a laugh at that. He ignored me.

She hesitated then her voice took on a flutter as she said, "I ... my husband is Winston Heinz. He's a contractor bidding on a project in Bradleyville, and he's done a very stupid thing. He's paying Mayor Costello a bribe to win the bid."

Say what?!

"I learned they plan to give the bid to someone else," she continued, still fluttery, "and, if he tries to expose them, hand a small portion of the bribe over to the attorney general's office then have him charged with attempted bribery. I begged him not to do it. I pleaded. But things are so desperate for his business, right now, he'll do anything. So I came here to take the money from them before anything can happen. Will you help me? Please?"

"What're we looking for?"

"Eight hundred-thousand dollars in bearer bonds."

"Eight hundred-thousand dollars?!" Daniel cried at the same time as me. Then he and I caught a quick glimpse of the old man peeking out of the kitchen, his eyes wide and wary. "For just a bribe?" Daniel continued.

"Yes," she said, breathless. "A man named Haddon brought it. In an envelope. I followed him, and when I saw him leave, I followed his trail to the cabin. Odd, but he drove away like a madman. And on this ice."

I spun on Daniel. "Drove like a madman?! He's gone for help! I knew you should've told the sheriff everything!"

"Dammit," Daniel muttered, "I was really hoping he'd just vanish."

"Hoping?" Mrs. Heinz asked him. "You mean, you saw him?"

Daniel nodded, absently, and held up the pistol. "That's where I got this."

Now she looked incredulous. "*You* took his gun away?"

"Oh, not exactly."

I smacked Daniel up back of the head. "Will you shut up an' lie for once!?"

Daniel continued with, "He ... just left it with me."

If her expression had been insinuating before, now it was damn near predatory. "You're more interesting than you look," she purred. And I wondered just how many innocent young lads, be they gay, straight or bi-curious, had been led astray by that very comment. "So where are the bonds?"

Daniel shrugged. "He hid them before I knew he was here."

The woman's eyes glittered with greed, for an instant, as she looked around. Then she regained control, turned to Daniel and said, oh-so-plaintively, "Then they're still in the cabin. We have a chance to have the mayor charged with bribery, instead."

"Problem is, Haddon's gone for help," Daniel sighed as he headed for the landline. "I better call the sheriff."

"No!" she cried. "We must find the bonds, first!"

"Those guys could be back at any minute," Daniel snarled.

Before he could get the phone, Mrs. Heinz grabbed him by the shirt and slung him across the back of the couch, face up, and flopped on top of him in a position that Carmen and I had made use of on more than one occasion ... and 'nuff said about that. Then she turned up the helplessness by megawatts as she begged, "Please, Ace, you're big and strong and have great legs; you can take care of yourself while I'm just a poor, defenseless little woman fighting to keep her husband from being sent to prison and her children from losing their father and being turned out into the street because we can't pay our mortgage or grocery bills. You can't refuse to help someone in such a desperate situation."

Daniel barely kept the curtain wrapped around himself as I snottily sneered, "Oh, it's *The Perils of Pauline*, here."

"No shit," Daniel silently replied.

Then while he tried to untangle himself from her, Van stepped onto the staircase landing. Of course, it creaked.

The woman jolted off Daniel and spun about to glare up at Van, only a little flustered. "What's the meaning of this?" she sputtered, vaguely indignant.

"That's what I've been asking myself, all night," Daniel

replied as he stood up and pulled the curtain tight.

"And the answer'd freak you, baby," I said.

"Times ten," Daniel muttered, then noticed two buttons on his shirt had been popped off. "Aw, man, I like this shirt."

The woman stayed focused on Van as he sauntered down the staircase. "Who are you? How much did you overhear?"

"Nothing, really," said Van, gently glancing at Daniel. "I was in the bedroom and heard voices, so I came out to make sure Ace is okay. What do you need help with?"

The woman hesitated. "Um, nothing. Nothing." Then she turned to Daniel and whispered. "Please don't tell him who I am. My husband would kill me if he knew I'd come."

Daniel sighed and nodded, then smiled at Van and said, "This is Miss O'Brien."

Carmen appeared by the table, slamming it with her fist. "Hey, she can't be me! I ain't that old!"

Daniel and I both snapped, "Carmen!"

Carmen huffed and vanished as Van fought back a smile and shook Mrs. Heinz's hand.

"Carmen, I'm Van Shostakovich, Ace's brother. Just dropped in to see how he's doing, make sure he's keeping warm, not too drunk on coffee, all of that."

Damn, this dude was smooth. Maybe just a bit too smooth.

Daniel nodded in agreement. "He, uh, even brought me some chicken soup. I'd offer you some, but we ate it, excellent soup, too, it had carrots in it, and I like soup with carrots, not carrot soup, no, there's something about soup made from carrots that's just too bizarre, like it's carrot puree or carrot juice and that's not for me, just Bugs Bunny, but soup with carrots in it, that's different, they just add color, don't you think, like celery and tomatoes and ... and ... and ..."

Van and Mrs. Heinz watched Daniel, nonplussed, as I softly said, "Dan-O, you're jabbering."

Daniel nodded. "I know; I can't help it. Somebody stop me before I jabber, more!"

Van stepped over to Daniel and guided him to the stairs. "Ace, you really should get dressed. You're shivering."

"Huh?" Daniel asked, responding more to Van's touch than his words. Which was not a good sign. Then he nodded. "Oh. Uh, right. I was about to take a shower when Haddon showed up, and I've been trying to get it back together ever since."

Van just nudged him up the stairs. "Come along, big bro'."

"Big?"

"By a year and two months." And he winked at Daniel.

"Oh," said Daniel. "Okay."

"If you'll excuse us for a minute," Van said to Mrs. Heinz.

She went to the banister. "Um, is this really necessary?"

"I'm just going to find something to wear," said Daniel. "I'll send Van down with some brandy. He can keep you company."

I heard the old man huff at hearing that. So he thought *he* had dibs on the dribbles.

"Oh, and Mrs. H— ... uh, Carmen," said Daniel, "if Haddon does show up before I get back, go in the kitchen. There's a door at the other end of it and you can get out through there and ... and I'll deal with whatever happens. Okay?"

She nodded, wary. Van just patted my guy on the back to keep him moving on up.

Daniel led Van into the bedroom, me right behind them. My guy turned on the lights then picked up the bottle of *Dvin*.

"Are you all right?" Van asked, and for the first time I caught honest concern his voice.

Daniel looked at him with complete innocence. "Hm? Yeah. I am. Really." But I knew he was nowhere near sure about that.

Obviously, Van wasn't convinced, either, but he just shrugged and said, "Well ... don't trust that woman. I went to school with the Heinz boys and she is not Mrs. Heinz."

Daniel handed him the bottle. "That a fact? Why don't you heat some water? There's a nice size pot on the stove and the bag by the hearth has tea, honey and packets of lemon juice."

Van followed him. "Wait, wait, wait, you knew?"

Daniel nodded as he picked up his pants. "I played along to find out what she was after," he said. "That, uh, that's why I did the jabber thing. Over the carrot soup. To keep her off guard."

I smiled. "I'd say bullshit on that, but I kind of like the reaction it got."

My guy just smirked.

And Van noticed the torn pants. "Wow, what happened?"

"Hm? Oh, Haddon."

"He did that?"

"Don't worry," said Daniel, with more than a hint of wicked in his voice, "it wasn't *that* much fun."

Van got wary and asked, "Do I want to know what you mean?"

"Nope," Daniel said then poked his head through the hole in the crotch and sighed. "At least they'll keep my legs warm."

Van eyed Daniel with a hint of awe. "Damn, Ace, you really do live up to your books. Is every aspect of them from your own experience?"

Daniel grinned at him, sweetly. "A writer never reveals his secrets, even when he does."

Van smiled back. "C'mon, you can trust me."

"Yeah," I sneered, "you've known each other a whole thirty minutes."

Daniel took the pants off, looked straight into Van's eyes and made himself say, "First tell me why you're really here."

Oh, shit. Going for the be-honest-with-me tactic. Give the guy a chance to explain himself. Time for careful.

Van blinked. "I did ... I'm ..."

"C'mon, you trust me." And Daniel batted his eyes at him.

Van hesitated then nodded. "That payoff – I think there were two others. I heard this one might happen and ... and then Orlando called me about the bet, so I came up to see if I could ... could keep you away from here."

Not even barely believable, but what's nice is, my guy wasn't swallowing it, either. "Why?"

"Daniel, these people're dangerous."

"You came alone."

"I ... I didn't plan to confront anybody." Uh-huh, and that's why you got a pistol on your ass, right. He kept on with, "The fact that Haddon was already here surprised me. I just planned to use my column to rant about the corruption in our little town. Maybe get the Attorney General to start investigating; or even get Costello sent to Washington, where she can steal from the whole country instead of just us."

Aw, now I just had to pop in with, "Still bullshittin'."

"Okay, don't tell me," Daniel sighed, resigned. And I could see he was letting it slide not because he didn't want to accept the possibility that Van was a *bad-boy*, but because he honestly was not seeing any kind of duplicity in him. And I sort of understood why. The guy all but radiated integrity of the kind that makes you want to like him and be around him. Still, it was obvious he wasn't being honest.

Van huffed and leaned against the dresser, looking casual but sexy in that dude-next-door kind of way.

"Well, what do *you* think I'm up to?" he asked.

"Doesn't matter," Daniel sighed. "Just look for that envelope."

"I'm not supposed to know you're searching for anything."

Daniel dropped the shower curtain, more than a hint of provocation behind his eyes and movements.

"I didn't say *search*," Daniel smiled. "I said *look*."

I leaned against the other side of the dresser, sneering, "Some reporter. Even I know the difference."

Van took in a sharp breath and looked my guy up one side and down the other, which gave him hope but added to my worries, then he said, "Okay, what if I find it?"

"Tell me, and I'll handle Mrs. Heinz."

"You're over-dressed for her," the guy smirked.

"I thought she liked the bubbles," Daniel smiled. "But it doesn't matter; I also have an arsenal. Which makes me more dangerous than you, right? I mean, it's not like you have one of these." And he held up the pistol. "Right?"

"Well, not exactly," Van said, his voice dripping with insinuation as he shifted into a new pose that made him look like sex incarnate even as he sort-of-kind-of lied. "So, I guess I should be glad you're here, *Ace*. You're such a big strong man, and I'm just a little guard dog. Imagine you being willing to help this puppy keep his town from being robbed and ruined. I whimper at your feet." And he batted his eyes.

Daniel felt something grab him hard behind not only his heart but everywhere else, and it got really obvious that I'd lose this fight if my guy wasn't so fucking loyal to Little-Lord-Perfect. He had to take a long, deep breath before he could whisper, "And who's been a major distraction. So maybe you should get to work. Earn your Kibble. And let me dress."

Van blinked. "Oh. Well. Okay, boss," he said, his voice soft. "I ... uh, guess I'll get the operation underway."

He turned and headed out the door, bottle in hand.

Daniel watched him go. Noted the hint of the pistol under the loose sweater. Watched his casual little jaunt of a stride. Felt how comfortable the guy was with himself in ways my guy had never been. He really did like this dude one hell of a lot, despite only having known him for half an hour, which indicated the connection was stronger than mere lust or need. It wasn't even simple loneliness or a longing for happinesses past. No, it was almost karmic. A moment or two more like this and my guy would fall headlong into Van's flirtation, so I had to stop it, here and now.

"Dan-O," I said, "wake up! He's a sneak who's after somethin'!"

"Don't," Daniel snapped, rubbing his forehead. The first hint of one of his headaches made itself known – not migraine bad but close enough, and usually brought on by moments of confusion, like this. He looked around, lost, then absently picked up the curtain. "There's more to him than that."

"That's what you kept thinkin' 'bout Tad."

"And there was," he murmured as he headed for the bathroom.

I followed. "Okay, you guys were in sync the first year, year an' a half, while Mr. Glorious was makin' ...*Moccasins*."

"Stop. Please." His headache was building. "I don't want to deal with this, right now."

"Buddy, when're you gonna face reality? It wasn't your sister pullin' her shit and showin' Sir-Perfect just how crazy your family was that ran him off! It was the minute he got the rights to ...*Tristan* and ...*Madam* that things started a crash and burn between you two."

"No, I think it was over with Tad before that," he said, turning on the shower. "He'd never have lasted with me."

Say what?

"I'm not what he needs to feel complete."

Say *what*?!

"How long've you believed that?" I asked.

"I dunno," he sighed as he leaned against the counter and let the pistol drop onto the sink basin. "Maybe from the moment I saw him."

"Why didn't you let me in on it from the start?"

His hands toyed with the curtain. "And have you tear us

apart even faster than before?"

"I never have …"

"You did it with Jarrod!" he snapped, dropping the curtain to rub his neck.

Oh, uh, Jarrod's a guy he got involved with in at Iowa State, who looked so much like the perfect Mormon missionary, you'd have thought he was Mormon even though he wasn't. At least, I don't think he was. I mean, his undies came from Target, not the Tabernacle. But man, you want to talk about a guy who had secret corners to his soul? Jarrod was the epitome of a hard drive in desperate need of some serious de-fragging. He and my guy hooked up after the mess with mom, when Daniel and I were using the writing workshop to perfect *...Moccasins*, meaning he got caught in a couple of back-and-forths between me and Daniel over the plot and character and ... well, you know what I mean. So from the beginning he was unsure about my guy's mental stability, even though his is the one that really should've been called into question.

"His was fine," Daniel snapped, his hands beginning to shake. "It was you bugging me when he and I were together that made him begin to think I was a budding serial killer, ready to feast on his flesh after I feasted on his flesh."

"Dude, he was a young Repugnican who couldn't decide if he was gay, straight or wanted to fuck donkeys, and you were ignorin' *...Moccasins* to be with him all the time and, shit, even Carmen was gettin' antsy about it; just ask her and …"

Holy shit – that's when it hit me. Van looked a little bit like Jarrod.

"Not that much," moaned Daniel. "Like cousins, maybe."

"An' you kept it hidden from me," I said, actually hurt.

"I can't have you control me anymore, Ace."

"Like Jarrod did? Like Tad did? Like your mom did? With you always doin' what they want an' never what you want?"

"Instead of what *you* want?"

"Dan-O, I'm you! What I want is what you want! Shit!"

"I know! I know."

"So you'd rather let scum like Tad and Jarrod be more important to you than you?" He sighed. Meaning, *yes*. "Oh, that's *dumb*!"

"I ... I know," he said, overwhelmed.

"Things were never that great with either of those guys!"

"At least Tad tolerated you being in my head."

"Only 'cause he wanted something," I growled.

"Who doesn't?" he whispered. "I don't think it's possible to be with someone and them not want something from you. Something more than you. Maybe that's all I'm worth." He pulled off his shirt and briefs.

"Aw, shit," I sneered, "you keep pullin' this kind of crap an' I'm gonna have to agree with you on that!"

Daniel bolted up and snarled, "Ace, will you just ... just fuck off! Just stay the fuck away from me!" And he kicked the door closed in my face.

To say I was shocked ... well, I was shocked. Of course, I knew he was really just freaked out by how confused and lost and unsure he was, again. Like he'd been right after that stay in the padded room. Maybe I'd gone too far, pushing him like this, but I knew my guy. Knew if he was beaten up any more like Tad did near the end ... emotionally, not physically ... he'd do a crash and burn into despair. He was already thinking he didn't deserve happiness, and that would bleed into everything he did. But I needed him to have at least some sense of confidence to bounce my stories off of. Because that's me, you know? That's my character – all sure and confident and ready to do battle with the world for what's right and sexy. So the fact that he was setting himself up for a hurting at the hands of what was probably gonna be just another nice set of pecs made me decide to do anything I could to keep it from happening, again.

And that's my only excuse for what I did next.

Daniel disappeared into the steam and let it whisper into his lungs. Clean. Warm. Caressing. Peaceful. Despite the Dali/Seuss fishies. Well, for a moment, anyway, because suddenly it hit him, "I wasn't even gonna take a shower. I was just gonna pull my pants back on. Shit, what the hell is wrong with me? I got no way to dry off!" And his mind slammed into this nasty loop of *I'm losing it; I'm totally losing it*, mixed with Depeche Mode's *A Pain That I'm Used To*. And don't even think of asking me to explain where this came from; my guy's mind works in mysterious ways, to put it mildly.

He leaned against the wall. Let the water pummel his chest and muttered, "Shit, I'm batshit crazy. Tad was right to drop me. He never should've asked me to help him. He should've known I'd fuck it up. That something'd fuck it up. And he won't be nice about it. He won't be nice at all."

Which, of course, brought His-Grandificence forth from the broiling steam, in that scarlet Speedo and as gorgeous as the devil, himself, snarling, "Why should I be, you two-timing mouse? Tossing everything aside to help a piece of meat like that Van character? Do you think he gives a shit about you!?"

"Are you telling me you ever did?" Daniel snapped back.

"Danny! What do you think I am?!"

"A figment of my imagination, in every concept of the phrase!"

"Careful! Just cause I'm not real doesn't mean I can't feel!"

"You mainline ice-water. Just ... just go away, will you?! I can't handle this, right now!" He turned to let the water wash over his face.

Carmen appeared beside him, now in a clear raincoat and boots, holding an umbrella to keep the water off her.

"Danny, Danny, it's okay, baby" she purred. "You're just

off balance from all the crap that's been goin' on. It'll be all right once things simmer down."

"Oh God, I hope so," Daniel murmured, still unsure.

"Sure," she nodded, then frowned. "Unless it *is* Tad behind it all. Unless it's him doin' this to mess with you."

"C'mon," Daniel wailed, "that doesn't make any sense!"

"But wouldn't that be just like him?" Carmen whispered.

"No," Tad whined. "Why would I do that?"

Daniel turned to let the water pound his neck. Tad's response was too logical to ignore, even in the middle of his current psychotic break, and …

Wait a minute!

"Oh my God, Carmen," he gasped. "What if that guy ... the Cheeto-eater ... what if he never was involved? I never met him. Everything's been through Tad. What if it's all just bullshit?"

Tad frowned, confused. "I don't understand."

"Simple, Tad," Daniel snarled. "You told everybody that twenty-one-year-old dickhead was adapting my books, only what if you jumped the gun and didn't have a contract with him, yet? What if he turned you down, after you spread the word? You'd look stupid, and you hate for people to think that about you. Then you get an idea; you write these crappy scripts yourself then get me to agree to rework them, then fuck it up for me and tell people I ... I'd demanded the right to adapt my own writing. That I'm the one who ruined everything. Oh, shit, I can just hear you. *Guys, I wanted to use the best, but Danny and I have a history, and he's a writer and I thought he'd do okay. I guess I shouldn't have tried to be a nice guy. But don't worry, I'll get it fixed.* And that's why he wanted me out of town, so I wouldn't hear about it till it's too late for me to counter his lies. Which makes it all my fault. Son-of-a-bitch!"

"Uh, Daniel, since when am I smart enough to think up something like that?"

"Oh, Taddy, you always had smarts enough to stab somebody in the back," Carmen smirked.

"No, no, he's right," Daniel sighed. "That is way too complicated for him. Besides, why would he go through all of this crap to do it? He could mess me up a lot easier back at my apartment, and I'd still be out of the loop. And ... and it would also mean Van's part of it, and I ... I'm not getting that vibe off him, that ... that scumbag-kind-of-shit attitude."

"Maybe you just don't wanna see it," Carmen said. "He is sort of leadin' you on. Maybe he's Tad's new boy an' he's just helpin' his bed-buddy out."

"No, no, it's something else that's got him playing these games," Daniel said. "He acts more like a cop than a crook."

"Oh, right," Tad snapped. "Right! *Me*, you'll think all kinds of crap about; but the second Mr. Too-fuckin'-cute-to-be-believed might be involved in something that's not so very nice, you do back-flips to make him look good!? Why? Why?! Why?!"

And that's when the light of Daniel's consciousness flashed on my comment about the rights to his books, shifting it from abstract awareness to solid as a rock. Now he could see how everything had been all, *You're my guy, Danny*, till he'd signed the option for the rights over to Tad just three weeks before his sister had called. Then things had really started downhill after he got back from her place, even as Daniel was struggling to polish *Cadillac...* and plot *Dirty Baker's...* and keep from crashing into despair. Suddenly, Tad was working so much, they saw each other maybe once a week. And every time Daniel'd raised the idea of going away together, he'd had some excuse not to. Which started building the subliminal awareness in the recesses of my guy's brain that he was losing him, which sent him into a such a depression he'd finally needed Prozac, so he could function, because deep inside he knew his ... my ... our wariness about Tad's motives were true. That his caring had always been a really good act. That the books had been the only reason he entered Daniel's life, and the belief that Tad had needed more than he could offer was nonsense. Once Tad got what he wanted, he'd shrug any guy off. And then, just over six months ago, came the final break.

Allow me to offer some background here.

It was during Gregory Taylor's Birthday party, at this bar in Hell's Kitchen. My guy obsessed for days over getting the right gift for *the man who gave his life direction*, so he was already pretty uptight about the whole thing ... and yes, I know it was really just the tension between him and Tad making itself known in another outlet, but try and convince Daniel about that at the time; just try. Didn't help that Tad was in a mood, too.

Over what, I got no idea 'cause he never talked about shit like that, though right about then is when he was in deep negotiation with Cheeto-eater about writing the scripts, and it wasn't going well.

Now the bar was nice enough for a pony joint — meaning lots of pretty boys wanting to be someone's pretty toy, all lounging around on non-stop chrome and leather in that subdued kind of lighting that hid just about any flaw anybody could have, real or imagined. The problem was Gregory's Current-Crush booked the entertainment, something whose IQ barely understands *Yes* and never understood *No* should ever be allowed to do, no matter how hot they look in CK's.

So what did Crush decide on? A drag queen faking Faith Hill. In tassels and chandelier earrings. Talk about a crime of fashion; Carmen's words, not mine. Faith's partner was a drag king playing ... you got it, Tim McGraw. In cowboy boots with British riding heels(!) and a too-tit-tight T-shirt of the athletic kind that made even me cringe, big-time. Meaning, yes, we were both with our guy. They were snarling out some sexy-sassy-stupid duet thing full of twangs and moans, and I couldn't help but pop off with, "Jeez, sounds like two dogs matin'." Carmen laughed, and Daniel spit it out loud before his politeness filter kicked in. *Tim* heard it, and they got into a fight, so we got banished by Crush, to Tad's mortified mortification. Gregory apologized, later; but the damage was done.

You see, sometimes that happens with me and Dan-O, since I'm him and he's me; I speak the crap he's too polite to, and he usually just keeps quiet to keep anyone from knowing what he's really thinking. But Prozac let his inner *Miss Manners* hit the snooze bar in his brain, so he was paying less and less attention to controlling my snark and more and more of it was slipping from thought to voice. I mean sure, he'd stopped taking the crap a few weeks earlier, but it wasn't completely out of his system, yet. Or maybe it was, and he just didn't give a shit, for a change. I don't care; either way worked for me.

Of course, Little-Sir-Perfect snarled at my guy about it being all *the end of the world* and *how can I do business now* and yap, yap, yap, like a pissed-off Chihuahua. But after some bitching back and forth, Daniel convinced him he was sorry, and they wound up having some so-so make-up sex, which only made things worse.

I like the way Carmen put it, best, "Fuckin' Tad couldn't fuckin' get it up, so he fuckin' blamed it all on Danny and fuckin' told him he wanted to fuck other people, the fuck."

Told you her English is better than mine. And French.

Now let me translate – it took Tad a long time to ... oh, *get done this time*, shall we say? And he popped off with, "Prozac's made you lousy in bed, too."

To which Daniel popped back with, "Since when does a piece of meat complain about how it's cooked?" Okay, so maybe it's a bit too subtle a slap for Tad to figure out, but I so loved that line, I made sure Carmen got to use it in *Dirty Baker's...*

Anyway, those two little comments kicked a slow-building rift into a chasm ten miles deep, and they both exploded. And the break-up happened. And Dan-O hid in the bathroom from Tad and me, both, for an hour, scaring the fucking shit out of me. Seriously, if he'd wound up hurting himself, I swore I was going to find some way of getting born into a Sumo wrestler and spend my entire existence tracking Tad down so I could sit on him and crush him to death after I'd taken a shit and hadn't wiped my ass. But my guy finally pulled back from the abyss of despair, and Tad walked and that was that. Would've been perfect if fantasy Tad'd vanished, too. But, no such luck.

"I didn't really know you, then," Daniel whispered to his imaginary Tad, the shower's steam billowing faster. "But I do now. I finally fucking see you and know you. What a fucking idiot I was."

"Hey, Danny, just a minute," said Tad, "we had good times, too. Don't slap me just because you have the hots for Mr. Perfect Ass, downstairs, when all his hots are for God knows what!"

"Now calm down, Tad," Carmen purred, "you know how Danny gets over his type, with that sweet, innocent, deer-caught-in-the-headlights look. Brings out the wicked in him."

"Oh, for God's sake," Daniel snapped as he turned to let the water pour over his head, again. "Stop thinking, stop thinking, stop thinking," now looped through his conscious mind. Didn't help, but at least bad, sad, beautiful *Depeche Mode* was gone.

"You're right," Tad sneered. "Van's just out to get what he can get, and then he'll be gone, and Danny'll be mine, again."

Daniel rubbed his temples. "Oh, shit, oh, shit, oh, shit, I am losing it; I am finally fucking losing it!"

And now it was time for me to make my grand entrance through the steam, back in my trench coat and Joe Cool to the max. "Losin' what, Dan-O? We're still here. We'll always be here to pick you up when you crash and burn. We're the only ones who really understand you, who really care."

"I never dropped you, Danny," Tad purred. "You can face that, now. You grew so erratic after the trip to your sister's. Nice one minute, pissed off the next. Like it was my fault. I didn't know what to make of it, buddy, and that's despite my knowing how you write. After months of that nonsense, I had to back away. And you know it was the right move."

"For you," Daniel whispered, his eyes jammed shut.

"Ain't that always how it's been?" I asked.

"Careful," Tad snapped.

Daniel fought to ignore us, whispering, "I. Have gone. Completely. Insane."

"C'mon, Dan-O," I purred, "what's insanity but another way to help you deal with the crap in the world? Shit, like when you got mixed up with that little fuck, Jarrod." I swung around to grin at Carmen and Tad. "I swear, that little shit must've invented the idea of doublin' back on who you are, insistin' he ain't queer while all but beggin' to be chased by little ol' Dan-O here …"

"Stop calling me that!" Daniel roared. "I sound like a side-kick on a fifty-year-old TV show, and I hate it!"

We all looked at him, shocked. For the first time, I heard serious anger behind his words. Carmen and Tad felt it, too.

"Hate it?" I said. "You hate it?"

"Dammit, Ace, go away!" Daniel growled, holding his head in pain. "Just … let me sort this out, myself!"

"As if you can! You need my help for this and …"

"I don't need shit from you!"

Now wait just a minute. "That's bullshit, Dan-O … *Daniel.* An' how … how can you do this to me? Yellin' at me to fuck off an' … an' now you hate the nickname you gave me to give you? After all I done for you?"

"What have you done for me?" he gasped, barely in control.

"I saved you, you little shit! When you were about to lose it in that hospital, I came in an' gave you a reason to keep goin'! I chose you to tell my stories, an' ... an' I helped you find your way back an' I protected you as best I could against those assholes, an' ... an' ... an' this is how you repay me?!"

"But you're taking over my life!"

"Aw, right, right, blame me for tryin' to give you some kind of direction an' help you make it through the day an' keep writin' an' ... an' everything!" I snapped back at him, my heart torn in half.

He finally looked at me, his face contorted in pain. "But, Ace – you're me! Part of me! Why do you keep making me feel like I ... I'm worthless, even to myself, and don't know what I'm doing and belong back in that padded room?"

"'Cause you do!" I snarled, instantly wishing I hadn't said it, but I couldn't help it; the idea that my guy was turning on us made me lose control. Then I stupidly added, "Treatin' me like this."

Daniel got this look on his face; it's the kind of look that gets guys knifed. "Only because of the crap you keep pulling on me!" he snarled. "You and Carmen and Tad, messing with me when I'm talking to people, making me seem crazier than I already am and ..."

"Hey, Danny," Carmen said, her voice a bit scared, "me an' Ace're only tryin' to ..."

"Trying to make sure I spend my life alone! Trying to make sure you're the only things I have!"

"Dan-O, when have I ever tried to come between you an' anybody. Even Tad?"

"When have you NOT, with your stupid little comments and non-stop snarking? I wish I'd never met you! *Any* of you!"

Aw, man. I backed away from him, barely keeping control as I muttered, "Aw, this ... this ... this is more than a man can take."

"You're not a man, Ace," he said, fighting to keep his voice even. "You're a character I made up in a book!"

"Six books, dammit," I cried, "AND a movie!"

"For cable!" he shot back. "And it was melodramatic

CRAP!"

The ultimate insult to a fictional character. That's when I knew I had gone too far. I had pushed too hard. And now he was breaking with me. Tears streamed down my cheeks to mix with the water pouring over me. "So you're takin' everything from me?" I whimpered. "You ain't leavin' me nothin'?"

Carmen took my face in her hands, horrified. "Danny," she gasped, "you made him cry!"

"I ... I'll be okay," I blubbered. But I couldn't stop.

Daniel crouched down to cower in a corner, letting the steam put a hint of a wall between him and us as he muttered, "Oh, God, this is bad, this is bad; I'm way beyond padded room. I need an exorcist."

"No, you just need a kick in the ass," Tad snarled.

A scream burst from downstairs, instantly followed by the sound of someone falling. Daniel jolted and looked around, lost for second, then remembered where he was and moaned. He rose, turned off the water and grabbed the curtain as he absently stumbled into the bedroom.

"Right," I muttered. "Little-Lord-Daniel off to save the day. NOT!"

"You're a real bastard, Daniel Bettancourt!" Carmen yelled after him. "Just see if I'm in any more of your books!"

I spit out, "Me, too!"

"And let's not even talk about your dreams, bitch!" Tad chimed in.

Daniel stormed back, wrapping the shower curtain around himself, but only to grab the pistol, muttering, "That would be a blessing." Then he headed back to the door, still dripping.

I sat on the edge of the tub, defeated. He was gone. I'd driven him off. Now me and Carmen were separated from the guy who'd brought us to life, and I had no idea what to do next.

"You'll think of something, Ace," Carmen whispered, real fear in her voice. "You always do."

Do I? Not without Dan-O as my backup. He'd been my rock. My way into the world. Without him, my mind was a blank. So what could I do, now? Shit ... what could I do?

I was lost.

Pistol in hand, curtain barely hanging on his hips, water dripping everywhere, Daniel stormed onto the landing to find …

Mrs. Heinz chasing the hermit around the room with a fire poker. The old man had the bottle of brandy and was whooping like a chimpanzee as she shrieked, "I'll rip your beard off when I catch you!"

Daniel rolled his eyes and started down the stairs. The hermit climbed up part of the fireplace and raised the bottle to hit her with it, but since Daniel was close, he yanked it away.

The old man spun around. "Now just a damn minute!"

"What's going on here?!" Daniel snapped. Then he noticed Van seated on the entryway steps, a hand pressed to his forehead, blood flowing down his face. "Van, what happened?"

"It's too stupid to tell," Van muttered.

Daniel snarled at the old man, "Did you hit him?!"

"No, Ace!" Van said. "No, when he grabbed for the bottle I tripped over the steps, here."

"That's my whiskey!" the old man growled.

"It's brandy!" Daniel absently snapped.

Mrs. Heinz snarled, "I don't care if it's Pabst Blue Ribbon Beer! That's no excuse for you to sneak up on us!"

"Are you okay?" Daniel asked Van, heading farther down the stairs.

"Yeah. I ... I forgot the old fart was in the kitchen and ... and ... and that's a *stupid* place to put steps!" snarled Van as he rose and went to the closet to pull out a sheet. He tore a strip off one end.

Daniel eyed him, worried. "You ought to get that looked at; you may need stitches."

"No, it's not that bad," the guy said. "Head cuts always bleed like crazy. But that ruins this sweater."

"Put seltzer water or ginger ale on it," Daniel said. "Keeps the blood from setting."

"The voice of experience?"

"No, it ... it's just something my grandmother told me."

"You have some?" Van asked as he tied the strip around his head.

"Maybe there's some in the wet bar in the kitchen."

"I'll check in a minute."

"Don't wait too long," said Daniel, then he jolted and leaned over the banister. "Oh, let me have the rest of that sheet."

Van handed it up to him. "So – you took that shower?"

"Yeah, I ... uh, I had a brain freeze," Daniel said, using the sheet to dry off. "Not unusual for me, lately. So if I understand it right, little ol' Herman, here, tried to grab the bottle and run and ..."

"My name ain't Herman," the old man shot back.

"What is it?" Daniel asked.

"None of your damn business!"

"None of this is!" Daniel nearly shrieked. "But that doesn't keep people from dragging me into it! HERMAN! Hermit!"

"Don't you yell at me, boy! I'll knock you upside the head!"

Daniel whipped the sheet over one shoulder, gripped the curtain with the hand holding the *Dvin* and raised the pistol, all in one surprisingly fluid motion, and snarled, "Wanna try?"

Herman climbed down from the fireplace, casting Daniel a wounded expression. "Well, if you're gonna be like that."

"I'd shoot him, anyway," sneered Mrs. Heinz. "Put him out of our misery."

Herman glared at her. "See why I don't like women? They's just plain mean!"

"Pot calls kettle black," Van shot at him as he was about to enter the kitchen.

Daniel grimaced and took a step back to regain control. "I'm gonna pull on something and be right back."

But a vehicle was heard approaching.

Van, Herman and Mrs. Heinz looked at the door.

Daniel just sighed and sat on a step halfway up, moaning, "Now what?"

"Sounds like a snow-cat," Van said, warily.

Herman nodded and added, "Headin' this way."

"How opportune," Daniel muttered.

Mrs. Heinz backed away from the door. "What if it's Haddon and his friends? You took too long. Now it's too late to do anything about …"

"Oh, stop!" Daniel snapped. "I'll handle this. Everybody up to my room."

Van hurried over to the stairs. "Daniel, you should really let me take care of it."

"Don't be silly," Daniel said. "You're wounded, and I've got this." He held up the pistol. "And if things do get crazy, you can jump out the window and run when I can't." He motioned to his extreme lack of clothing. "Besides, they won't do anything dumb if they think there'll be witnesses."

"You so sure about that?" Van asked.

Well … no, but that didn't keep him from saying, "Just turn off the lights and get upstairs."

Herman huffed. "I ain't goin' in no room with …"

"You *know* where you can go!" Daniel snapped.

Herman blinked. "Well, no need to get rude."

Daniel's snarl became a vicious glare. Herman quietly slipped into the kitchen.

"Daniel, you're being awfully casual about this," said Van.

Because the entire situation just didn't make sense, Daniel thought. Seriously, all of this happening tonight of all nights? Problem was, he couldn't figure it out, yet, and needed time to think. So he just draped the sheet over his shoulders and said, "What should I do? Freak out and hide in a closet?"

Van almost smiled then shrugged and said, "Come, Mrs. Heinz. Sounds like my bro's got a plan." Then he continued up the stairs.

"Don't forget your coats," Daniel said.

Mrs. Heinz grabbed them then turned off the light and stopped. "The lava lamp."

Daniel finally noticed someone had turned on the lava lamp, and it was happily glooping its red gloop up and down in its casual fashion, adding serious weirdness to the moment.

"Well, it'll have to keep on going," said Daniel, because it was too late to turn it off now.

She shrugged and followed Van upstairs.

Daniel stayed where he was, halfway up the steps, partly

hidden by the fireplace's chimney, pistol at the ready, and watched the entrance in the reflection of the French doors.

"Use Dad's cabin," he muttered. "It's the dead of winter. Nobody around for miles and miles. So much quiet, you'll go nuts. Thought the bastard dumped me because I already was."

On the landing, Van cast him a glance then followed Mrs. Heinz into the bedroom and peeked out to watch. The woman snuck up to look out over his shoulder.

Van cast a whisper back at her, "What took you so long to get here?" Apparently not realizing Daniel could just hear him in the room's deathly quiet.

She sighed and whispered back. "You did notice it's snowing?"

"Then you shouldn't have come in."

"You were supposed to wait for me."

"I had to move. Haddon went in and didn't come out. I didn't know Daniel already had the guy under control."

"He really does think he's on top of things."

"That's what's got me worried."

"What do you mean?"

"Some of the things he's said ..."

"So what's the plan, Van?"

"Keep playin' it on the fly."

"With these idiots?"

Then silence.

Daniel just sighed. As much as he wanted to keep faith in the dude, he just couldn't. Not till he knew what he was really up to, and now he strongly suspected it would be something he did not want to know. Which hurt.

"I bawled out my ids for being right about my libido," he muttered, "Psychosis, thy name be Bettancourt."

The snow-cat stopped then footsteps approached. Daniel forced himself to focus on that and tried not to shiver. He chuckled as he thought, "Couldn't I at least have remembered to grab my shirt?" He slipped deeper into the damp sheet, trying to keep warm. "Okay, uh, they're not trying to sneak up, so it probably isn't Haddon's guys. Just let 'em come in and do their business and keep nice and quiet and maybe they'll just go away." Then he snorted at himself. "Dream about it, Daniel."

A key jiggled in the door and it slowly, slowly CREAKED

open to reveal a young, slim, boyishly-good-looking guy and a woman who seemed so much like a Wagnerian Valkyrie, you'd swear she was going to break into an aria from *The Ring Trilogy*. The man started to enter, but Madam Valkyrie bowled right past him and headed straight for the kitchen, sending him into a skid. The only reason he didn't crash to his butt was he had a death-grip on the doorknob so he used that to steady himself. He cast an evil glare after her then shoved the door closed with another CREAK and scurried over to the hearth.

"Haddon wasn't kidding," he said. "There is a fire."

Daniel crunched tighter against the chimney.

From the kitchen, a powerful female voice responded, "Don't belabor the obvious, Max." And Daniel actually wondered, *Could she be a Coloratura or a Mezzo-Soprano? Yeah, focus on what's important.* A moment later, she burst from the kitchen, digging through a manila envelope. "Oh, excellent. Excellent, indeed."

Mezzo. Sure as snow.

Max saw the envelope and squeaked in surprise. "Is it all there?" And from this high angle he looked about fifteen.

"Indeed it is," replied the Valkyrie, then she grinned at him in a way that did not bode well. "Not a bad haul for one night, wouldn't you say?"

Max spun around to focus on the fire. "No, no, no. Not bad, at all. No."

"Indeed," the Valkyrie said as she closed the envelope, her smile still dangerously aimed at him. Then her voice took on this cooing tone as she said, "Surprised they're still here?"

He turned to look at her, frowning. "Huh?"

"The bonds," she said, circling around on him. "Aren't you surprised they're still here?"

This look of deliberate-innocence filled his entire body. "Uh, um, what do you mean?"

Daniel rolled his eyes then noticed Van and Mrs. Heinz were peeking farther out of the bedroom to listen. He sent them a mental warning of, *Stay where you are!*

The Valkyrie's eyes went cold, and if Daniel had thought of Mrs. Heinz as a lioness, she was now designated kittycat in comparison to this beast, especially when the woman growled, "I refer to your new girl."

Max backed away, wary. "New girl? What new girl? I don't know any new girls. Couple of old ones but ..."

"Gretta Bergstrom. The woman you've seen three times in the last forty-eight hours."

"You had me followed?!" Max said, indignant.

"Naturally," sneered the Valkyrie, "once I learned she's served time for fraud."

Max huffed. "You're full of it, mayor! Gretta's a great girl! She's smart and kind and makes killer hashbrowns."

"She's also a bit old for you," was the Valkyrie's reply.

Which made the woman now known as Gretta straighten in anger and almost storm onto the landing. Van barely held her back.

Daniel noticed and had to fight to keep from snapping at them, *Don't move, you idiots*!

Then the mayor pulled a semi-automatic pistol from her coat, huge, polished and gleaming. Max froze.

Daniel tensed and readied his revolver, and noticed Van reaching around his own back. "For his gun," he thought.

"I almost believe you," said the Valkyrie. "Indeed, I do. But I also know you had a copy of my key to that door made so that *great girl* could get this for you." She held up the envelope. "Ten percent should have been more than enough, Max, indeed it should."

She raised the semi-automatic in Max's direction, and Daniel got ready to crash their party and ...

The door to the kitchen squeaked, and someone was heard scurrying away.

The Valkyrie spun about in nearly operatic horror, almost losing her balance. "Was that her?!"

Max squeaked, "I-I-I-I-I didn't hear anything!"

She bolted to the kitchen door, her weapon trained on Max. "Who's in there?!" No answer, of course. She motioned to the guy. "Stay there! You move and ... just stay there!"

She stormed into the kitchen, and you could almost hear the shrieking chorus of *The Ride...* as she went. Daniel actually wondered if she might also be into Gilbert & Sullivan. She'd make a great *Daughter-in-law Elect*.

Max very nearly followed her then jerkily circled the couch, almost catching a glimpse of Daniel peeking from behind the chimney, but then he focused on the fire. Through the French doors, Daniel could barely make out Herman's yellow pants plowing through the pristine snow, just past the deck, plumes spurting around him like waves as his little legs chugged. Daniel smiled and shifted to keep watch on the main room.

The Valkyrie came back in, warily, muttering, "He got out through the kitchen door. Footprints everywhere. Must have been that hermit. And he could be a witness." She frowned. Obviously, that was not something she wanted to worry about, so she smiled at Max and said, "As I was about to say, had these bonds not been here ... well, all that matters is, you're fired."

Max laughed. "You can't do that; I'm civil service."

"It's that or jail," she responded. "I strongly recommend against you behind bars. Unless it's your dream to participate in some very gay porn." Which triggered Daniel's indignation. "No, I strongly urge you to go find work with some other idiot. In some other town. Preferably some other state."

"But I like it here," he said, confused.

"Then go like it in Texas!" she snapped. "I understand they prefer having crooks in office down there."

"Noooo, I went to Dallas in August, once, and it was hot."

She raised her gun. "I could send you someplace hotter."

"Okay, okay, okay! I'll move to Kentucky. How's that?"

That made her straighten up, confused. "Why Kentucky?"

"I like the sound of it," he replied, too-too-seriously.

Okay, this'd gone on for too long, so Daniel rose. "I don't," he sneered. "You'd miss joining your boss in prison."

Max and Madam Valkyrie jolted and looked up at him. She started to raise her pistol, but Daniel aimed his right at her.

"Stop," he said. "My manners flew out the window about ten minutes ago, so I will shoot you."

Gretta hopped onto the landing and leaned over the railing to sneer, "Shoot her, anyway," her voice a bit too happy at the prospect.

The others jumped and looked up at her. Van cast her a glare and snuck his pistol back to its holster. Which Daniel noticed out of the corner of his eye.

Max grinned and danced for the stairs, chirping, "Gretta, you're okay!"

But the Valkyrie grabbed his collar and yanked him back like he was a sack of potatoes. "So, you *were* going to double-cross me!" She put a lady-wrestler choke-hold on him, and he gasped.

Van bolted down the stairs, past Daniel, Gretta sauntering along behind.

Daniel just sighed and fired the pistol into the ceiling! Everyone jumped and looked at him.

"You two want to kill each other, do it on your own time!" he snarled as he descended the stairs and turned on a light. "This is my time, and I'm not wasting another minute of it! So, to put it gently, Mayor Costello, back away from the boy!"

He motioned to the Valkyrie, who almost stepped forward, her politician's smile suddenly evident, even as her death-grip on Max did not lessen.

"Ah, you know who I am," she said.

"Yes. Let. Him. Go." She did. He fell to his knees, gasping then Daniel motioned to Van. "Would you please get the gun and envelope?" Van hesitated then did so, barely hiding a grin. "Thanks. Okay, Madam Mayor, you're going into the closet."

"I don't want to go into the closet," she replied.

"Please!" Daniel spat, indicating the proper door.

"Hardly appropriate, indeed it's not," she sighed as she slipped in to mingle with the sheets.

"Van, will you prop a chair against the door?" He did. "Now the love birds'll want some time alone, so how about the basement?"

Gretta cast a glance at Van, who gave her a blank look back. She huffed and turned to Daniel. "Ace, please, I don't think you understand …"

"My dear Mrs. Heinz," he sighed, "or Miss Bergstrom, no difference – I've written better con-women than you."

Meaning the lovely long-legged Angelina in *High-Heeled Moccasins*, whom he modeled on that bellboy named George, who took him for a thousand bucks before he vanished back to Jersey and wound up on a reality show under another name and set of enhanced pecs.

He herded Max and Gretta to the basement door. She cast a quick, irritated look at Van, who smiled, sweetly. Which Daniel noticed, of course. Then the door was closed and locked. He hoped it meant the guy was on his side, now, but knowing for sure could come later. He stormed over to the phone, saying, "What's that sheriff's name?"

"Candelaria," said Van, watching him with a hint of awe.

Daniel dialed 911. "Would you bring down my shirt and pants?"

"You want my coat?"

"Thanks, but wool makes me itch."

Van quickly hopped up to the bedroom as that voice came on the line, still loud enough to be heard in Hoboken.

"'Mergency operator!"

Daniel winced then said, "Uh, I need Sheriff Candelaria, right away, please."

"Whoa, not so fast!" the voice snarled. "This number's where that 'mergency call did *not* come from, an hour ago!"

"Yes, I know that but I'm ..."

"Ya wanna know how much trouble ya got me into, playin' practical jokes like this!? Sheriff thought I made the call up 'cause I want a raise! Well, now I got ya on tape! And makin' fake calls in the middle of the night's a misdemeanor punishable by a fine of not less'n two hundred dollars nor more'n ten days in jail, so ya can get yourself ready for a stint behind bars, ya little weasel!"

Daniel stared at the phone, incredulous, something about the woman's voice tickling his memory. But he brushed it aside to yell, "Fine! Arrest me! But to do that you'll need to call the sheriff!"

"No way I'm botherin' him! He's in sleep! A-bed! Like you oughta be!"

"Call him anyway!" Daniel snapped. "This an emergency!"

"Says who!?"

Say what!? What kind of emergency operator was this bitch? "Says me!"

"And who're you?!"

"I ... I'm Daniel Bettancourt. I'm calling from the Bentley cabin and ..."

"Cain't be!"

Daniel blinked at that one. "Why not?"

"Ain't no place by that name in our neck of the woods!"

"Well, THAT is where I am and THIS is where I be and

Mrs. Serff BROUGHT me here, so it must be real!" And that was it! She sounded like Mrs. Serff, just at ten times the volume. It jolted Daniel, and he had to make himself say, "I mean, it ... it's the first of three cabins near a lake at the end of a road, so tell him I'm holding three criminals up here and ..."

"Ya are?"

"That. Is what. I've been trying. To tell you," he said as Van came down with his clothes, the pea coat slung over one shoulder.

"All by yourself?" Daniel nodded, as if she could see him. "How?" she asked, as if she actually could see him nod.

"I ... I have a gun and they ..."

"I thought so! Got a permit for that gun!?"

Daniel was starting to freak out. "Uh, no."

"Why not!?" she snapped.

"It's not mine?" he half-sputtered as Van helped him remove the sheet and put his shirt on.

"Then why ain't ya got a permit for it?"

"Why would I need a permit for a gun I don't own?"

"Ya got one now, don't ya!?" she snapped back at him. "So ya better get a permit before ya start holdin' people at gunpoint an' callin' the sheriff to come pick 'em up! Not havin' a permit for a gun ya got but don't own is a misdemeanor punishable by a fine of not less'n five hundred dollars or more than thirty days in jail," she rattled off in one breath. "You'll get picked up, instead!"

Daniel looked at Van and whimpered, so the guy calmly handed him his pants and took the receiver away, whispering, "Allow me." Then he said into the phone. "Hi, is this Betty?"

Oh, good, he knew her. Knew her name. She was real.

"Van, baby, where ya been hidin' yourself?!" Still screeching loud enough to be heard in Hoboken.

"Oh, here and there, chasing stories," he smiled. "How 'bout with you? How's things?"

"Oh, there's lots going on, baby," squawked Betty. "Joe Jackson asked me to go out a night I ain't working all night!"

"Grab him, honey. He's one slick mortician."

"Yeah, an' the goop he puts in his hair cuts the smell of formaldehyde like ya wouldn't believe!" They shared a chuckle. "So, who's the freak!?"

"Oh, just an article I'm working on." Which made Daniel sigh. Maybe he was on his side and maybe he wasn't, again.

"Is he weird or what!?" squawked Betty.

Van glanced Daniel over with a smirk. "Oh, I wouldn't say that. A little baskety, maybe, but ..."

Daniel blinked. "Baskety?"

Her voice took on an insinuating tone. "In a good way or a bad way?"

Van smirked. "Lots of ways. Listen, Betty, we did have some trouble up at The Lyons' Den."

"Oh, that's where ya are! I thought it sounded familiar!"

"Could you send the sheriff up?"

"What happened!?"

"Let's make it a big surprise. But bring backup."

"Cool!" she squeaked, joyously. "I'll call the SWAT team! They need the practice! An' I'll make sure they got the key!"

Meaning, number seven. Imagine how Mrs. Serff'll react when she finds that out. And who will Homer beat up, first? The bad guys, the mayor, the lava lamp maker? The possibilities were boundless.

"Thanks. Later." Van hung up and smiled at Daniel. "Just gotta know what to say in this part of the world."

Daniel frowned at him. "I'm baskety?"

Van shot back with, "I'm a distracting guard dog."

Daniel snarled, despite himself. "Times ten."

"Woof," Van grinned back at him.

"But you do know her?" he asked, pointing at the phone.

"From the cradle. Why?"

"Nothing. She sounded like someone I met."

"That's not unusual, upstate, with the accent and all."

"Oh. Okay." Daniel steadied himself and looked around the room. "So, you ... you called this place The Lyons' Den. I think Haddon called it that, too."

"That's how it's known here," Van said, his eyes locked on Daniel.

"Now I get your Biblical reference, from earlier."

"I wondered why I didn't get more of a reaction."

"Why's it called that?"

"Simple. It was built by some guy named Lyons, for his mistress. His wife got it in the divorce. Sold it to the Bentleys."

"Isn't that the way it always works?"

Van gave him a frowning smile. "You believe in clichés?"

Daniel half-smiled. "Just considering my experiences."

"There's nothing in your bio about you being married."

"Wasn't, but I've been through ten divorces." Van grew wary. Daniel smirked, "My parents each got married five times."

"Oh," said Van, then he frowned. "Wait ... that adds up to nine divorces. I mean, if they were married to each other when they had you."

"Couldn't I be a bastard?" asked Daniel, all Mr. Innocent.

"No, never," said Van, and his voice held real tenderness in it.

"Tell that to Tad," Daniel smirked. "He lets people think that's why he dumped me."

"Does he?"

"Well, I heard it from Gregory Taylor, so the source isn't what you'd call trustworthy, but it fits. Who wants to admit they were involved with a psycho popping Prozac like Tic-Tacs?"

Van frowned. "You really like to beat up on yourself."

"I like to be honest," Daniel said, his mind drifting. "In my family, truth's the only way to keep from getting lost."

He'd learned that long before his seventy-two-hour stint in the hospital, though it was when the first doctor he saw in there bluntly asked him if his fits of paranoia were constant or occasional that it came in handy. Instead of trying to dance around the question, he'd bluntly responded, "Well, doctor, if people *are* out to get you, then you're not really paranoid, are you, even if you are. Because it's only if you are and they aren't that you're nuts. But if you are, and they *are*, you're still nuts, just in an acceptable way," and he'd offered up a crooked smile and the doctor had laughed. That shifted them into thinking maybe, just maybe, it wasn't him in need of a lobotomy, no matter what the judge said.

So from that point forward, Daniel had made it a rule never to answer a question unless he could be truthful and honest and real in his response. He didn't want to get tripped up by claims of inconsistency. And don't think that the lie Daniel told Tad about the scar on his face means anything. When Tad found out the truth and reminded Daniel of it, his response had been, "So what? Like Walt Whitman, *I am large; I contain multiples.*"

"That, I already knew," Tad had snapped back.

But he quickly caught on that Daniel really was consistent about it when dealing with projects Tad was working on. If he liked it, he'd say so. But if he didn't, he would politely say nothing, and that nothing would damage Tad's confidence more than any direct criticism ever could.

"Hmm," Daniel whispered just loud enough to hear, "I wonder if that's why we broke up?"

"Because you were on Prozac?" Van asked.

"Hmm?" Daniel responded, vaguely.

"Is that too personal a question?"

Daniel looked at him as if seeing him for the first time, then snapped back to the present. "Oh, no. No, I ... actually, I'd stopped it weeks before, but Tad didn't know. No, I'm just wondering if one of the reasons we broke up was that I stopped lying to him."

"You lied to Tad?"

"A few times. Not much. When he caught me in one, I stopped. I think it messed with him. He couldn't handle honesty, he was so used to people lying. That's how he figures out what they really want."

"If that's true," said Van, "then he's an idiot."

Daniel cast him a crooked grin. "No, I'm being simplistic. There were lots of things going on. Lots." He drifted for a second then chuckled. "Or it could be he finally just got sick of dealing with all the people in my head."

"You mean, Ace and Carmen?"

"To name a couple. Some move in, some move out, depending on the story. Guess that makes me the perfect definition of schizophrenia."

"The thirty-three faces of Daniel," Van said, chuckling.

Daniel laughed. "Almost. Like I told you, I talk to my characters, and they talk back, but that's how I write. They have to tell me the story. If they don't, I can't write it."

"Who brought you the battleship and her attack group?" Van asked, gently.

Daniel thought for a moment then said, "Carmen. She liked the idea of a murder being caused by lies and unfounded gossip. What she didn't like was how the old ladies took the story over and ran with it. But you can't tell your characters what to think, say or do; it interferes with the whole process."

"How much of your writing is informed by your own history?"

"As little as possible," Daniel said. "My characters work with me; my father, mother and sister, and everyone I know – they work for themselves in ways I have no control over."

"You see yourself as powerless?"

"I dunno," Daniel said. "Sometimes. Mostly it's just ... I'm all on my own. And lately it's made me so, so weary." Then he looked at Van, surprised. "I'm telling you things I haven't even told my therapist."

Or Ace.

"I feel privileged."

"You should," Daniel grinned. "You want to hear about mom's best divorce?" Van hesitated, then nodded. "It was her second one, when she was between husbands. She dumped Dad for him. Then the guy dumped his wife for her. Then mom decided he was tedious because he was so earnest and wanted to get married before they actually went to bed. That's when I learned that if there's anything my mother absolutely refused to tolerate, it's tedium. In herself. Her husbands. Her kids."

"I'd hardly call you that, if tonight's any measure."

"I'm not," Daniel happily said. "My schizo ways kept Mom on her toes. And finally she used it to break free from my control."

"Your control?"

"When I was nineteen, I was put in charge of her finances. Which was no problem so long as I gave her what she wanted. But when I questioned some expenses, in the space of five seconds I shifted from being *My Demented Danny* to *You Psychotic Fuck*."

"Jesus."

"It wasn't so bad," Daniel said, a faraway look taking over his eyes, "once she broke the trust and blew it all in Mexico."

"She still there?"

Daniel shook his head. "A facility in Maryland."

"Facility?"

"Something in her broke when she went broke," Daniel murmured, "and she's now living with hubbie #2 in the same house occupied by Ozzie and Harriet. I'm David; my sister's Ricky."

"Yeah, right," Van chuckled.

The faraway expression left Daniel's eyes, and he turned a sharp gaze on Van. "Don't ever assume I'm joking."

Van blinked. "Jesus, Daniel, how'd you turn out so decent being in such a crappy environment?"

"I'm not," he said.

"I'd argue with you on that," said Van, uncertainly.

"You don't know me."

"I know you well enough."

"Well enough to tell me why you're really here?"

Van blinked. "Huh? We've been over this!"

"C'mon, Van, something's going on between you and Gretta. What is it?"

"You don't believe that I'm ...?"

"I don't know who or what you are," Daniel said. "I look at you, and I don't know what to think or act or say. I don't know anything. I've never been good at reading people, but you ... you, I'd like to know. Understand. Trust."

"You don't ...?" Van seemed at a loss.

"Please. Just be honest with me. Tad never was, not completely. He always kept this wall up that he used to hide his sneakiness behind and ... and I just want the truth. What're you up to?"

Van hesitated, and Daniel gave free rein to the strongest, meanest, most hurt-puppy look he could muster. Hardly fair, but it worked. Van sighed and slowly held up the envelope. "These things're good for anybody who signs them. And eight hundred-thousand is a lot of money. Tax free. Might help us find our own peace."

Us? Daniel gasped in a sharp breath, and his mind froze at realizing that Van was all but saying, *Let's run off together. Leave the world behind. Just you and me, and Gretta be damned.* And the look on his face was so open and honest and pure, Daniel knew it was an honest proposal.

And, as perfect timing goes, that is when a weird little whine, coming from a distance, broke the spell.

Daniel did not move, so Van slipped over to the main window and peeked through the curtains. "Two ski-mobiles headed up the road."

"I guess helicopter's next," Daniel whispered out, with a smile.

"Wouldn't be surprised," said Van. "Whoever it is, they're in a rush."

Daniel nodded. "So we know who to expect." He rose and eyed Van. "You drove up, right?"

"Yeah, but I'm snowed in, by now."

"Oh." Daniel began to circle, slowly, looking at nothing. "The snowcat ...?"

"Max probably drove it up," said Van, watching him, warily. "He ... uh, he knows how."

"Do you?"

"I don't have the key."

"Right." Daniel stopped circling. "But you do know this area?"

"Daniel, what're you ...?"

"Just tell me."

Van hesitated then said, "I've lived here all my life."

"How far is it to town?"

Van jolted. "I'm not leaving you alone!"

Daniel's heart all but jumped for joy. Here he was giving Van the best excuse possible to split with the cash all on his own, to prove his offer to share the bonds with Daniel was a lie, and his instantaneous response was to refuse to go. Maybe hope could be allowed, after all. Daniel grinned as he said, "It's the best way, Van. It gives me a three-fold argument against them doing anything – you've gone for help and the sheriff's on his way."

"That's only two."

Daniel rolled his eyes and dropped the curtain, revealing everything. "And I'm still not dressed for travel," he said with a crooked smirk. Van huffed, exasperated, as Daniel dipped down to pull the curtain back up around himself then added, "Plus I've got an arsenal." He twirled a pistol in each hand. "So that's four. Or five. One for each gun?"

Pistol!

Van heaved a deep breath and pulled on his coat. "Well, I can't go out the front; they'll see me."

"And the kitchen door faces the road. So it's out over the

deck," Daniel said as he opened the French doors.

Van stopped right behind him. "I feel like I'm running away."

"From what?" Daniel laughed. "Being bored to death by more jabbering?"

"I kind of enjoyed the jabber," Van sighed.

That comment hit Daniel in too perfect a way, so without thinking, he pulled Van into a kiss that was so gentle, so tender, so right, it seemed to fill his soul with dreams of home and love and support and caring and the joy of a future together, forever.

As for Van, no forcing of the tongue by this guy; merely acceptance of lips to lips and body to body and gentle embraces. And when they parted, it was so reluctant on both their parts, Daniel could have wept.

Van let out a long slow sigh. "Wow, just when I think you're a playful little kitten, you turn into this wildcat."

"I can be whatever you want once this is done," Daniel said, Van's comment tickling the déjà vu in his brain.

"If you can say that," Van whispered, "then you're anything but powerless." And there seemed to be pure admiration in his eyes.

Daniel's heart nearly burst from the collision of emotions and he held the guy close. He finally whispered, "Be careful."

Van nodded and said, "You, too. Ace." Then he headed out to the deck, leapt over the railing and slashed off through the snow into the darkness.

And no matter how much he wanted to believe otherwise, deep down inside Daniel had this nagging, terrifying feeling that he'd never see the man, again.

Uh-Oh Means You're Nekkid

Daniel could not move as he watched Van dance into and out of the night's shadows. He fought to believe in the guy, a man he barely knew, but he wasn't so delusional that he couldn't admit he was flying on faith, yet again. And thanks to the fact that such faith had been trashed and trampled far too many times, one aspect of his inner being instantly popped up with this automatic snarl of, "Here you go, aiming for another crash and burn."

"That's proof of insanity," he murmured back. "Doing the same thing over and over and expecting a different outcome."

"You got that right," the damned voice agreed.

But no. This time ... no, this time it was different, and that kiss had sealed it. Because instead of it bringing him mere hope, it brought a moment of sharp clarity, and he realized Van was unlike anyone he'd ever been with, before. Yes, his face had aspects of Jarrod's bone structure, but his eyes were open and accepting, not careful and always aware. He had something of Tad's figure, true, and some of George's Italian-stallion swagger, but only hints of them. The fact was, Van entered his mind's eye as someone fresh and new and unconnected to anyone else in his past, and he had to acknowledge he hadn't felt this strongly about anyone since ... well, since *Star Wars* with a boy named Kenny, who may have had the same vaguely surprised expression and smile that was as inviting, but who was the polar opposite of Van in looks.

Daniel jolted at realizing that was nearly half his life ago. Back before he'd finally had to accept the truth of human duplicity in his mother, sister, father, step-fathers, friends and lovers. Back before he'd learned to hide a piece of himself away as protection, something he could have of his own to return to when his world collapsed, yet again. Where, like a cat hiding under a bush after a vicious fight, he could be silent and still and unthinking and able to let his psyche repair itself in its own time.

But this time he'd opened himself up completely to Van, and now he was terrified of all that could mean and all that could happen and how easily he could be crushed, and to his surprise it made him more than joyous; he was excited at the prospect. Ecstatic that he could care about someone so damn much, he ached for him no matter what the truth might turn out to be. So damn much that it was acceptable to hope and pray and fear for his safety. And dream. Because this time it would be different. He knew it. He just plain knew.

"Oh, God, please come back to me," he whispered, shaken at this sudden explosion of uncontrollable feelings and ...

A skimobile's light flashed over some trees and almost seemed to point at Van. Daniel stopped breathing. "Did they see him?" he muttered, now shivering more from nerves than the cold. "Did they?"

But Van slipped into the darkness one last time, and their whine continued to approach from the front of the cabin, so he relaxed, closed the doors and leaned against the table, weak.

"No," he muttered. "No time for this. No time."

He took in a deep breath, straightened up and grabbed his slacks to inspect them. The two legs were joined together solely by the zipper. "Worthless," he muttered. So he tied the sheet around himself like a pair of *Aladdin* pants then considered leaving his shirt unbuttoned and sitting cross-legged on the couch by the lava lamp and greeting whoever came through the door with, *Welcome, sahib*!

"Naw," he murmured, "That's Indian and Aladdin was Persian. Can't be mixing metaphors or characters or whatever the hell it is. Okay, so what do I do? What can I do!? Stall 'em. Keep 'em busy till Van gets back. But how?"

That's when I decided it was time to bring myself back into the fray – half because he needed me to bounce ideas off of and half because ... well, it's just as much my story as it is his, dammit. But I didn't arrive from my happy place. No, sir, I popped in with plenty of 'tude, snarling, "Oh, chill; I'll help you. Not that I should, after all the shit you've given me, tonight. But if they kill you, I start from scratch, so I got no fuckin' choice."

"But you do got a way with words," Daniel snarled back.

"Oh, bullshit on that," I snapped. "And will you cut the worryin'? We been in worse jams. Like in ...*Tristan*."

Daniel snorted at the memory. We'd finally figured out this asshole sheriff was messing with a couple of drug rings and was planning to blame the murders on the Tristan character, so I set out to get some positive proof by videotaping him overseeing a delivery from a little fast-boat off the Louisiana Bayou. But I got caught and he was about to shoot me, and not with a camera, when the members of one gang came roaring up. You see, early that morning I'd told my contact with them all about what was going on in their own backyard. Well, their guys were armed; and the sheriff's guys were armed; and everybody was locked and loaded and then the other gang appeared, also armed to the gills and ready to fire. Then on top of that, four fishermen with AR-15s popped up, thinking we were gonna take their fishing space, followed by one pissed-off Cajun grannie manhandling a twelve-gauge shotgun from a nearby house, who thought we were all burglars. Everybody wound up pointing their pistols, rifles, shotguns, Uzis and nasty words at everybody else with me in the middle of it all in an open field on a moonlit night with nothing but my little ol' camcorder and a Walther PPK.

"Surprised the hell out of me," Daniel said.

"How d'you think I felt?" He was about to snipe back at me when I said, "All right, all right, I know, I know, I know, you know. But it was you who got me talkin' so fast and weird, I had everybody convinced I was with everybody else. So they got so busy snappin' an' pissin' an' moanin' at each other, Carmen had time to bring in the cops. So ...?"

"So keep the argument going till the sheriff gets here. Question is, how?"

The snowmobiles' whine died. Daniel tensed.

"Simple," I said. "Inventory!"

"Inventory!?"

"Daniel! Rule #1 for the end of any mystery! C'mon."

"Right! Right. Uh, let's see, I got three people locked up, two pistols, Van gone for help, and the sheriff en route."

We hope.

I nodded. "Now there's two ski mobiles, and each carries two people. That's four guys, total, and better count on each one of 'em havin' a weapon, so even if you keep both them pistols out, they won't do you no good."

"So ... so hide them where I can get to them," Daniel muttered, looking around, "just in case."

He slid the automatic under the couch and shoved the revolver into the pail holding the hearth tools.

"No, no, no, no, that's the first place they'll look!"

"How will they know I've got ...?" Daniel started then cut himself off. "It's Haddon's pistol. Shit."

He grabbed it out and dropped it behind the woodpile.

I eyed it. "That's still iffy."

He groaned, dropped a log on top of it and huffed, "It'll have to do." Then he jolted. "Oh, I got an idea." He scrambled into the kitchen, grabbed his laptop and brought it back to the table to fire it up. I met him there, warily wondering, "You think this'll work?"

"Got a better idea?" Daniel chirped. Well, no, so he cast me a smirk of triumph then smiled as the screen came to life. "Y'know, you surprised me in that book, Ace. It's the first time you let me let the story go the direction it wanted instead of taking it down all those dead-end alleys."

"Hey! Those alleys're half the fun!"

"Okay, okay. And they did lead us to some ... *interesting* places, and you did say things I'd never even thought of."

I shrugged. "That's how it works, sometimes."

"Yeah," Daniel said. "Daniel Bettancourt does great in fantasy while reality slaps him about like a toadie's toad. What does that say about me?"

"All it says," I moaned, "is that, well, in that story, you finally let yourself trust yourself."

"Trust you, you mean."

I rolled my eyes. "Daniel! I'm a guy in a book! All I can say or do is what you tell me to say and do."

"Which're things I don't have the nerve to do in reality."

I smacked him in the back of the head, snarling, "You mean, too polite! So cut it out, or I'll make damn sure you do get back together with Tad. Then you'll really have something to whine about."

"I'm not whining," he whined. "I'm just ... just ..."

Scared. Right. But suddenly it was not from what was

arriving on those skimobiles.

He was on a new road.

He was eying a folder titled *CBC* on the laptop. His file for *The Cocoa-Butter Conspiracy*. The outline set in Florida. He'd suddenly realized that most of what'd happened tonight seemed to come straight from his notes on that story, and suddenly the whole night was beginning to make sense, and he froze.

What if everything that had happened tonight wasn't real? Was just part of his mind breaking down? Oh, that had to stop.

"Daniel," I said, "you're not slipping into psychosis."

"But, Ace, what if that is it?" he whispered back. "What if I'm imaging the whole night in my head? What if I've vanished into one of my stories to the point where I can't tell fact from fantasy or …?"

"All right, that is *not* a place we need to start from, buddy, not right now. No, sir."

"But the whole night ..." he murmured, growing still and quiet, "... everything tonight, it's been like this story ... or ... or one of my stories ... and my dreams and ..."

"*Bull*-shit," I sneered, trying to make it a joke. "If this was just in your head, it'd make a hell of a lot more sense."

"Not in first draft."

"Don't get logical on me! Not now!"

"Can't help it. It's the honesty in me."

"All right, so let's say you *are* lost in fantasy-land," I snickered. "What're you doin'? Hidin' in a closet, scared to make a move?"

He hesitated then said, "No."

"Right. You're still …"

"Facing it."

"Head on. Like you always have, when you needed to. Like you have me do. You know why? 'Cause I'm you and you're me. Meaning what I got in me you have in you, up here." I tapped Daniel's head then patted him on the spine. "And right here. So together we can keep facing down the bullshit and, when it's over, that is when we'll figure it out."

"You really think so?"

No, but no way was I letting him know that. All I said was, "Watch."

A twig snapped, outside. Neither of us jumped; we just

looked at the front door.

"They're sendin' a guy 'round the kitchen door," I said. "In case you try to escape."

"Yeah, like I'd know where to go," Daniel sighed. "Well, if this doesn't get resolved soon, I'll just plead insanity with Tad. That way he'll have no problem getting people to believe that ... that I'm ... at fault ..."

His voice dropped off, and he frowned, confused. I looked at the computer screen, and there in the top menu bar of his Mac was the upside down cone showing he had a wireless signal. He had fucking WiFi!

He grabbed his cell phone and opened it up. No bars.

"Ace," he whispered, "how?"

"You can't. Not without cell-phonage or a kick-ass relay."

Of course, that is when we heard a pair of Clydesdales crunch up to the door. Too late for questions; time for the game to begin.

"Shit!" Daniel growled then he focused on the laptop, using the reflection in the French doors to keep a wary watch on the entrance.

It finally, slowly, painfully CREAKED open, Haddon pushing it. Seems Max and Costello neglected to lock it after they entered. Behind Haddon was a massive set of pure muscles, six feet tall and wide and thick and every square inch of it bulging with testosterone, bundled up against the cold in a way that made him ... or her; I'm not sexist ... seem even bigger and meaner and more ready to rumble. But what was this behemoth holding? An M-16? No. An AR-15? No. An Uzi? No. It was the dinkiest, stupidest little air-rifle I'd ever seen, with a sniper scope!

Seriously!

Man, I just had to snark, "Must've left his slingshot at the dry cleaners."

Behind them both came a man who was barely five-foot-five but had such a huge presence, you'd have thought he was five-six. He slowly strutted into the place, black knit cap on head, mittens as big as flapjacks on his hands, boots the size of Rhode Island on his feet, looking more like a five-year-old who'd been dressed by his overly-protective mommy for a day in the snow than the big, bad, butch bear he obviously thought himself to be. He motioned for Haddon to close the door. It CREAKED shut even louder.

"Man," I said, "an entrance Cagney would've loved."

Daniel smirked and quietly said, "I was thinking Edward G. Robinson; he's shorter." Then he dimmed the laptop's screen as the twin to the first set of terrorific muscles appeared from the kitchen, also holding a rifle that was just as adorable as his buddy's. And we were not talking small in proportion, here; the damn things really were kid-sized.

"Shit, Daniel," I said, shaking my head, "here's proof it's not in your mind! I mean, c'mon, squirrel shooters with sites? Here? Now? With those two? Not even Elmore Leonard's that crazy."

"You so sure?" Daniel whispered, then he rose to face the men as he jauntily said in what had to be the world's worst British accent, "Gentlemen, good evening! Had you bothered to knock, I'd have been happy to let you in."

"Who're you?" Pint-sized snarled.

Daniel crossed to warm himself at the fire as he said, "I? Why, I ... I am Mayor Costello's boy toy, sir. Can't you tell?" And he opened his shirt to emphasize his naked torso.

I busted out laughing. "Oh, that is fuckin' wicked."

"He's full of it, Mr. Heinz!" Haddon snarled, and I'd already figured that's who the little puffball was. "He's the guy what jumped me, earlier tonight!"

Daniel cast him an incredulous glance. "I? Why, I have never seen this gentleman before in my life, sir. And do I appear as though I could jump anyone?" And the sheet shifted lower on his hips, and I have to admit — if I'd been a noodle hound that treasure trail would have caught all my interest.

Heinz just nodded, his eyes never leaving Daniel. "Uh, huh. If you're the boy toy, why ain't you dressed?"

Daniel frowned. "Really, sir? Must I explain what a boy toy is for?" Heinz indicated that would not be necessary, so Daniel continued, "Besides, it *is* nearly eleven in the evening. I've just had my bath and *was* planning to grab some much-needed rest. Mayor Costello does like to, oh, get started early, shall we say?" And he batted his eyes at the men.

"That's another lie," Haddon snapped.

"And how might you know that, I wonder?" said I, casting

the guy a smirk.

Heinz frowned at Daniel. "Wait, Costello's here?"

"Yes, sir. As is your wife. Hope you don't mind."

Heinz huffed. "My wife's at home, asleep."

Daniel feigned some truly serious shock. "Oh? Oh, dear. Then whom have I locked in the basement with the other toy boy?"

Oh, this was too perfect. "Dude, your actin's worse 'n Tad's an' twice as fierce."

"Now that was just mean," he smiled back at me.

Heinz glanced around the room. "Where is the basement?"

Daniel sweetly indicated, "Behind door number one, sir."

Heinz made a motion with one hand and Terror-Twin-1 opened the door. Max and Gretta came out, him wiping lipstick off his face, her looking like a very untrustworthy kittle-cat that had just ingested a nice big bowl of cream and was wondering where to spit her next hairball.

"Max Benitez," Heinz smiled, snarled, sneered and shot, all at the same time. Don't ask me how; I don't know nothin' 'bout the laws of physics.

"Uh, Mr. Heinz," said Max, sheepishly. "Fancy meetin' you here."

Pint Sized turned to Daniel. "That's my wife?" Daniel shrugged, in answer, so he nodded. "Okay, where's Costello?"

"Door number two, sir. Over there." And Daniel sweetly pointed to the proper location.

Another motion from Heinz's hand and Terror-Twin-2 removed the chair from under the doorknob to open the door. Mayor Costello came out, straightening her clothes. "I suppose you think it's funny, toying with a dangerously claustrophobic mind, indeed you must, but let me assure you, young man ..." Then she noticed Heinz and froze.

"Hello, Jo," said the way-smaller man, "what d'ya know?"

"Oh, uh, Winston," said the Valkyrie. "What brings you to this location?"

"Haddon," Heinz snapped. "He had the first run-in with — what *is* your name?"

Daniel gave a little cock of his head and said, "Well, actually, sir, my name is ..."

"C'mon, Daniel, be yourself," I said.

"They wouldn't believe it," Daniel barked then laughed and dropped the accent. "Okay, I'm Daniel Bettancourt."

Heinz gave him a wary look. "The writer?"

I proudly stepped forward, patting my guy on the back. "Guilty, guilty, guilty."

Heinz sneered, "I read one of your books. It was crap."

Uh, what? Say what!? Crap?!

Haddon glanced between them. "Wait, that bullshit story he told me wasn't bullshit?"

"Nope," said Heinz, almost gleefully. "That *Ace Shosta-what-zis* guy's the dumbest son-of-a-bitch in mysteries."

"I'm dumb?!" I snapped. "Me!? What, what, what, you readin' your lack of brains into mine?!"

"All he does," Heinz continued, "is fuck his secretary and wait for the killer to make a stupid move."

Oh, I did not like this man. "I guess that means you prefer *Agatha CHRISTIE*!" I snarled. "Pretty proper British people standing around with no life and boring verisimilitude!"

"Whoa." Daniel looked around for pen and paper.

"Over there," I snapped, pointing to a notepad and a pencil in the telephone nook.

Daniel grabbed them and wrote my little spew down, dust billowing off the pad as Costello calmly said, "Now is not the time for rudeness, Mr. Heinz, indeed it's not."

"Like hell," the twerp sneered. "I always wanted to tell a big-name writer his work sucked."

Big-name? Since when?

Daniel jerked to a halt at that to glare at me.

"Hey, hey, hey," I sniped, "focus on what's important."

He huffed and kept writing.

Max looked between the others, asking, "Excuse me, but what're you guys talkin' 'bout?"

Daniel finished writing as he absently said, "It's simple. I told Tad Bentley I'd rewrite eight really crappy scripts for a meeting on Monday, so I came up here for solitude and peace, but wound up with half the county barging in on me, making damn sure I can't get anything done." He set the pad and pencil by the lava lamp, smiling sweetly at everyone. "Clear enough?"

Heinz frowned. "Wait a minute. If nobody's supposed to know you're here," he turned to Costello and kept on with, "how'd you know you could get in?"

"Ah, Winston," said Daniel, "allow me." He took three keys from his shirt pocket and dropped them on the hearth, one after the other after the other. "Not to mention Her Honor's and three more that I know of," he whispered, winking at Costello.

Damned if the Valkyrie didn't wink back, jolting him! Maybe Haddon and that boy toy crap wasn't so far off the truth.

Heinz snarled at Costello. "What the – you ain't supposed to have a key till Mike, here, drops his off! What the hell're you pullin'?!"

"How 'bout a *crap writer* gives you the scoop?" Daniel said, still spooked by Costello's wink. "She planned to come early, take the bearer bonds and, when she got her *official* key, come back and say the money wasn't here. Blame it on Haddon or Max or somebody."

"That's a lie!" Costello cried. "Indeed it is!"

"Makes sense to me," said Heinz, glaring at the woman.

"Me, too," said Haddon.

"Me, three!" Max quickly chimed in.

Costello waved the whole thing off, imperiously. "Winston, Haddon called Max and said someone had been up here. We thought it was the hermit, so he and I came to make sure neither he nor anyone else got to the money. Indeed, we did."

"Anyone else who?" Heinz sneered, spit and snarled.

"Her, for instance," said Costello, indicating Gretta. "Max had a key made, so this scheming bitch could sneak in and steal us blind."

Gretta rolled her eyes and lounged across the top of the back of couch. She was having way too much fun with this.

"Careful with her, Daniel," I muttered.

"No shit," he nodded.

Max bolted over to Costello and poked at her with a finger. "No, you were gonna steal the bonds and blame me and Gretta!"

"That is a lie!" Costello shrieked back at his roaring, and Daniel figured her range was about one octave less than Callas'.

"No, you're lying!" Max roared even louder. Wow, tenor.

"I think you both are!" Haddon added, smirking.

That's when Gretta rose and whispered, "HEY!" The others looked at her as she added in her pleasant, insinuating voice, "Don't you think you're *all* missing something?"

"What?!" Heinz, Costello, Max and Haddon said.

"A brain?" I asked. Sorry, couldn't help it.

"Van," said Gretta, gently.

Okay, here it comes. Daniel tensed and edged closer to the woodpile.

Heinz frowned at her. "Who?"

Costello grimaced and gasped, "The other man who was here!"

Max jolted around. "Oh, right! Right! That guy."

Now maybe it's just me being my paranoid little-ol'-self, but I just had to nudge Daniel and point out, "Van's lived here all his life, but nobody knew who he was?"

Daniel nodded. He'd already noticed that.

"Where is he?" Haddon asked no one in particular.

Gretta sighed. "Gone. Probably with the bonds."

Costello turned to Heinz, rasping, "He knows everything."

Heinz stiffened. "Everything?"

"Everything," Max nodded in agreement.

"Indeed," said Costello.

I nodded and casually muttered to Daniel, "Normally, this'd be a good time to run."

"Yeah, but where?" Daniel muttered.

The whole room turned to look at him, in perfect unison.

"Yes," Heinz nodded. "Where is he?" And suddenly he looked like a rabid rabbit who saw Daniel as his next carrot.

My guy took an involuntary step back and bumped against the mantelpiece. "Oh, uh, he'd be in town, by now. He has a car."

"Preposterous!" Costello cried.

"His car's outside, snowed under!" said Haddon.

"He's probably hikin'!" Max snarled.

Heinz turned to his men. "He'll have left a trail!"

BAM! Daniel dropped to grab the pistol from the pile of wood, but the log on top of it got caught and he had to fight to get it off. Haddon noticed and jumped him, grabbing his arm as he finally rose, pistol in hand. They twisted around. Max grabbed Daniel from behind. The Terror-Twins piled on and they all crashed to the floor between the couch and hearth. Gretta screamed in shock as Costello scurried aside. Heinz just watched and waited.

My guy fought like a madman, kicking Max back over the couch and sending a few good elbows into Haddon's side, but the Terror-Twins finally pinned his hands behind him and yanked him to his feet. His left eyebrow was cut and blood trailed down his face. The *Aladdin* pants had fallen away and his shirt was torn at the shoulder and collar. The two sides of beef then slammed him against the mantelpiece, knocking the wind out of him and holding him there. Daniel gulped and grimaced, in pain.

Heinz calmly strolled over, took the pistol and held it on him then motioned for the Terror-Twins to do the release thing.

"Stay put," the bastard whispered at my guy.

Haddon struggled to his knees, winded and irritated. "I oughta knock the shit outta you," he gasped.

"Not now, Mike," Heinz muttered. "Later, maybe."

Haddon growled but sat on the back of the couch, rubbing his shoulder.

Then Heinz noticed Max, lying face down on the floor on the other side of the couch, playing up how winded he was. "You okay, Max?" he asked.

The twerp nodded and slowly rose.

And from the corner of his eye, Daniel saw him sneak the pistol into his coat pocket.

The pistol my guy'd hidden under the couch!

Shit.

Daniel looked away, shaken, then caught a glimpse of Herman peeking through the kitchen door. They exchanged nods and the old man quietly slipped away.

Heinz nodded to his men, "Go." The Terror-Twins grabbed their too-cute rifles, yanked the front door open and bolted outside, reminding me just too damned much of *Dudley Do-Right*. Cartoon reference; Google it.

A moment later, the skimobiles began to whine, again.

Gretta picked up the sheet, almost licking her lips as she purred at Daniel, "You're more interesting than you seem."

"Huh?" Daniel sort of let whisper out; he was too lost in trying to figure out his next move to pay her real attention.

"Nice, um, ass along with nice legs," she said.

"Indeed," said Mayor Costello, in a voice that cut right

through my guy's brain and creeped him, me and Carmen out. She'd hopped out of the shadows when Daniel got hurt and was watching, worried, over by the table.

Daniel nodded. "Uh, right. Right, I ... I'm not dressed. Uh ... let me just run upstairs and ..."

"Put your hands on the mantel." Heinz snarled.

"But I ..."

"ON THE MANTEL!" Emphasizing each word with the pistol.

Daniel took hold of it, shaken.

Gretta tore a strip from the already torn sheet and used it to dab at the blood on my guy's face. "I'd wrap you back up," she purred, "but it seems I'm a gay man trapped in a straight woman's body, so why would I want to do that?"

Oh, for cryin' out loud, this was over the top. I snuck up on his other side and whispered, "Keep it in perspective, Dan-O. Remember, sheriff's on his way."

"So where is he?" Daniel whispered.

Costello turned to Heinz, concern in her voice. "Winston, this was uncalled for, indeed it was. Now the young man's been hurt, so it's gone far enough, indeed it has."

"Naw, it keeps going till the fat ..."

"DON'T say it!" Costello snarled.

"Yeah, yeah, yeah," Heinz sneered, spit, snipped, sniped and ... aw, you get the idea. "Now as I see it," he continued, "we have two options here – end it or go to jail."

Max jolted. "Jail?"

Haddon just nodded, now stretching to work out the pain.

Costello seemed lost. "But ... but ..."

Gretta slowly turned her focus to Heinz. "Oh, no, no, no." She moved closer to him, her sex-appeal tuned up to mega-molten-lava as she sighed, "I will not go back to prison."

Max jolted, again, and squeaked, "Back?!"

Gretta rolled her eyes and sneered at him, "Max, grow up! Madam mayor told you all about me."

"But I ... I thought ..."

"No, you didn't. You never think." She turned her electric gaze back and down to Heinz, her voice purring. "You're the only man with a brain here. You're the only one who knows."

"I call bullshit on that," I sneered.

Daniel nodded then realized everybody was focused on Gretta so used the distraction to dip down, rub his leg as if it hurt and surreptitiously grab a little packet of lemon juice from the grocery bag. No one seemed to notice.

"What does he know?" Costello asked Gretta.

"Better this end in a whisper than a bang," Heinz purred back at her, holding up the pistol. "Considering how cold it is, outside."

Uh-oh, this was not going in a good direction.

Then Pint-Size slowly crossed to Daniel, muttering, "And how quick you'll die of exposure if you've locked yourself out of a nice, warm place like this." He had to all but stand on his tip-toes to put the pistol to my guy's temple. "With nobody around for miles. Naked."

Then he jolted down and tore Daniel's shirt off his shoulders and down his arms, nearly sending him to the floor! Shit, the little fuck was stronger than he looked. Daniel almost dropped the lemon juice and had to grab a stone in the hearth to keep from falling on his ass, burning his left hand.

Heinz chuckled and tossed the shirt's shreds into the flames, letting them dance happily around it.

Daniel didn't even try to cover up; he just stared at Heinz, shaken, holding his burned hand in a way to keep the juice packet hidden. "I liked that shirt," he said, fighting to keep a tremor out of his voice.

"I didn't," Heinz said.

"Now, Winston," said Costello, "let's not get carried away, here. You do have a tendency to go overboard and ..."

"Not this time," he snarled. "'Cause nobody'll know what really happened. Cut on your head? That means you might've fallen and not been able to regain your senses in time to get back inside. So sad. But you know it's an easy death, freezing. You just go to sleep."

"After shivering your ass off!" Daniel and I growled out at the same time.

Heinz pressed the ice-cold pistol under Daniel's chin and forced him back to the French doors as Costello, Haddon and Max exchanged stunned glances.

Daniel fought to maintain control of his voice. "You, uh ... this ... this is getting out of control, Heinz."

"It's murder," Costello said. "Indeed it is."

"No, Jo, it's just an accident," Heinz replied.

"C'mon, boss," said Haddon, "you really need to think this one through a bit better, okay?"

"Why? Things like this happen all the time."

Daniel gulped. "Trust me, you don't want to do this."

"Yeah," I sneered, "'Cause the sheriff's on his way!"

Daniel bumped against the table, muttering, "He ... he should've been here by now."

"Who should've?" Heinz asked.

"Van," Daniel snapped, staring Heinz straight in the eye. "When he comes back with the sheriff and they find me out there and you in here and ..."

Heinz laughed, circled Daniel and pulled one of the French doors open, sneering, "They won't. Outside."

Daniel hesitated then took hold of the table and said, "No."

Heinz cocked the pistol. "If you don't ..."

"You'll have a shit-load of blood splatter to explain."

I perked up. "Oh, Dan-O, I like that line and ..."

"Not NOW!" Daniel snarled, as he surreptitiously tore open the packet in his hand.

"Yes, NOW, you little faggot," Heinz snarled, "'cause I don't give a shit how you die."

"FAGGOT?!" Daniel growled. "Who the fuck you calling a faggot, you dumb fuck?"

"Hey, who the fuck you think you're talkin' to?"

"You, you son-of-a-bitch!" Then Daniel squeezed the juice into Heinz's eyes! The smaller man cried out and stumbled against the French door as Daniel grabbed him, only the pistol fired into the air, nearly hitting Daniel. He yelped and ducked under the table.

Everyone else froze.

Heinz regained his balance, furious. He rubbed at his eyes and tried to get a good aim at my guy as Daniel scrambled about to keep the chairs in-between them. It was getting dodgy until Gretta finally bolted over and grabbed Heinz's arm.

"Winston, don't be an idiot," she snapped. "Look at him. He can't travel like that. Where's he going to go? You've been the only man with a head on his shoulders, so far; don't lose it now. Wait until your men return, then have them take both him and Van down to the lake and throw them in. Stripped to nothing." And the way she said it suggested she'd enjoy that spectacle way too much. "Then they won't be found till March or April."

Heinz let her draw him back, still rubbing at his eyes as he said, "The lake, huh?"

Gretta's voice took on a more seductive tone as she led him to the fire. "Wouldn't that be easier to away with? Come on. I have eye drops in my purse. Let me wash your eyes clean. Give you time to remember that you're the only one who knows what all of this means. You're the only one who knows what we really have to do to bring it to a *satisfactory* conclusion." And the purr behind her words made promises no red-blooded heterosexual man could resist, and maybe even some red-blooded gay ones.

Max noticed and got this weird tone to his voice as he said, "Get away from him, Gretta."

I glanced at him. Boy, were his eyes green, and not from envy, lemme tell you.

She kept her focus on Heinz, pulling some eye drops from her purse. "I know you'll see this through, no matter what. You'll do what you have to." She caressed his arm. Fondled the revolver. Then she bent his head back to drop in the saline solution.

"Get away from him!" Max snarled like a pissed-off ferret. "I mean it!"

Gretta shot a disdainful glance back at him. "Will you stop it!?"

Max pulled the automatic pistol and pointed it at her! "Get away from him, Gretta!"

Haddon jumped. "Where the hell'd that come from?!"

Costello spun back into Valkyrie mode and cried, "Now just one moment! That is *my* pistol, indeed it is, and ..."

"It's mine now," Max growled, aiming the pistol at her.

She side-stepped back, startled. "Uh, Max, really, this ... this is far too much, indeed it is!"

Daniel crawled out from under the table, glancing between them all, once again traveling the déjà vu road. "It is *The Cocoa Butter Conspiracy*," he muttered.

No shit. Part of that story revolved around the son of a

corrupt judge killing his girlfriend over another guy. But Daniel'd about decided to drop it because it didn't fit. Like now. A jealous rage going on in the middle of attempted murder and possible kidnapping? Really?

Heinz just scowled at Max. "Now cut that out! We got this under control."

Gretta's voice became soothing and gentle as she slithered away from Pint Size. "Well, baby, this shows a whole new side of you."

"Oh," said Max, "now it's *baby*. Now it's all me." He held up the pistol. "So what're you sayin'? The only thing you love is a man with a gun?"

"Pistol," I snarked.

"Don't be silly," Gretta cooed. "We're in this together."

Costello stepped forward, swooping along in mezzo-soprano-mode. "I knew it! I knew it! Indeed I did!"

Max shook his head, his eyes hurt as he muttered to Gretta, "You lying bitch. I really thought I meant something to you. Now? Now I bet you were in it with Heinz. So were you gonna steal the bonds back for him and lay it all at my feet?"

Gretta shook her head and said, "No, baby, listen to me …"

"I did," Max snarled. "That's my problem."

Daniel tensed. That was the character's last line! "Max DON'T!"

Max fired the pistol, hitting Gretta in the chest! She crashed over a couch, bounced and landed on the floor, face down. And still.

Everyone froze for a second or forty-seven or so until Haddon finally whispered, "Oh, shit," in shock.

I backed up next to Daniel, shaking my head in disbelief. "Well, at least they can't say she froze to death."

Costello leaned against the mantelpiece, murmuring, "This was unnecessary, indeed it was."

Max stared at the body, blankly, then hiccupped and cried "Oh, God," as he crashed to his knees. "I shot her! Gretta! Gretta!"

Daniel started over, but Heinz shoved him back with the point of the pistol, snarling, "Stay there!" Then the twerp slithered around the couch to check Gretta's pulse and finally snarled at Max, "You stupid son-of-a-bitch. She's dead."

Max wailed, "No, no, no, Gretta!" He walked on his knees over to her and would have taken her in his arms, but Heinz yanked him up and shoved him across to the opposite couch. He bounced into it and out of it and landed back on his knees, as if in prayer.

"Don't get any blood on you, you idiot," Pint-sized snarled.

Costello just muttered over and over, "This is not good, indeed it's not."

"Shut up!" Heinz snapped. "Let me think."

"Perfect!" I chirped. "He's so out of practice, he'll go into meltdown and it'll all be kewl, again."

"Dream about it," Daniel muttered.

"Okay, I ... I got it," Heinz sneered. He shoved his pistol in Costello's hand.

"What're you doing?" she cried.

"Keep him there!" Heinz snarled, pointing to Daniel. "If he makes a move, shoot him!" Then he turned to Haddon and said, "Help me."

He took Gretta under the arms and nodded to her feet. Haddon slipped an arm under her knees.

The Valkyrie kept the pistol trained on Daniel as the men hauled Gretta to the stairs. Crimson blood soaked her blouse.

"What're you doing?" my guy asked, completely confused.

Heinz sneered at him. "Holding a killer at bay. You forced her up here at gunpoint. Tired to rape her. She fought you. We came to stop you, but we were too late."

Costello rolled her eyes in disbelief. "Oh, my-my-my."

"You stupid son-of-a-bitch," Daniel snapped, "I'm gay."

"You're also naked," Haddon said, popping his head around the chimney. "An' you got powder residue on your hand."

"You did fire the pistol," said Costello, "indeed."

No, my guy fired Haddon's pistol, not the Valkyrie's, and a comparison of bullets would show it was the latter pistol that shot her. All he'd have to prove is the timeline.

"You think I could?" my guy sighed.

"*Puh*-lease," I sneered. "Considering how dumb this crew is, that'd be cake."

The two men lugged Gretta across the landing and into Daniel's bedroom, and he heard them toss her on the bed. Then

Heinz strutted out and back down the stairs, saying, "Besides, the mayor, her assistant and a respected contractor will say you did it."

"Heinz, there's too many people involved," Daniel sighed, "and Van'll be ..."

The skimobiles were heard, approaching, their whine sounding a thousand times nastier than when they'd first come.

"Back already," sneered Heinz. "Say, maybe we'll work this as a three-way. She walked in on you and Van, so you shot her to keep her quiet. Then shot him. Then drowned yourself in the lake. That sounds even better."

Damned if it didn't. Daniel felt his heart sink.

"C'mon, Daniel, keep the faith," I muttered. "They didn't find him. They couldn't find him. He's still runnin'."

The vicious whine ended. Daniel took in a deep, ragged breath.

"But it's the story," Daniel whispered. *The Cocoa Butter Conspiracy.* You escape but you're on one of the Keys so get caught and brought back and I couldn't work up an ending that left you and Carmen alive."

"C'mon, buddy," I said, growing more and more nervous. "That was in a partial first draft. We'll come up with something. I'm you and you're me and ..."

"I know, Ace, I know," Daniel nodded, almost smiling. "We'll think of something. We always do."

But he wasn't sure, and I was coming up blanks, too.

Then the front door creaked open.

And the Terror-Twins entered.

Holding that manila envelope.

And they were alone.

Daniel's heart damn near stopped. "Where's Van!?"

All he got was a smirk out of Terror-Twin-1 as the guy handed Heinz the manila envelope. The second one held up a .38 pistol as he sneered in a deadpan voice, "He was packin'."

BAM! Daniel's chest nearly exploded. "Oh God, Ace, I got him killed," he gulped. "I got him killed."

"Dan-O, Dan-O, calm down," I said, "calm down, we don't know that, yet!"

But he wasn't hearing me. "I got him killed, I fuckin' got him killed." And he careened straight over the edge of batshit crazy and turned a vicious glare on Heinz.

I said, "Don't!"

But he screamed, "You son-of-a-bitch!" and slung a chair at him! It shattered on the hearth next to the bastard! Then before anyone could even react, Daniel jumped the table and crashed into Pint Size, hollering like a madman!

They bounced over the couch and onto the bloody floor, kicking Max aside. The Terror-Twins scrambled to yank Daniel back, but he was twisting and screaming so much, they couldn't get a grip. They wound up having to grab his legs to pull him away from the twerp, one for each since he was kicking so furiously. Then one slammed a boot into Daniel's left side. My guy cried out in pain, giving them a chance to force him to his feet, twist his arms behind his back and shove him, face down, across the end of the dining table. To put a cap on it, Terror-Twin-2 jammed Van's pistol to my guy's head and barked, "Stay!"

Daniel stayed, but only because all of a sudden he could barely breathe. And it wasn't from cold, fear or adrenalin; it was from pain shooting through his entire body to the point where he could barely see. He gulped in air and gasped, "Ace."

Oh, shit. Shit. "Dan-O, you think they broke a rib?"

He nodded.

Max and Costello helped Heinz to his feet. His nose was bloody and his face was screwed into a look of the purest anger. "You little shit!"

"It's your own damned fault, Heinz," snapped Costello. "I warned you that you were going too far, indeed I did."

"So let's end it," the bastard growled. "Throw the little fuck in the lake."

The Terror-Twins glanced at each other then yanked Daniel up. He cried out in pain then kicked one of them in the knee, making him howl. My guy almost wriggled away, but the second twin still had him from behind so dragged him, kicking and hollering, to the French doors and …

The main door slammed open and a big brusque Sheriff bolted in, pistol at the ready and yelling, "Drop him!"

Well, being totally devoid of brains, Terror-Twin-2 did exactly that. Onto the end of the table. Making Daniel's side explode in pain. He cried out. Curled into a near-fetal position, his feet hanging off the table's edge. He was facing the French doors so only heard the Sheriff holler, "Now what in Sam Hill's goin' on in here!?"

But then in the reflection of the door's glass he saw a figure enter behind the man and heard, "Daniel?"

It was Van!

"Oh, shit, Dan-O! DAN-O!" I all but shrieked.

My guy couldn't speak; he just gulped in air and gasped and forced himself to roll over, so he could see for himself.

And sure enough, there Van was! In his pea coat and red muffler, looking around with his beautiful deer-caught-in-the-headlights expression, calling, "Daniel?"

He'd gone for help!

He'd kept his word!

He could be trusted!

Aw, man, even I was close to tears. That'll show you, you inner doubter voices ... guys ... things.

Van finally saw my guy and his face nearly went white. "Daniel," whispered out of him, then he scowled, spun around and yanked one of the thick curtains down from a window and brought it over, the material billowing behind him.

"Here, this'll warm you," he said as he wrapped it around

Daniel, his face a storm of emotion. "What happened?"

"I thought I got you killed," my guy murmured, still half afraid to even touch him for fear he'd just vanish, his shaking out of control – half from cold, half from pain and half from disbelief that Van was really there and all right, and to hell with the rules of math.

"No, I'm fine," the dude whispered, brushing my guy's hair back from his face. "It's you who's all beat to hell."

"But they had ... they had ..." He looked at the manila envelope. It was still in Heinz's hand. Van saw it.

"They almost caught me," he said, "but I got away by tossing the bonds at them."

"Your gun."

Van pulled out a sleek little Walther PPK and said, "Right here. Why?"

Aw! The Terror-Twins ... the stupid fucking Terror-Twins lied, hoping to make their lord and master think they'd done what they'd been ordered to do, like that hunter in *Snow White* with the wicked queen. Suddenly, Daniel was laughing out of control, which only cut him deeper with pain but he just couldn't stop.

"What is it?" Van asked. "What? Jesus, there's blood everywhere."

My guy nodded, unable to speak.

"Okay, cut, we gotta cut this! Daniel needs a doctor."

"Oh, calm down, Van," said the sheriff. "I already put in the call for one. Now, let's take inventory."

"Inventory," my guy choked out.

"Like at the end of any mystery," I nodded.

He laughed even harder, starting to cough and gasp. But through the tears, he noticed the Sheriff had collected the pistols from Heinz and Costello, as well as the .38, and put them all on the table. And that cut into the funny, because we both thought, *What the hell is wrong with this character? You don't leave weapons around for just anyone to grab hold of.*

The sheriff looked about the room, focused on Daniel and said, "All righties, I know everybody here but this fella."

"Uh, sorry," said Van. "He's Daniel Bettancourt." Then he said to Daniel, "This is Sheriff Candelaria."

"You sure. About that?" Daniel gasped, back in control.

Van just frowned.

"Well," said the sheriff, bolting over to shake Daniel's hand, even though he could barely let go of his sides, "this is an honor, Mr. Bettancourt. I love your books."

Hah! I sneer at you, Heinz, and spit on your mittens.

"'Specially *The Dirty Baker's Dozen Plus Two*," the sheriff continued. "That bit between Ace and Carmen in the cookie dough – whooh." He shook a leg at the memory.

Oh, and did my sneer then become a smirk. Remembering Carmen covered in chocolate chips while I had to deal with shortbread. But it got me one of the best lines of my career.

"Who'd of thought catchin' killers'd make ya diabetic?" I happily murmured. "That was some damn good writin', Dan-O."

Oops, I just realized my name for him was slipping out, again, but Daniel just smiled, like he didn't mind me being all superficial and unconcerned about him for a moment. Which made me beam with happiness. He wasn't pissed at me. I could call him by the nickname he'd given me to call him by, which made me joyous because I can't be pissed at a guy who's not pissed at me, not matter how pissed I am at him.

"What brings you up here?" asked the sheriff.

"Murder," said Heinz, a bit too quickly. "He killed a woman."

The sheriff slowly turned to lock at him. "What?"

Van rolled his eyes. "Dammit, Heinz, it's over!"

"Not so far as I'm concerned," he snapped back at him.

"Help me up," Daniel winced to Van.

The guy gently guided him into a sitting position on the table then he noticed Daniel's side was beginning to bruise. "Jesus," he muttered then grabbed the sheet off the floor to tenderly wipe at the blood, true concern in his eyes. "How'd this happen?"

"Uh, Gretta did that when he tried to rape her," Heinz said.

Max jumped up and nodded his head like a monkey in heat, all but singing, "Yeah, yeah, yeah, I saw it all! I saw it! All of it!"

Daniel rolled his eyes and forced himself to say, "Could they have. Made up. A more ridiculous. Story?"

"Considerin' how dumb these bastards are?" I asked.

Van glared at Heinz then looked around. "Wait, Gretta. Where's Gretta?"

Daniel frowned at him. "Bedroom."

Torn, Van hesitated, his eyes locked on Daniel's, but my guy sent him on his way with a fluttery *be gone* motion of his hands, so Van said, "Don't move." Then he ran up the stairs.

Daniel watched him go, whispering, "Walther PPK."

Oh, shit. Then I got it.

"My pistol in ...*Tristan.*"

He nodded.

Shit! Just when everything's gonna be all right, something like this pops up! Dammit!

Heinz jumped over to the sheriff, pointing to Daniel. "Listen to me, Candelaria, that man shot her!"

Haddon joined him. "I'll back you on that!"

Max jumped up and scurried to be part of the cabal. "And he's blamed everybody else in the room for killing her!"

Heinz added, "He kidnapped her up here and ..."

Max cut in, jerkily. "I saw it and I told Costello."

Costello sat on a couch arm by the fire, to warm herself. "Don't mix me in this," she said like a total diva. "It's complete foolishness, indeed it is."

The sheriff waved his arms, shouting, "Okay, okay, okay, everybody pipe down!"

Heinz took in a deep breath. "Dammit, listen ..."

"If there's any listenin' to do, here, you'll do it!" The sheriff cut in. "Let's start with who she was, first."

Daniel's focus was finally back, despite the aching in his side, and he eyed them all with uncertainty as I said, "C'mon, Dan-O, it's not in your head. You wouldn't let Van be the only guy interested in ..."

"Gretta Bergstrom," said Heinz. "She was one of my ... of my secretaries."

Van backed out of the bedroom, seriously angry. "Whose idea was this?" he muttered.

Heinz pointed to Daniel, snarling, "Your little friend!"

Daniel shook his head, numb and barely focused. "Van. Max got jealous. And shot her."

"No way!" Max screeched. "I'd never hurt Gretta! I love her! Gretta!!" He flopped back on the couch, kicking and bawling like a five-year-old. "Gretta! Gretta!"

Costello rose and moved to the other side of the hearth, muttering, "Excuse me."

Van slowly crossed the landing, eyeing Max, confusion in his eyes. Daniel watched him.

And suddenly he saw the light.

And he understood everything.

And what I heard him screaming inside was, he really, seriously was finally, totally and completely caught in one of his ... my ... *our* stories!! It was all a fake! It was all unreal! Holy shit!

"Psycho Daniel," he growled, "qu'est-ce que c'est? Ha-ha-ha-ha-ha-ha-ha-ha-ha-ha." As the *Talking Heads* would sing.

The Sheriff stood before the fire, his focus on Heinz. "All righties," the man said, "when did it happen?"

"Before I arrived," said Pint Sized.

"Ten minutes ago," Daniel absently added, still processing the revelation. "And he's been here twenty."

Well, I guess if you're going to be part and parcel with this new and way-too-weird story, you may as well keep it going.

The sheriff looked at him. "Then who just came up on those skimobiles?"

"Those two guys," Van muttered, his eyes locked on Daniel as he indicated the Terror Twins. "They came after me."

"You were kidnapped up here, too?"

"No, I came on my own. So did Gretta."

"How do you know that?"

"I was here when she arrived."

"But you just got here."

"This time. Not the first time."

"First time?"

"Yes. I first arrived about a quarter past ten."

"So it *was* you made a call to the emergency operator!"

"No, that ... that was me," Daniel said as he slowly, painfully shifted off the dining table and headed for the fire, holding the thick black curtain around himself like a shroud, smiling in such a vacant way, it would have shut everyone up if they'd been paying any attention.

"I talked to Van when I called back," said Candelaria.

"Sure as snow," whispered Van, his eyes now locked on

Daniel. All right, all right, at least *he'd* noticed my guy's new attitude.

"Then you made the call," Candelaria snapped.

"No, I told you," said Daniel, his grin growing. "I made the call. He took the call."

"Why would he take a call you made from up here when he's up here, too?"

"Because," said Daniel, "I took your call then he took your call."

"My call?"

"Your call," Van nodded.

"You did?"

"I did."

"He did."

"Indeed," I chimed in.

The Sheriff shook his head. "Whoa, whoa, whoa! All this explainin's got me confused!"

"Oh, you can come up with a better line than that, Daniel," my guy said as he all but collapsed on the hearth.

"Fits in with the stupid," I said.

"To say the least," Van said.

Say what? Can he hear me, too? I cast him a look. Daniel glanced between me and Van, and noticed the worry in Van's eyes. My guy sighed. The dude looked so sweet and caring.

"Why couldn't you be real?" Daniel murmured, hurt.

Heinz noticed and warily pointed to Daniel. "Be careful of that man, sheriff. He's trying to cause confusion so he ... he can escape."

Candelaria just snorted. "I got the SWAT team surrounding the place. Nobody gets in or out till I say so. And if somebody's been killed, that won't be till the coroner gets here with the state police. Now where's the body?"

"Up here," Van absently said, his eyes still on Daniel.

The Sheriff started up the stairs, saying, "All of you work on your stories. Maybe they'll make sense by the time I come down."

Costello shook her head. "I wouldn't count on it; indeed I wouldn't."

I squatted beside Daniel. He was making a fresh inventory, and it was spooky. From the political corruption to the payoffs to the girl Ace met who might or might not be on his side to the innocent guy caught up in the middle to a murder by passion to double-crosses and backstabbings and country cops – shit, everything that happened tonight really was like a loose play on every damn one of his books, especially *The Cocoa-Butter Conspiracy.*

Shit! That's when the last piece fell into place.

"The eight-hundred-thousand!" I gasped. "The diamonds the Macaw swallowed in ...*Madam*."

My guy nodded. That clinched it. There was only one possible explanation.

"This isn't live," he sighed with a crooked grin then looked at me. "It's padded room."

"No, Dan-O, it ... it's Tad pullin' a joke on you, that's all. Yeah, it's gotta be."

"How?" he asked. "How?"

"He knows the stuff you write, and he's got connections, and he ... he ... "

"He doesn't know anything about *CBC*. I never told him I was working on it."

"No, Dan-O, c'mon, you're headin' for that secret place you got, and I don't like it when you hide there."

"So you think all this is live?" He looked at me, that little-boy-lost look in his eyes, and it tore me up. Something was screwing with his brain and he was looking to me for an answer, only I didn't have one to give.

"I don't know what *live* is," I had to admit. "I'm you and you're me. To me, everything you think's real, well, is real."

Carmen came over, worried, Tad with her, in his Speedo.

"Same here, Danny," she said.

"And I'm just your fantasy of how you wish that jerk'd be," offered Tad, "so I can't add anything to the discussion."

"But you're hurt!" I said. "If this wasn't real, you couldn't have got hurt!"

"Couldn't I?"

Oh, shit. That scared me. "Dan-O, what're you sayin'?"

"We'll see, Ace," he whispered. "We'll see. Let's give it just one more test. If it really is that story, then what happens next is ..."

The sheriff stormed out of the bedroom, snarling, "She's

not there!" Van followed him out, irritated.

And Daniel sighed. In *Cocoa-Butter Conspiracy*, he'd thought of having the *dead* girlfriend and boy actually be informants for the FBI who were getting set to go into witness protection. So they'd faked her death and would fake his, soon after but got found out and vanished and ...

And now there was zero question. It *was* all fake. It was all in his head.

Everyone kept chattering, only bits of it cutting into his consciousness as he leaned against the hearth, shaking, numb, his side now just a dull throbbing ache.

The sheriff glared down at the room. "So what're you people trying to pull? Where'd you put her?"

Max tore at his hair. "No, no, this can't be happening!"

"She was in that room!" Haddon said. "We laid her there not fifteen minutes ago!"

"You moved her after she'd been shot?!" the sheriff cried.

"Where could she have gone?" Max wailed. "Gretta!"

Daniel started to giggle at the guy's silly hysterics. Van quickly came down the stairs, his eyes back on my guy.

"The window's open," Candelaria said, watching Van oddly.

"She got away," Daniel said, gaily.

"How?" Heinz asked.

Daniel gave him a conspiratorial look. "Herman."

"Herman?" asked the sheriff.

"The hermit," Van said. "I forgot about him."

"But one of my men would've seen them and alerted me."

Daniel smirked and gulped in pain, "Sure as snow."

"The basement!" Heinz said. "There's an outside door!"

Van squatted beside my guy. "Daniel, you're sweating. Are you in pain?"

"No, not possible," my guy said.

Van growled at the Sheriff, "Where's that doctor?"

"Oh, hold on, Van!" The sheriff pulled out a walkie-talkie and called into it, "Houston, come in; we got a problem." Then he started down the stairs.

A deep-fried Southern voice responded, "Yeah, sheriff?"

I rolled my eyes. "Dan-O, really, Andy Griffith in upstate New York? This can *not* be in your head!"

"Story's set in Miami, Ace," Daniel whispered.

"What story?" said Van.

"This one," my guy said, absently.

"I want you to find an outside door to the cellar of this cabin," the sheriff said. "Enter and search it."

"We got a warrant?"

"Don't need one."

"Yes, we do."

"Says who?"

"*Criminology Made Simple*. I read it, last week."

At the same time, Van took my guy's face in his hands, tenderly. "Daniel, are you referring to a story you wrote?"

"No, I didn't write it," said my guy. "It's not any good. So I didn't write it."

Van was at a loss for words.

"Don't need a warrant if there's a crime in progress!" snapped Candelaria.

"So we got a crime in progress?" the Southern Voice snapped back.

"Yes!"

"What?"

"Murder! Which is what I'll do to you if you don't come search this cellar, right now!"

"Well, if you're gonna be like that. Gee."

"Over," snapped Candelaria, as he reached the bottom of the stairs. "You just can't get good deputies, these days. Now let's figure out what the hell this is all about."

"Don't you know?" Daniel asked. Then he absently motioned to the manila envelope. "Eight hundred-thousand dollars. In bearer bonds, this time. Next time ...?" He shrugged.

The sheriff jolted over and grabbed the envelope away from Heinz.

Pint Sized snarled, "Hey, those bonds were stolen from me, sheriff!" Then he pointed to Van and Daniel. "They took 'em!"

Max nodded in agreement. "Yeah, they're in it, together!"

Haddon chimed in with, "They're homosexual lovers!"

Oh, please! "Again, Dan-O, this can't be in your head; you'd *never* come up with a dumb-assed line like that!"

"Way too Fifties, baby," Carmen agreed.

"And fucking insulting," Tad nodded.

But Daniel had slipped into his secret zone, and I couldn't tell what he was thinking or feeling, anymore. Not anything, except ... except mixed into it was this numbness and sadness and suddenly I was sick with fear.

"Dan-O," I said, softly. "Buddy?"

"Let's lie down on the couch," Van said. "Okay? Daniel?"

He ignored both of us.

Costello sighed at the others, "Will you stop it? It's over, so let's make the best of it."

"That's easy for you to say!" Heinz snarled at her. "I have a business about to go bust because of you and your schemes!"

Haddon nodded. "Sheriff, the only way you can get a government contract in this town is to bribe that bitch!"

Daniel chuckled and pulled out an imaginary note pad and started writing. Van's face nearly went white.

Costello stormed over to the rest of them, snarling, "Like I had to twist your arm to do it?! You've been attempting any number of illegal contrivances to get into my good graces, indeed you have!"

"For years!" Max added.

"You tellin' me this is a bribe?" the sheriff asked.

Daniel absently sighed, "Brilliant observation, sheriff."

Van gently nudged my guy, whispering, "Daniel, please, lie down. You really don't look so good."

"Gotta document. The padded room," Daniel muttered.

"I don't understand."

"If I've lost my mind, I want it on paper. So I can find it, later. See?" And he showed Van the imaginary note pad.

Van burst out with, "Okay, that's it! We gotta cut this out! We gotta CUT it …!"

But Daniel put a finger to his lips and went, "Shh, it's time for the proof." Then he forced himself to his feet and stumbled over to his laptop, everyone's eyes on him as he brightened the screen and looked at the program window. It popped up with the Garage Band set-up. Van followed him, just as scared as me, and I was about to let Daniel know when …

The cellar door slammed open and this deputy from the backwoods of nowhere shoved Herman in. Van jolted to look around. Daniel didn't even notice.

"Look what we found," sneered the deputy.

"Damn your hides!" Herman snapped. "I hate the police!"

Candelaria asked, "Did you find anything else?"

"Nothin' that means nothin'," said the deputy.

Max squeaked and pointed at the French doors. "Gretta! I saw Gretta!"

"Of course you did," muttered Daniel. "You always were the hysterical one."

Van looked back at him then looked closer at the screen.

Candelaria turned to the Deputy. "See if you can find her! I'll keep watch on this bunch!"

The deputy bolted outside, the door not even bothering to make a noise when it slammed shut. The others tried to follow him, but the sheriff pulled his pistol to stop them. "Nobody's goin' nowhere! Back up!"

They backed.

Heinz snarled, "Now just a minute, here!"

"You don't have to pull a gun!" Haddon whimpered.

Max bounced, nervously. "Who d'you think you are?!"

Costello shifted so the fire could warm her backside, muttering, "Completely out of his mind, indeed he is."

"Jesus Christ, Candelaria, this is ridiculous!" Van cried.

Daniel chuckled. "Oh, we're way beyond ridiculous and lost in reality by Dali."

I jumped and motioned to the note pad. "Uh, Dan-O."

"Later," snapped Daniel.

The Sheriff cast him a quick glance then grabbed the phone and dialed. "Uh ... you think so, huh?" he said.

"Guys, guys," Van said, moving to the center of the room, "this has got to stop, now. NOW! There's something wrong with Daniel! Do you hear me!? DO YOU HEAR ME!?"

"They can't," said Daniel. "They aren't real."

Van looked at him, stricken. "Oh, jeez, oh, jeez."

Candelaria spoke into the phone. "Uh, Karen? This is Milo. Get the kids out of bed and meet me out on Old Crandall Road. By the pond. Just do it! Now!"

Heinz growled, "You're taking my bonds?!"

"People, call it off!" Van cried. "It's gone too far!"

"No, it hasn't," said Daniel as he hit the play button on the Garage Band program. "It's part of the story."

They all cast a glance at Daniel, then the sheriff said,

"Damn straight. This is eight hundred-thousand dollars worth of bearer bonds! They're good for anybody who signs them!"

Van cried to the heavens, "Okay, Bentley, listen to …!"

"Gentlemen, good evening!" Daniel's voice in his horrible British accent blasted forth from the laptop. Everyone jumped and looked at my guy. "Had you bothered to knock, I'd have been glad to let you in."

"Who're you?" Heinz's voice said.

Daniel chuckled and rocked back and forth as he listened to his voice chirp through the laptop's speakers, saying, "I? Why, I … I am Mayor Costello's boy toy, sir. Can't you tell?"

His chuckles became nearly maniacal laughter.

"I've done it," he gasped, rising and backing away from the laptop. "I've finally done it. I'm lost in one of my stories!"

"He's full of it, Mr. Heinz!" said Haddon's voice. "He's the guy what jumped me, earlier tonight!"

Van waylaid Daniel, carefully saying, "No, listen, Daniel, this isn't really happening; the story you wrote … and … and Tad Bentley and …"

"I?" Daniel's voice kept on with. "Why, I have never seen this gentleman before in my life, sir. And look at me; do I appear as though I could jump anyone?"

My guy twisted away from Van, saying, "I know it's not real. Because Ace won. Ace and Carmen and Tad, they won."

"Wait," I said, "what d'you mean we won?"

"Nobody's real, anymore. Hell, I'm not even real."

What the hell? What was he doing? I still couldn't fucking read him! "Dan-O, what're you talkin' about? C'mon, you're scaring me, here."

I was standing beside Van, but my guy backed away from both of us, vaguely aiming for the French doors. Van and I paced him. Everyone watched us, finally realizing something had gone seriously wrong.

"Daniel, please, listen to me," Van said, "It'll be okay. You … you'll be okay, okay?"

Daniel kept backing around the table. Past the doors. His eyes locked on us as he circled closer and closer to where the pistols lay.

"I wanted you to be real; I wanted that so much," my guy murmured. "But it's okay. Why would it be? Why would you exist? Hell, I don't even exist. In order to not be okay then I'd have to exist, but I'm here in the middle of nothing and since none of this exists then I don't exist, and since I don't exist I can't be not okay, okay?"

What the hell was going on? Why wouldn't he let me back into his thoughts? "Dan-O, cut it out! This ain't funny."

"Danny," Carmen whispered, "what's goin' on, here?"

"Uh, careful, everyone," said Heinz, nervously, "he's been doing this all night and ..."

"I've been doing it all my life!" Daniel exploded, then he smiled and chuckled and said, "Or have I? Maybe *all* of it was just in my mind. Oh, oh, oh, maybe I've never really been here. Maybe I'm just a figment of your imagination, Van. Or yours, Heinz. Or Costello's."

"Dan-O," I snapped, "if you say we might be part of Max's, I'll throttle you."

"From *The Red Knife in Blue Jell-O*, right?" Suddenly, he flicked Haddon's revolver, sending it spinning across the table and off the other end, to the floor.

Why'd he do that?! What the hell was going on here?!

"That was our first story," he muttered. "I think."

"Yeah, Dan-O, it was. It was."

"No, Daniel ...." Van was shaking from fear for my guy.

"This is real," I said. "It has to be. All of it has to be."

"Does it?" he asked, more to himself than me. Then he jolted and knocked the .38 away, making it spin across the table and almost off the side. Then he looked at me and Van, his little-boy-lost expression at full power. "Isn't it better if I'm not real? You can't hurt somebody who's not really there, can you? And I am so tired of being hurt."

"Please," said Van, his voice shaking with fear, "listen to me. I can explain."

Daniel's chuckles returned, with a truly dangerous flavor. "Sure, you can. Sure as snow."

He grabbed the automatic! Van and Haddon scrambled to stop him, but Daniel danced around them and into Candelaria and tore the envelope away and shoved him into them, laughing the whole time. Then he raced upstairs, the black curtain billowing behind him as he yanked sheets of paper from the envelope and they flew everywhere.

And every damn one of them was blank!

Van scrambled after him, crying, "Daniel, wait! Listen to me! None of this is real! It's all fake! We're making it up!"

"I know!" Daniel shrieked. "I know! I'll prove it!"

The flying papers drifted to the stairs, getting underfoot and making Van slip. Haddon, Max and the Sheriff chased up the stairs after Van but only wound up piling on top of the guy.

Daniel raced into the bedroom and across to the bathroom, slamming the door, behind him.

Van untangled himself and scrambled up the stairs, and I was ahead of him because I couldn't hear Dan-O's mind and …

BAM!

The pistol fired!

And I couldn't feel Daniel!

I couldn't sense anything coming from my guy, anymore! No thoughts. No fears. No words. Nothing! Nothing but Carmen screaming and Van yelling, "Oh, shit! Shit!"

SHIT!

All right ... in fairness, I should let you know – some of what follows from this point, I learned later. But for the sake of continuity, I'm putting it down as if I saw it, myself.

First, shift location to a semi-portable editing suite containing a bank of three-dozen camera monitors, each labeled to designate every entrance, room, nook, corner, cranny and wall in The Lyons' Den, and each showing either a regular or a night-vision image of that location. And every damn one of them was active. Two even showed Van and everyone from different angles as they scrambled up the stairs. The only blank screen was labeled *Master Bath.*

Second, a man of the I've-have-too-many-donuts-in-my-life-to-give-a-shit-or-even-be-able-to-shit variety was set before those monitors, staring in horror at a set of three larger monitors above all the rest that had *Relay 1, Relay 2* and *Set-Up* under them. A series of levers and buttons and switches were below it all, and a cordless phone lay on a table, to his right.

Behind him, Tad ... as in, I'm-His-Real-Gloriousness ... jolted up from an overstuffed chair, his latest cup of coffee flying everywhere as he cried, "What happened to the master bath cam?!"

"Somethin's coverin' it," snapped the donut-eater. "Like blood, maybe. I told you to cut!"

On the monitors labeled Master Bedroom, Van ran in and slammed against the bathroom door, pounding on it. "Daniel! DANIEL!" Meaning, yes – there was also sound.

Tad bolted from the editing room, leaving his coat behind. He raced through a cabin similar to The Lyons' Den, but with dressing tables and lights and lots of warmth and food and crew people sitting around enjoying the craft-services ... oh, that's a snack table, for those not up on film lingo ... one of them being Mrs. Serff, who was positioned beside another cordless phone labeled, drum roll, please, *Lyons' Den*! They watched him run past but did little more than share shocked expressions as he clambered out the main entrance.

Well, it turns out Tad was in a cabin by a lake in a snowy forest. Meaning, yes – he was right next-door the entire evening. Moonlight danced between thick clouds, giving plenty of light to see by as he plowed through the snow over to The Lyons' Den. The front entrance, of course, was locked. He pounded on it, screaming, "Let me in!"

He heard a crash, upstairs, and stepped back. An upstairs window was lighted and open, and through it, Tad heard Van cry, "Daniel!? Oh, shit! Daniel!"

Tad stepped back to cry, "Van, it's Bentley! Let me in!"

Van poked his head out a window and spat, "You son-of-a-bitch!" Then he gasped and vanished back inside.

Tad shrieked, "LET ME IN!!"

Then he felt a pistol press against the back of his head and heard a voice sharp with pain growl, "You need a key."

Tad spun around to find Daniel behind him, shivering in the snow, his parka on, the curtain now torn into shreds and wrapped around his feet, the automatic quaking in his hands.

I popped up behind him, so pissed and relieved I could've slugged him and kissed him, both. "Oh, Dan-O, you little shit, don't *do* that to me! How *did* you do that?!"

And Carmen was right there with me, swatting at Daniel as she laughed, "You are such a sneak!"

Tad had to lean against a tree to keep from falling over from relief. "Danny? Oh, shit. Shit. You little fuck."

Daniel snarled, "I knew it. You son-of-a-bitch, it *was* you behind all this."

"Shit, Danny, have you any idea how much you scared me!?"

"I scared *you*?!" Daniel shrieked, his words clipped from the ache in his side. "I thought I was going crazy! That my stories were taking over my life! I was this fucking close to convinced, Tad!" he snarled, holding his thumb and forefinger pressed together. "But I set up my laptop to record everything, and it did! I got Haddon and Heinz and everybody *but* Ace! So it was real! You're all real!"

Van appeared at the kitchen door and hesitated, then he

carefully approached Daniel. My guy noticed but left it to me and Carmen to keep an eye on him.

Tad rolled his eyes, finally back to his asshole self. "Cut it out, Danny! If you think I'll accept this *you hurt me* crap after what you just pulled?!"

"How'd you do it?" my guy gulped, cutting him off. "Everything's just like the outline of that story I'm working on. But I never even told you about it! Never told anybody! So how'd you get my outline? How'd you set it up!?"

"Give me a fucking break," Tad sighed. "You were always working on something, and besides, it's on your laptop."

"When've you ever had access to my computer?" Daniel snarled.

"That last night we were together."

"When you dumped me. Because of what happened at Gregory's party."

"Yes. You'd left it on, so I took a peek while you were in the bathroom."

"Talking myself out of downing a whole bottle of Prozac!"

Van jolted and cast Tad a vicious glare, and boy, was I glad to see that.

Sir-Great-And-Glorious blinked and gave my guy a cock-eyed grin. "Really? I thought you were just being little sir drama queen."

"You know how upset I was!"

Tad sighed and rolled his eyes in that way he's got and said, "Okay, fine, I stuck around to make sure you didn't do something stupid. You know, you said you were off the Prozac."

Ah, yes, Sun Tzu say, *When defense is weak, go on the attack.* Or was it Aesop?

"I was," Daniel muttered. "I am. I ended it weeks before we broke up."

Tad shrugged and gave Daniel his best *Okay, I screwed up* look. "Sorry," he said. "But that's why I stuck around. And I figured while I was waiting, I'd go online. Do some work. But I saw the file, checked it out and got an idea, and set up remote access. Anytime you were online, I could sneak a peek at what you'd done with it, and I could see you were having trouble with this story. But that's what made it work."

"Made what work?" Then my guy grimaced in pain.

"The pilot I came up with for a new reality show," Tad chirped, not noticing or caring that Daniel was quaking from pain and cold. *Writers for Reel.* We get a real writer, fix it so he lives one of his stories and see how long it takes him to catch on. Bravo has the screamies for it."

Oh, not really.

"Jeez, that sounds dumb," sneered Carmen.

Van grew closer. "Daniel, we ... we're actors. All of us. From an improvisational theater in the city. I read your books and got a feel for the characters you write. We used your outline for the basic plot, and since you're gay, I took the lead."

"Of course," said Daniel, almost sadly. "And Tad told you which buttons of mine to push, didn't he?"

Van hesitated. then gave a slight nod.

"Now ... now put the gun down," He said. "You're in pain. And you're a good guy; you don't want to hurt anybody."

"Stop it," my guy said. "It just has blanks." He lowered the pistol and stepped back, shivering and holding his side, the cold finally taking the pain into a dull ache. "I knew that when Gretta vanished," he continued. "No way she could have moved, not where she was shot. And Herman's not strong enough to carry her."

"No shit on that," said Carmen. "She could lose twenty pounds an' still be heavier 'n me."

"Mean Carmen," I purred. She sent me a giggle, in response.

"That's why I flicked the other two away," Daniel kept on with, "so I'd grab the right one when I made my break."

The door CREAKED open, and Haddon, Herman, Heinz, Costello, Max, Gretta, the Terror-Twins and the Sheriff peeked out, one after the other. Daniel pointed at them.

"Then I remembered Haddon said I'd fired the pistol. He wasn't around when I did that. And you, Van," he said, casting the dude a sideways glance, "you knew there were sheets in the closet before it'd been opened. But that only kept making me wonder how crazy I was going ... until I looked up at you. When you were coming down the stairs that last time. And I saw this little red light."

"Whoa, whoa, whoa, that was a camera light?!" I yelped.

Tad exploded. "Dammit, I told Sandy to cover them!"

"So," my guy whispered, "they're night vision cameras?"

"How else could we've seen all the action?" Tad snapped.

Daniel looked as if he'd been punched, and I grimaced, too, because now we knew just how nasty this was going to be.

"And ... and they're all over?" he asked. "In every room? As I talked to myself? As I jacked off?" Then he focused on Van, his eyes filled with pain. "As I spilled my guts to you."

Van winced and nodded. "I'm sorry."

"What're you sorry for?" Tad asked. "You got him to tell you things he never told me. Shit. Danny, it's like you didn't trust me or that I never really mattered to you. Do you know how that makes me feel?"

Oh, that bastard. Swear to God, if I could have, I'd have throttled him.

Daniel just looked at Tad, his wounded-puppy eyes lost in disbelief. Van was also rather taken aback.

Tad finally noticed and gave a slight grimace then added, "Listen, you have nothing to worry about. Night vision is very grainy, and we have to make it PG. Plus it's just a half-hour slot. But my bet is, once they see the raw footage, Bravo will want an hour."

"Yeah, and wait'll you do the blooper reel," Daniel sighed back at him. He cast another glance at Van. Pulled his parka tighter. He quaked from the cold. "And you agreed to this."

"Our contract said we had to play the part till you called us on it," Van replied, barely able to speak. He really seemed ashamed of it all. "Or Bentley called cut. Otherwise, no pay."

"That explains what you did when you came back," Daniel muttered.

"Yes. But, Daniel, listen to me. We had it all laid out for me to run the story and lead you along, but you took over. Threw everything off. Rewrote the whole script. You really lived your books."

"I always live my books," my guy muttered.

No bullshit on that, buddy, because I'm you and you're me.

"So all I could do," said Van, "was follow your lead. Try to keep up. I really fell into the part."

"Yeah, perfect type-casting, all the way around."

"I don't understand."

"Nothing. It's just – well, Tad cast you because he knew it'd throw me off. Y'see, you're just my type and ..."

"Now, now, wait a minute, I thought I was your type," Tad joked in his best insinuating voice.

"No," said Daniel, "you're my punishment."

Tad stiffened. "Excuse me?"

"C'mon, Daniel, let's go inside," said Van, getting a bit closer. "We'll get a doctor and have you checked ..."

"Wait, you're hurt?" said Terror-Twin-1. "You mean, you weren't faking that, too? You really are hurt?"

"Oh, for God's sake," Van exploded, "look at him! When did he have a chance to go for makeup?"

Tad looked closer. "Now, Danny, are you sure you aren't being Mr. Drama, again?"

"I dunno," my guy said. "I may only have a broken rib. Ruptured spleen. Something like that."

"Aw, shit," Van spit. Sorry, couldn't resist the rhyme.

Terror-Twin-1 moaned, "Oh, man, I thought you could take a hit; we're taught how to take a hit in class."

"He's not an actor, you idiot!" Van cried. "I tried to tell you! Tell everybody! And I couldn't understand why Bentley wasn't calling cut and ... and ..."

"Why would I?" Tad asked, hopping over to my guy. "It was fantastic. That's what made it so good, Danny, that you really did live it, for a while. So what's feeling somewhat achy in the morning? Isn't this coolness defined?"

"Jesus," Daniel muttered, keeping him at arm's length, "you really do mainline ice-water."

"Excuse me?!"

"Forget that shit, asshole," snapped Carmen. I barked out a laugh, at that.

"Daniel, please," Van said, putting a tender hand on my guy's shoulder. "Let's get you warmed up and into some clothes and have you checked out at a hospital and ..."

"No, just one thing more," Daniel whispered, numb. Then he looked at Tad. "So ... is there a camera out here, too?"

Little-Sir-Perfect nodded. "For when you arrived. We had them in my car and that pickup, as well. Oh, Danny, some of your reactions were, they were simply priceless."

"Then how about a priceless finish?"

"Are you kidding me?" Tad said. "You turning everything back on us is the perfect ending."

Daniel smirked. "I got a better one. Did you know blanks can kill at close range?"

He jammed the pistol against Tad's forehead! The bastard froze. Gretta and the Valkyrie screamed. Van yelped and yanked Daniel to the ground so fast I barely knew he'd done it! They crashed into a snow bank and my guy cried out in pain and the pistol ...

Clicked!

Van gasped and jolted back onto his knees, stunned. Daniel slowly rolled onto his good side then held up the bullet clip in his other hand.

Tad could not move. All he could say was, "Shit."

"Can I get up now?" Daniel muttered, painfully. "I'm about to get frostbite in places I don't want. Or will you shove me down, again?"

Van slowly rose, shaken. He offered Daniel a hand, only to have it slapped aside. Instead, my guy forced himself to his feet and breathed deep then staggered into the cabin. And the look on his face seriously said: *Step away from the maniac.*

Inside, he collapsed on the hearth, still quaking. He put his legs up on the stones to get them closer to the fire and rubbed his calves, despite the pain. I was right with him, now in my best night-sneaking-around attire; Carmen sat behind him, in a skirt-suit, rubbing his back. Fantasy Tad sat on his other side, still in his Speedo. And if you think it looked like we were standing guard, you'd be right; we were.

The cast of characters slowly wandered in, uncertain and keeping a wide berth around my guy.

Tad followed a moment later, pissed as shit. "Danny," he snapped, "that was bullshit! This was all in good fun. And we'll make a massive amount of coin, so what do you ...?"

"Fun for you," snapped Daniel. "Money for you. That's the way it always works for rich bastards like you."

"Hey, hey, HEY! I'm cutting you in on it."

"For what? Ten percent? Twenty, maybe? You think I think it was worth it?!" He grimaced then noticed Van was entering. "What about you, gorgeous? Was it worth it to you?"

Van slowly closed the door, no creaking, not looking at

Daniel. "I told you, it ... uh ... it was a job."

"Are you really getting paid? All of you?"

The cast glanced about at each other as Gretta smirked, "Guild minimum."

"Damn, you're getting fucked, too," my guy chuckled.

"Cut that shit out, Danny," Tad snarled. "Everybody here gets residuals."

"Meaning, fucked worse than me," Daniel snarled at him.

Van looked at my guy, honest contrition in his eyes as he said, "If I'd known about ... about everything, I wouldn't have done it. Playing a part as a joke on a guy is one thing. I mean, we ... I ... we needed the work, but this? I really am sorry."

Daniel's expression softened. "Okay, it's okay," he sighed. "I know what it's like to need a job."

No shit there.

Van cast him a grateful near-smile.

Fantasy Tad rolled his eyes and snarled, "Now there you go again. Too-cute-to-be-believed hands you a line of golly, *I really am sorry* crap and you swallow it whole."

Daniel waved his hand ...

And the creep vanished.

Startling me and Carmen, both. A very good sign. Then my guy looked at the all-too-real Tad, snarling, "So the meeting?"

His-Gloriousness was still irritated so snapped back, "That was bullshit to get you up here with a ticking clock."

"But the scripts I'm working on, they're really dog-meat."

"I know. That Cheeto-eating bastard actually *did* fuck them up. Would you like to hear something ridiculous? You know that movie he's so famous for writing? Once they began shooting they saw it was pure garbage so they hired an eighty-year-old screenwriter who was big in the fifties to redo it, and *that* is why it turned out good. So once word got around the twerp was adapting two of your books, no one wanted anything to do with the project."

"Of course," Daniel sighed. "So the option's dead, and the project comes back to me."

"I don't blame you for not wanting it," Tad muttered.

"But I do. I'll make them work, like I said I would."

I all but jumped for joy. "Dan-O! That'd be so kewl!"

"Oh, Danny," Carmen sighed, "we'll kick some real ass."

Tad squatted by my guy in his best big-brother mode. "Now, Danny, cut it out. I'm not holding you to ..."

"Are you buying the rights, Tad?"

"It'd be a waste of even more money," he snarled. "And my investors would rip me a new one. I could barely talk them into accepting this pilot in a tradeoff."

"Then kill the option."

"They won't let me. Part of the deal was I have to see if someone else'll take the project off their hands and get them back their seed money."

"I'll talk to them," said Daniel. "If they'll work with me, I'll get them repaid."

"Oh, come on! Do you know how hard it is to raise serious cash for a film, these days?"

"Do it," my guy said, "or I won't sign a release for this."

"If you don't sign," sighed Tad, still in big-brother mode, "no one gets paid."

"Wrong," said Van. "We just won't get paid residuals."

Tad rolled his eyes then shrugged and said, "Okay, fine, I know everybody's a little upset, so let's take some time off. Danny, do you still want to go to Bermuda? We could spend a couple weeks, on my Amex. Relax. Put all this in the past." Then he let this tender look slip into his eyes, one none of us had ever seen before. "You know, I meant it when I said I missed you."

"Did you?" my guy murmured, wary but not wary enough.

Tad nodded, his ice blue eyes beginning to sparkle like they always do when he's about to win. "It's funny, but when I was around you, I was never lonely."

"You weren't?"

"No," Tad chuckled, "thanks to the company you keep."

Wait, was that a sneaky slap at my guy's mental minions?

He brushed his fingers up Daniel's chin and to that scar on his cheek. "Sometimes you don't miss what you have until you don't have it anymore. But two weeks on a warm beach? Away from all this snow? Give things another shot? Just you and me? Je tu dois au moins cela."

Son. Of. A. Bitch. *I owe you that much*? He's saying my guy's not really worthy of him!? In crap French?! After what he just pulled?! Oh, God, please, please, please give me real hands for just five seconds. Just long enough to snap His-Great-and-Gloriousness' neck!

But then Daniel smiled and sighed. And what I was reading was – shit, he was thinking it might be nice. And I was close to snapping, spitting, snarling and slinging nasty words at him to try and stop him when he pulled Tad in for a kiss that kicked fucking ass. So deep. So meaningful. So passionate. So pure. So practically porno. Still love alliteration. Shit! My guy's inner servant was kicking in! He was fucking willing to take the bastard back!

Van turned away, as did the rest of the actors. Except for Gretta; she licked her lips. Which made Carmen arch an eyebrow and smirk, "You got *that* right, bitch." Then she eyed Daniel and Tad and licked her own lips and, man, was this little horn-doggie conflicted, because her motor was up to red-line.

But Daniel finally let go, and Tad let out a deep breath as he whispered, "Whoa, Danny, I knew you could kiss, but that? That was end-of-the-world. So when's good for you?" he asked, actually seeming eager. "Tuesday, next week? I can have Sandy set it up and maybe even use my miles."

"Dream about it," said my guy, and the tone of his voice was so solid and sure, Carmen and I jolted for joy. "That was a taste of what you ain't gettin', no more."

True confusion came to Tad's face. "What do you mean?"

"You're a self-centered asshole," said Daniel, "and I have enough of that shit in my family; I don't need it in my lovers. We're through."

"Who the fuck're you kidding, Danny?" Tad smirked back. "Look at me. You can't give me up. No one can."

Daniel just smiled and shoved him back to fall on his ass. The look of shock on the bastard's face was worth that whole night, all on its own. Then my guy painfully rose and staggered over to Van.

"So, is there a snow cat here?" my guy asked.

Van nodded. "I'll take you down. Bradleyville has a good clinic, and I'll see to it they take good care of you."

"And you'll hold my hand as they tape me up?"

"You weren't supposed to get hurt," Van said, quietly.

The pain in Van's eyes cut straight into Daniel's heart. "I really scared you," my guy said. Van barely shrugged, and

Daniel's anger melted away. And lemme tell you, I didn't mind a damn bit. In fact, I very quietly pointed out, "You ever see this kind of caring in Tad? Or Jarrod? Ever? Hm? Hmmmmm?"

My guy finally sighed, "Van, I went too far with that suicide fake. I'm sorry."

Van shook his head. "No, no, you had the right."

"Didn't make it right." Then he looked Van straight in the eye. "I'm okay if you are."

It took a moment, but Van finally smiled his acceptance.

Daniel's expression shifted to nervous. "So all those things you said, you were just acting, huh?"

Van took in a deep breath. "At first."

"Really?" my guy whispered, barely able to breathe.

Van nodded. "Until I started wanting to protect you."

Daniel's heart swelled. "Maybe I need protecting, because I don't even know if Van's your real name and I'm about to ..."

Van smiled. "It's my real nickname. For Donovan."

Even Carmen liked the sound of that so said, "C'mon, Danny, c'mon, you'd be beautiful together," as she nudged him.

"Donovan," my guy smiled. "I like. And I promise you, I'm not as crazy as you think. At least, I hope not."

"Anyone who can say that is definitely sane," said Van.

"Careful," Daniel said, taunting him a little, "I might be fooling you."

"You're not," Van whispered. "Sure as snow." Then he pulled my guy close and kissed him, long and deep, with nothing but tenderness and caring and need and promise and hope and love and support.

And Daniel finally felt like he'd found home.

The Joy of D&D

Van held Gretta in his embrace, deep in a kiss. She was barely wrapped in a shower curtain and the cut from a bullet wound in her arm gently bled. They were on the roof of a bleak and abandoned high-rise overlooking Biscayne Bay, with the sun just beginning to glow over the Atlantic's horizon.

She finally whispered in Van's ear, using her best Bronx growl, "C'mon, I took a bullet for you; is that all I get in return?"

Van gave her his cockiest Ace Shostakovich smirk and said, with a gentle, loving tremble to his voice, "Baby, that's just a down payment."

It was sixteen months later, in a movie theater in LA. A packed audience was watching a screening of *The White Snow Conspiracy* with Van playing me and Gretta playing Carmen. It pretty much followed events in The Lyons' Den ... except the snowstorm was a hurricane. And there was no isolated cabin; just empty condos and half-finished office towers dotting the city. White Snow referred to a billionaire albino who was using money laundered through Bermuda to buy off politicians and judges and cops, left and right, in all senses of the phrase. It had action, romance, suspense, sex, me almost having to go all the way with a guy to get some info ... thank you so much, Dan-O, and may I do the same to you with a girl, some day, you little shit ... and the perfect ending moments after the albino went falling to his death from the top of that rickety condo tower. A bit too *Die Hard* for me, but Daniel mitigated it by saying, "Hitchcock used it all the time, so shut up."

I did.

Then *I*-Van lifted *Carmen*-Gretta into my arms and headed down the sixty-two flights of stairs. Do not ask how we got up there; it's complicated. Cops herded Haddon, Max, Heinz, Herman, Costello, the Sheriff and the Terror-Twins, all under new names, of course, ahead of us and the camera swooped away and the skyline of Miami looked exquisite in the early morning light and the credits began to roll.

And one of the first names up was my guy's, as producer and writer and all that jazz. Man, I couldn't have been more proud than if he was my child. Who'd of thunk he had it in him?

Not Tad, but then, he was no longer part of this.

Of course, the audience applauded; it was a preview for the cast and crew. The movie was set to be released nationwide in two weeks, no cable, not yet.

The lights came up and Van, Gretta and the others stood to accept it, then Van pulled Daniel to his feet to join in with them. My guy just smiled.

People crowded up to him, Van and the other actors to discuss all sorts of things and share memories and all that crap, and it took Daniel a good twenty minutes to sneak away from them all. I stayed by him, just like I had through the writing and the deal-making and the shooting with a director who really did think he was Orson Welles and had a huge crush on Gretta, and who had to be reminded, constantly, that I ... well, *Van* was the star of the picture, because the twerp would've put her dead center in every shot, scene and cinematic moment, the little snot. Meaning, yes – he was the director version of the Cheeto-eater, but with an ego the size of Texas ... and an eye for making even two people talking in a room seem tense; so at least he did have talent. And I've been there through post production and the gathering of distribution deals in the U.S. and overseas. And I'd be there for the festival premier, Saturday, and the red carpet premier the following Tuesday. And as unreal as I am, I was damn near exhausted!

Because in the middle of all this, we also put out a new book titled *The Toadie's Toad* about a gay screenwriter who's blamed for killing the director and producer who mangled his screenplay. And please don't ask if it's based on anything like reality because it isn't.

Honest.

I swear.

Plus we got the funding to shoot *...Tristan* and *...Madam* for a new mystery series on PBS and were set to start production the end of the month.

Of course, now that we had the luxury of looking back, I could see the only reason the film got done, let alone got done in less than two years, was Daniel had this new *I don't give a shit what you think; it's a great project and it'll make back ten times your investment* attitude that made even Tad's investors think he knew what he was doing ... despite the fact that he was just reading it in a book. I guess since he'd already been through the first five stages of hell, he figured that was enough to prep him for stages six and seven – dealing with the arrogance, attitudes and insanity of Hollywood and distribution. So they dumped Tad and went with us.

And now it was done, and he was blank. And I didn't care, because I was prouder than shit for both of us. And for Carmen, too, since she helped a little, even though she swears she had to do it all, herself.

But don't tell her I said that.

The crowd finally shifted its focus to the actors, since they're the ones everybody wants to fuck, giving Daniel a chance to quietly slip outside for some fresh California air. Yes, I know that's an oxymoron, but we were in Santa Monica, right near the ocean, and the night breeze was almost perfect in its coolness. We wound up sitting on a bench across from the theater and watched people and traffic and life whip past at warp speed. My guy didn't like LA. Didn't like having to have a car and drive everywhere. But he'd be done with it in ten days and could go back to his beloved New York chaos, which would be especially great since Tad was now based on the West Coast and locked into pulling together a new season of *Writing for Reel Time*. Season One had been a hit, especially Daniel's episode; it tripled his books' sales within a week of airing and now Gregory was begging him to do a signing tour for *Toadie's Toad*.

But that could be decided later. Right now, he was just sitting and enjoying the lovely thought of lying in his own bed, again, when Van joined him, holding a bottle of Cabernet he'd stolen from the party. He silently offered Daniel a swig. My guy took one, smiling.

"Not bad," he said. "I had better where I tended bar."

"You chose this label."

"Really? How cheap-assed of me."

Van chuckled and squatted before down to lean in between his legs, a little drunk from both the wine and the evening. "Miss that?"

"Never," said my guy as he gave Van a peck on the nose.

"How do you really feel about the movie?" Van asked.

Daniel took in a deep breath and said, "Vindicated."

Van laughed and rose and pulled him up with him to wrap his arms around him. "Honest, as always," he whispered.

Daniel held him just as close. Molded his body against Van's. Loved the feel of him. The warmth of him. The tender caress of his hands. The touch of his lips. All so right, so real, so pure, he couldn't help but sigh, "Who ever would've thought I'd find peace in the arms of a freaky actor?"

Van shot back with, "Pot calls kettle black." He patted Daniel's ass. "Let's go home."

"Can't," said Daniel, "not till next week's premier."

"You know what I mean," Van murmured, then he led my guy to the valet and handed over the ticket. "So where you wanna go to shake this off? Prep to shoot ...*Tristan*? You still like Behr-muuuuuuu-dah?"

"God, no, they hate fags in the Caribbean."

"Bermuda's not part of the Caribbean."

"Let's go to Edinburgh. I'll show you Arthur's Seat." And shis look grew as wicked as they come.

Van grinned back.

"Yeah," I snickered, "you just want him to climb all them steps in front of you, so you can watch his ass."

I was off to one side, smirking, Carmen beside me, her arm entwined in mine, me in a tux and her in an evening gown to die for. But that's for later, if you know what I mean.

Daniel sighed and muttered, "Careful. Next movie I may turn you into a drag queen."

I laughed. "And freak my fans? Fuhgeddaboudit."

Carmen smiled at him and said, "What if I'm there, too? It's not gay if it's a three-way."

"Ooooh," said my guy, "that'd be interesting. That Faith-Hill-Tim-McGraw scene from Gregory's party in a Bertolucci sense and ..."

"Daniel." Van glared at him, miffed.

"Hm?" my guy said, completely into his little-boy-lost-look, again. Then he snapped to reality and shyly grinned. "Just Ace, making trouble."

"Can't help it, dude," I said. "It's how I'm written."

Carmen patted my butt with a soft little giggle then asked, "Danny, you ever gonna let me watch, you two?"

"That's up to Van," Daniel said.

Van rolled his eyes. "What? She askin', again?"

Daniel shrugged and nodded. Van took my guy's face in his hands and kissed him and whispered his lips over the scar on his cheek and looked deep into his eyes. His own eyes held nothing but love and support and acceptance and understanding as he said, "*No*, is a good word. Strong. Powerful."

Daniel caught his breath. Sixteen months and Van could still send him into the stratosphere with just a glance and the sound of his voice. All he seemed to want was to be just as important to Daniel as I was. Lately it'd been pretty damn close but now? At that moment? Now Van was ahead by a kiss on a scar. My guy sighed, and waved his hand.

I knew when to back off, so Carmen and I slipped into an alcove.

"Still there?" Van asked Daniel, softly.

Daniel just held him tight. "Returned to the shadows."

The guy chuckled. "Okay. But I mean it, when we do go to Scotland, no peeping Carmens. No Ace on your shoulder. Just you and me. Promise?"

"Promise."

Van eyed him. "You sure?"

Daniel smiled and whispered, "Sure as snow."

Their Mini-Cooper convertible arrived, and they got in and drove off, acting like all they needed was each other.

I just shook my head in wonder. When was Van gonna catch on? This wasn't the same as quitting smoking or drinking. He could never win, not completely, not against me and Carmen; better to make his peace and let us all be in my guy's life. Daniel understood that since I'm him and he's me, that's the way it'll always be. We're of the same world, same essence, same DNA, even, and he could no more cut me out of Dan-O than a sixty-year-old guy who's been biting his fingernails all his life can stop.

But he was working at balancing it all, I had to give him

that. And the truth is, I like Van. I really do hope it lasts till death they do part. Because my ... *our* dude is worth any peace that comes his way, even if it does take him off to that great big world of reality for stretches at a time. So let him be as one with his guy. Let him make me over in Van's image and Carmen into Gretta's. It didn't matter a bit.

"Oh, no, that's easy for you to think," she snarled at me, some serious sexiness behind her words. "You, he made younger."

Ah, Carmen. Total Yin to my Yang. I just held her close and let her slip her hand around my neck and dig her fingernails in a little, since that always seemed to shut her up, but don't tell her I said that.

Some day she'd catch on, too. What mattered most was my guy ... no, *our* guy was happy, which meant his batteries were recharging, and soon he'd be open to catching ideas from the ether, again. And when that game starts up, he, Carmen and I'll make mystery music, once more.

And if you think what happened in *this* story was weird, wait'll you see what happens next time.

The Author

Kyle Michel Sullivan was born in San Diego, California, and has lived all over the world, from London to Honolulu to Los Angeles. He attended Trinity University in San Antonio and The University of Texas at Austin for graduate work, then moved to Houston, where he wrote, produced and directed industrial and training videos while working on independent features. He's been an art director, editor, cinematographer, camera operator, storyboard artist, audio recorder and done ADR work on feature films – making him a serious jack-of-all-trades.

Except in his writing – on that, he's focused on becoming a master. He's written thirty-five screenplays (twenty-one of which are good), two stage-plays, several one-acts, a number of short film scripts, some short stories, a novella, a fable, and several other novels. He's won numerous screenwriting awards, sold two scripts, been optioned, done work for hire and had his novels published, then republished them under his own banner. He also sketches and paints, has sold some of his artwork and been commissioned to do others.

And he is still writing.

OTHER BOOKS BY KYLE MICHEL SULLIVAN

<u>General Novels:</u>
Carli's Kills
The Vanishing of Owen Taylor
David Martin
NYPD Blood (out of print)
Bobby Carapisi

<u>Adult Novels:</u>
Blood Angel
Hunter
The Beast in the Nothing Room
Underground Guy
Rape in Holding Cell 6
Porno Manifesto
How to Rape a Straight Guy